Weil  ʊʊ̄ᴜ̄ɪ̄ʟ̄

VOL.2, NO. 2   **ISSUE 32**

Fiction

Childhood's Dread, by Taye Carrol 3
The Other Neighbors, by Daniel Davis 9
Rare Air, by Mark Slade 15
The Children, by J.E. Álamo 22
The Radiant Boy, by Kevin Wetmore 24
The Whisperer in the Woods, by Peter Schranz 36
Sweet Oblivion, by Andrew Darlington 46
An Unsolicited Lucidity, by Lee Clark Zumpe 57
Black Carnival, by Bobby Cranestone 69
The Howard Family Tradition, by P. R. O'Leary 76
Hell in a Boxcar, by Scott A. Cupp 84
Jorōgumo, by Kelda Crich 91
Clay Baby, by Jack Lee Taylor 99
The Corpse and the Rat: A Story of Friendship, by Joshua L. Hood 102
Getting Thin, by DJ Tyrer 108
Maybe Next Door, by Richard LaPore 113
Containment Protocol, by Leeman Kessler 116
Under a Rock, by Lori R. Lopez 119
The Children Must Be Hungry, by L.F. Falconer 131
The Road to Hell, by Kevin L. O'Brien 137
Maggot Coffee, by Roy C. Booth and Axel Kohagen 141
Baby Mine, by Marilyn "Mattie" Brahen 145
In Blackwalk Wood, by Adrian Cole 151
My Longing to See Tamar, by Jessica Amanda Salmonson 162
Gust of Wind Made by Swinging a Blade, by Molly N. Moss 165

Poetry

Necromancer's Lair, by Chad Hensley 21
The Helm, by Chad Hensley 23
Ex Arca Sepulcrali, by Wade German 35
The Laughter of Ghouls, by K.A. Opperman 75
Ode to Ashtoreth, by K.A. Opperman 83
The Necro-Conjuring Sorceress, by Ashley Dioses 129
What Dark Gods Are Friends to Me? by Chad Hensley 144
Scarlet Succubus Shrine, by Frederick J. Mayer 164
Penelope, Sleepless, by Darrell Schweitzer 173

Publisher and Executive Editor
John Gregory Betancourt

Editor
Doug Draa

Consulting Editor
W. Paul Ganley

Production Manager
Steve Coupe

A Note from the Editor

Well, it's time for another issue of *Weirdbook*! This is #32 or, if you prefer, the second issue of our relaunch.

There wouldn't have likely been another issue of *Weirdbook* if #31 hadn't been such a huge success. The reception that #31 received was amazing, and it appears that we touched the right chord as far as pleasing the readers went. The critics even seemed to like it. Of course, this is entirely due to the wonderful stories supplied by our contributors.

This issue continues the work started in #31 and offers another cavalcade of weird that has been filtered and distilled through more than a double devil's dozen of voices…each of whom has a uniquely twisted way of viewing (un)reality.

Thanks for stopping by. I'm positive that you won't be disappointed.

Faithfully yours,

—*Doug Draa*

Childhood's Dread
by Taye Carrol

The dread comes in on red berries and frozen breath, when the leaves have gone from golden and ochre to brown dyed dead. The red sets a startled contrast to the brown, yet together they are somehow fitting, a sanguine sign of what's to come. That first morning when the lackluster color scheme can be denied no longer, is always a solemn one. I never know what signals the exact moment of the dreads fulfillment at the same time to everyone, but when the morning comes, the children are wrestled off early to school, still bleary eyed and too asleep to sensor their complaints fully. I've always been extra carefully quiet, well behaved on that morning, no matter how early I'm rushed off to school, cold cereal the consistency of peas there's no time to warm, still sitting like a lump of coal in my stomach even when in-room lunch begins. We try to pay attention, really we do, but it is hard, even for those of us who are older, who didn't cry and beg and hang on our parents hems when the bus arrived. I've always thought the unlucky ones are chosen that way, that it's always the ones who fail to act right, be good when the time comes, that tips the scale. I've never actually proven this but it helps keep my fear at bay throughout the long day until it's time to return home.

Today the early morning rituals will be my last as a child. Though children aren't allowed to help their parents with the daily sacrifice, can't even watch, almost everyone has at some point or another. They get bigger, the sacrifices, starting at the summer solstice as if the shortening days might never reverse themselves otherwise. With so many families now, the river and creeks it gives birth to, begin to look rusty after a while and when they finally freeze over the ice is a strange burnt reddish-brown color. Papa says that he can remember when there were fewer families when the ice was the color ice should be and the children skated on it before the solstice. Even before the strange colors in the ice, it was decided that skating or any boisterous activity, should be forbidden since it could lead to the children being less careful about how they acted. Sometimes now we sneak away to the edge of the woods and collect the leaves into piles to jump into. We're careful not to get caught, though I've always feared that even when we think we've gotten away with it, there were other eyes watching, keeping track of who hurt with words and who with fists, who shoved and who pulled, who shouted and who cried at nothing at all.

I've never wanted to watch what my parents do in the early mornings on the days we stay in bed, pretend disinterest to disguise my fear. I have become good at not counting the animals in our pen, and don't keep track of the births anymore, even when I'm made to help. Fear has made me careful, helped hone my denial. And so I don't try to follow my parents when they go to the gathering place to talk about grownup stuff and never, ever try to see what they do when they disappear into the woods with one of the enclosures inhabitants but come back without. The other kids talk about these things in hushed whispers and maybe they even know what they're talking about. More likely they don't. I think even talking big can get you in trouble, even if it were clear that you didn't really break the rules but are just pretending to. I think when it comes down to it that's as big a sin as if you actually did. The other kids call me goody two shoes since I always behave. Well, not always, but I am usually better than the other kids so to them it seems that way, I guess. It's a struggle, not wanting to be thought of as good all the time at least by the other kids, yet at the same time not wanting to tempt the attention of the Others, the ones that usually stay outside the circle enclosing the village.

The enclosure is nothing more that sharpened wooden pickets, painted poppy red, the color chosen to keep evil at bay. Though we're taught to think of the others as justice not evil. But when your parents disappear one day, a trail of russet smears frozen beneath a milky white crust leading from your front door into the woods, justice is not the first thing that most likely comes to mind. At first, papa said, the fence had been painted a deeper shade, more carmine than simple red, until it was decided that crimson was really more dead on. Now it is a bright poppy red, though each year after the first frost when time comes to paint the fence again, there are always those who argue for crimson and a few voices still who argue for the original carmine. Those last are usually the parents of the youngest children, the ones who still have years to go, who know there are still so many things that can go wrong. Not disaster wrong just childishly wrong, but enough to decide their fate. I don't think it matters really. I doubt it would even if we painted the entire fence white. Since the first families had settled here until now, there has never been a year without a reckoning, a harvest and two less mouths to feed.

The first families weren't really the first. Some had been here before us. We know because they are buried here. The first families were supposed to have picked this spot because of the ones already here, the ones in the ground. They were supposed to have been holy. It should have been a good omen in a time grown strange. Other areas all had their woes. Maybe not a reckoning and a harvest, but something. Maybe something even worse. Every group that left to settle somewhere else when the days had darkened into night and the stars fell from the skies looked for a place of safety, safe from the terrors of their now blackened homeland. Every group looked for signs that their place would not have to wait in terror each year. I don't think any found such a place. At least that's what papa says.

This year, like always, my mamma went with some of the women outside the fence to the old burial place. They go in the late afternoon, since the others only are known to come in the early morning. There they measure the distance between the graves of the holy ones buried there before the turn and the coming of the others, before the reckoning, the harvest. They measure with wick string, carefully making sure the length is correct, no extra due to it snagging on a headstone or rock. The length must be exact. Then they cut the string into lengths and use it for candle wicks, making the candles all night long to leave for the Others in the early morning of the winter solstice. They never come before then. It's as if they wait until the days begin to lengthen bringing with them hope of an early spring and perhaps even a winter without a reckoning. Then once hope begins to bloom, that is when they come. Many families say this is just superstition, the string and candles, that it increases the danger for the whole village. No one is supposed to venture outside the red fence. But each year since my sixth birthday, mama left the safety of the enclosure and each year she returned. I know I will do the same when my turn comes.

The day crawls by but then, suddenly, it is over. All too soon we must go home. Although we get to ride to school today like always, we are expected to walk home. It adds more time for the harvesting, I suppose, without forcing us to stay at school even longer, as if the day is not different enough. We quietly trudge and shuffle along by ourselves, no adult present to hurry our steps. For once even the boys curtail their antics, keep their hands at their sides away from pigtails and ticklish ribs, half-hearted murmurs the slightest of nods to their nature. We crest the big hill, the last rise leading to the valley where the houses sit, and there we stop as if we can decide to never face what is below.

From here the houses look post-card perfect, smoke coming from each chimney, ice crystals sparkling like diamonds on roofs and eaves. The smell of yeasty bread warms us briefly despite the cold, and we breathe deeply at the top of the climb as always, pretending for this instant that there is nothing but the everyday ordinary below. Here we can forget for a minute that for at least one or two of us, nothing will ever be perfect again. Then a long howling sound comes, not so close but just close enough for us to realize once more that it is that day, the day those parents judged wanting are harvested, have already been harvested. Our bodies grow tight and still. Perfectly still. It's as if we believe if we stand there long enough we can prevent what we know has already happened. The wind stirs, strengthens then pushes like a hand in the small of our backs, forcing us onward, a message that we can only delay the inevitable not prevent it, and it is time to move on.

We trudge down, down, down, towards the waiting houses. Even the boys now make no sound. Tonight, after the big dinner, after we have played with our new toys, those of us who have escaped for one more year will go to sleep in our own beds. Our parents will keep watch through open doors in case this is the year one of us will become too smug and figure what would it hurt to just catch a glimpse. If they could see our faces when the wind whips at our backs, they wouldn't worry. We will all remain in our beds as we always have this night, and once again we'll pretend nothing is different tomorrow, that the unlucky house is not gone, a new one erected in a slightly different place, one or two of us now living with different parents. No one wants to live in an unlucky house and yet there will need to be homes for the newly matched couples soon. This year I will live in one of those houses.

As we approach each house one or two of us peels off, eyes deadened and downcast, breath held to disappear through a door quickly opened and shut. Some don't go in at first. Those who know they were not as good as they should have been linger outside, regret and fear plain on their faces. This is why the scream doesn't come until later. When it is my turn, I quickly push open the door, enter and shut it carefully behind me lest it slam. I fear if I so much as hesitate I will never be able to move past the yard.

My eyes are drawn to the table in the entryway. The cups of tea and plate of newly baked mandlebracht, a traditional guests fare, are gone, wafer thin china put up for another year. No one uses wedding china except on this day, believing it bad luck to mix potential bad fate with hoped for good. Mom and dad stand in the kitchens doorway waiting for me and I run to them, remembering to breathe again. Before I think, I am crying, both of them hushing me since I don't have anything to cry about. Even though once tears could be because of either something good or bad, now they are reserved only for the bad. I look out the window at the other houses, and pretend everything is as perfect as the snow blanketed image upon which I gaze.

Then I hear it. The scream. Tim's scream. It is high and piercing for a boy, quickly descending into what sounds like someone drowning, then fades, the glass between us muffling the sounds of his anguish. He is not my year and for a minute I am relieved that none of the girls in my class will have to marry without their parents there. Quickly, my relief is replaced by guilt and I turn from the window only to be sickened as always by the gaily wrapped presents I now see sitting in front of my room. Though it's one more thing not talked about, I know my parents did not buy them, that the toys I unwrap will not be found at either of the two stores in our village. I move leadenly to the packages, push down the rising nausea that comes with the grotesque images of the hands that wrapped them, and quickly uncover the gifts inside. Forcing a smile that feels as if it will cause my face to shatter, I look up at my parents only to see a similar expression on their faces. I am too old for toys, have been for several years now but perhaps childhood for the Others is different. If they have a childhood. This year I get a pretend tea set. Even though every other year the gifts are different, each girl gets pretend china in their sixteenth year. their last reckoning as a child.

The gifts are probably supposed to make the day seem better than it really is. It's not supposed to be thought of as all bad. The day not the harvest. The family that is harvested well, of course it's all bad for them even though the kids still get left stuff. Then they have to pretend to play with it until they are collected by their second parents. Every family must choose second and third parents, just in case the second are taken also. I bet no one ever wants to be listed as third parents since they know they will have to care for a child or children who had doomed two sets of parents already. It didn't happen much but it did happen. Last year Katy and Emily lost their second parents and they were now on their third. That's probably why they seemed so quiet this whole year even in summer when most kids can forget the coming winter, the first frost and the dread.

Emotions swirl in my head and parts of thoughts, the bad ones about "unfair," and "evil," and "torturous," tamped down firmly before they can play out until simple relief overshadows all. I have made it through my childhood without dooming my parents. I am now an adult and pray I will be rewarded for my success by being allowed to live until I see this day as a parent myself. There's no ceremony, just your last reckoning in your sixteenth year. Well, eighteenth year for the boys. So that means when I am matched tomorrow, it will be with someone two years older than me, someone from outside the safe group of my class, someone I don't know, have perhaps just seen in passing. We'll go to the gathering place, and the chancellor will read from a list left for him tonight. He's older. So's his wife and it's always someone either without children or whose children are grown and have no children. This makes sure he won't take whatever knowledge he has of the others and bargain for his own family. No one knows if this is possible but there are stories of the first chancellor put into place the first year of the reckoning. After he and his family had disappeared, the Others left clear instructions on how it was supposed to be done and since then that is how it has been done. They also left instructions and names for the matching ceremony to be read by the new chancellor. Many families balked at the young ages of those who would be matched then shortly after married to each other. A few families outright refused. They'd all disappeared along with their children. That was the only year more than one pair of parents were taken and the only year they'd taken children also. After that everyone followed directions quite strictly. How the others know so much about us, who we are, our names, exactly how many in each year and who is to be matched with whom, who is supposed to be part of the reckoning, is not known, or if it is, it's never spoken about. If I thought about it too closely I would have to conclude that we are always being watched and so I don't think too closely.

It will be some time before I am up for reckoning even if I have a baby next year. They don't take the parents of babies, after all what could a baby possibly do that you could blame its parents for? This is the beginning of the carefree years, those when my parents are past having to fear for themselves and don't yet have to start fearing for me and for me the same. The other families who are still slaves to the dread will resent us, hate us even, but for now we don't care. My parents hold each other tightly and for the first time I see what they must have looked like as newlyweds, each one an only child and so both carefree having come through the dread with both sets of parents intact. My father's eyes find me at the table where I still sit trying to figure out something else to do with my tea set. He gestures to me and I go to where he and my mother stand. They draw me into the circle of their arms and for once I remember not to cry. We stand in front of the fire watching the list of alternate parents, no longer needed, burn. Once even the ashes are gone I can pretend the list never was. For at least this moment, I finally know what it is to be a child. I close my eyes and sigh, held close within the circle of my parents arms and, just this once, just for a moment, indulge in the joyfulness of a future defined by the possibility of "what if?"

▲

The Other Neighbors
by Daniel Davis

Parker blamed the rabbit.

Technically, he was supposed to be minding Rupert. Technically, Rupert was supposed to be on a chain. The fence wouldn't be built for another two weeks; who knew that the fencing business had such a backorder? Until then, Rupert had to stay on his chain, or on a leash, or preferably inside.

Problem was, Parker hated messing with the chain. He had to carry Rupert out to the center of the yard, the terrier struggling against the restraint, bend down while still keeping the dog still, and thread the clasp on the chain through the ring on Rupert's rabies tag. Then he had to repeat the process when he was ready to go inside. It hurt his back. And he hadn't planned on being outside long; just a quick dip onto the patio to see if he had enough propane to light up the grill for dinner. He'd promised Eileen pork steak, and she liked it as black and crispy as a charcoal briquette.

But Rupert snuck out onto the patio, and Parker didn't think much of it. *Okay, fine, you've got twenty seconds, pal.* As he turned for the grill, however, his eyes swept over the yard. Caught the rabbit at the far back, near the tree line. Sitting there, watching them. As if waiting. As if saying, *Game on, bro, come get me.*

Rupert accepted the challenge.

Parker let out a monosyllabic yell, part curse, part shriek. The terrier yipped and yapped, paws flying, dancing over the grass. The rabbit hesitated. *Go the other way*, Parker thought, almost shouted. *Left or right, left or right!*

The rabbit turned and darted into the trees. Three seconds later, Rupert followed.

Parker brought up the rear. The thought of leaving the dog to his fate never even occurred to him. An impossibility. Though she had never accused him, *would* never accuse him, he and Eileen both knew that he was the one responsible for her last dog's death. He'd backed over it with a car one night at their old house. Not technically his fault; the dog was supposed to be in the back yard. Someone, perhaps a neighborhood kid, had left the gate open. Nothing to be done, maybe no blame to be passed around, but when Parker saw Eileen's tears, he knew he'd hold it against himself for a long time to come. And he had, and he did, and he didn't hesitate to chase after Rupert.

The trees scratched Parker's face. He almost tripped on a root, and had to think hard about the last time he'd walked anywhere other than plain flat ground. He hadn't been in a forest since his childhood downstate; suburbia had tamed him, had taken nature away without him noticing. He wiped a cobweb from his face and spat out bits of dried leaves. And to think, he'd once *liked* the woods.

* * * *

Rupert barked from a distance, growing fainter. Parker trudged on. Still hot in the shade. Dirt from the leaves and branches clung to his sweaty forearms. At least he'd been wearing his shoes; he never went out back barefoot, not since the time as a kid when he'd stepped on a nail. Almost lost his big toenail as a result; Parker had never gotten the image of his battered and bruised toe, swollen and *wrong*, out of his mind.

The rabbit hadn't run straight ahead; it had doglegged to the right, perhaps seeking a burrow, or hoping to lose the terrier in the thick underbrush. No such luck. Rupert could squeeze his way through anywhere, and Parker was big enough to bludgeon a path forward. He wondered what the neighbors would think, hearing him. Then he looked over his shoulder and wondered where the neighbors were.

He'd never come out here. He didn't think Eileen had, either. He'd seen some kids playing here, he remembered waving at them, but that was it. They'd only been in the neighborhood a month now, but he didn't remember anyone mentioning anything about the trees. Or what was beyond them, for that matter. Parker had just assumed more houses; when he and Eileen had driven through the neighborhood, that's all he'd seen, house after house, with the trees as a backdrop. He'd never stopped to think that maybe an entire *forest* was at his backdoor, because this was the middle of town, in good old Civilized, USA. You didn't have forests popping up out of nowhere.

The trees weren't that expansive; he knew this instinctively. He'd simply been away from nature so long that a little seemed like a lot. He wished it didn't, however, because his paunch was already catching up to him, too much barbeque and beer. Eileen kept herself in shape, said she'd need to be fit for whenever she got pregnant. For the first time, Parker thought maybe she meant for *him* to get fit with her. Maybe he would, after this. Maybe Rupert and the rabbit were all the inspiration he'd needed.

After a while, surely just a few minutes, the barking changed direction, coming now from Parker's left. He turned, and eventually the space between the trees began to widen. He could make out the back of a house, the open expanse of a yard, and just like that, the trees were behind him and he was bathed in sunlight again, wiping debris off his clothes and wondering if he could pass for the Wild Man from Borneo. He felt something crawling against the back of his neck, and slapped himself silly before he realized it was just a leaf. He looked up to see if anyone was watching.

No one was. In fact, the yard didn't look as though it'd seen any attention in weeks. The grass had grown up over the tops of Parker's tennis shoes. A rusty playground stood a few feet away, the swing creaking in the slight breeze. The house itself, a two-story job not dissimilar from his own, had yellow-turning-brown siding, dirty window frames around streaked glass. The screen on the back door was ripped. Even from a distance, Parker could tell the wood in the porch was rotted through.

He glanced at the homes on either side. Chain-link fences separated him from properties just as run down as this one.

"Guess we chose the right side of the tracks," he muttered. "I mean, trees."

Rupert barked up ahead, from around front of the house. A subdued bark now, not as eager as before. Not triumphant, either. The rabbit must've reached its burrow, and the terrier now stood over the entrance, wondering where the prey had disappeared. Rupert was cute, Parker had to give him that, but the dog wasn't much on brains.

"All right," Parker said, raising his voice a little and clapping his hands. "Come on, boy, let's go home. Come on."

He approached the house, eying the windows in case anyone was watching. He didn't want to give the wrong impression; he felt like someone who lived in a place like this might get the wrong impression fairly easily. But he saw no one, no fluttering blinds or curtains either. Perhaps they were at work. Not everyone got the summer off; most folks, especially from homes like this, worked hard the whole year 'round.

Parker paused, frowning, and shook his head. He was being too judgmental. He could do that sometimes. He knew nothing about the family that lived here; he had to remember that. Thinking like this didn't hurt anyone, but thinking sometimes led to actions, and actions *could* hurt. He taught ethics every other semester, for Christ's sake. He should know better. *Lead by example*; wasn't that what he'd been told in college?

Then again, he taught Health Ed on occasion, too. *Eat a five servings of vegetables a day to avoid a gut like this.*

Much to Parker's relief, Rupert stopped barking. Parker shook off his self-criticism as he rounded the side of the house. He could judge-slash-pity himself later, with a slab of pork in his belly and Eileen curled up next to him. Right now, he had one task: to retrieve the damn dog and head back home, and never mention this to his wife.

A brief yelp wiped the smile from his face. Rupert dashed around the corner, in full panic mode, running right between Parker's legs. Parker spun around, saw the dog race across the yard, yelp once, and dart back into the trees. All in the span of five or six seconds. Rupert hadn't run so fast when he'd taken off after the rabbit.

Parker opened his mouth to say something, realized the dog was out of earshot, and shut his trap. He hung his shoulders, prepared to head back. A wasted trip, but with any luck Rupert was already back in his own yard, cowering beside the door, pissing the patio in terror of whatever had set him off.

What did *set him off?*

This thought was followed perfectly by the crunch of a branch. *Snap.* Parker almost jumped; he'd taken it for granted he'd been alone, he'd just assumed that, because the house *seemed* empty, it was. Stupid, again. Foolish and intolerable. He smiled, shook his head in self-mockery, and turned around.

They stood in the afternoon shadows cast by the house. Three of them, adults, maybe parents and grown child. Two female, one male, dressed in loose, tattered clothing. That's all Parker could say of them. All three were pale, skin sagging from their faces, mouths open wide, eyes even wider. Tangled, mussed hair that hadn't seen a comb or shampoo since the last presidency. They stood perfectly still, so immobile that Parker thought maybe they were Halloween decorations, the owners so lazy they left them up the whole year. *Wouldn't bring the property value down much*, Parker managed to think, even as his smile faded.

Then the man moved. *Man.* He shambled forward, made a grumbling sound from deep in his throat. Reached out with one arm, fingers grasping in desperation. Behind him, the women shuffled. The younger one clutched something in her fists, something furry and brown and red. At her feet lay what may have been severed rabbit ears. Her mouth, Parker noticed, was stained dark and ugly.

"No," Parker said. He took a step back. He pointed at where the shadows disappeared into sunlight. "No. Stay. You can't."

The man could, stepping into the light easily.

Of course: vampires weren't real. This was.

Parker cried out, turned, and shouted again. He'd been so focused on the three in front of him that he hadn't heard the other, an elderly female, coming up from behind. She clutched at his shirt, pulling herself forward. Her mouth filled with sharp things that couldn't possibly be teeth but were. She said something, not words, but Parker understood too well. He shoved her away, his hand making contact with her bare arm, skin so impossibly hot, as though she'd been standing in the sun all day waiting for him. He shoved again and she fell, choking and chomping.

The man grabbed him from behind. Sharp fingernails bit into Parker's back as his shirt tore. He felt the man's breath against the side of his face, warm and sticky and maggoty, then felt a searing pain in his ear. Parker didn't think, he just jammed his elbow into the man's chest. The pain turned into a deafening roar, and Parker's vision went black even as he tore free and stumbled, falling to his hands and knees.

The other two were there to catch him. Hands and mouths tugging at his hair, his clothes. More, too, more of them. Above his own screaming, he heard Rupert, returning to save him, barking and snarling. From beyond the pain, Parker willed the dog away, swore he wouldn't let another of Eileen's pets die because of him. He wouldn't be responsible for that, *just run, Rupert, save yourself.*

Perhaps, by some divine mercy, Parker got through, because eventually he didn't hear Rupert any more, and a little while after that he heard nothing at all except the chewing.

▲

Rare Air
by Mark Slade

It was Bernstein that introduced Meg to Howard King.

Not only was Meg annoyed by the many stories Bernstein was telling about his Mother's youth (as old as Lew Bernstein was, you'd think his Mother would already be dead.), but there was a very loud and obnoxious man screaming at the top of his lungs to punctuate his pornographic story about a recently widowed woman he had bedded.

"Lew, darling, who is that loud man over there?" Meg said over top of her martini glass.

Bernstein turned quickly. He saw a short, bald man with over-size framed glasses in a checkered blazer sitting at a table full of other successful men laughing at his dirty jokes. Bernstein readjusted himself in his seat, took a sip of his white wine. "Oh, that's just Howard King." He said nonchalantly. Bernstein returned to his salad made specifically for him with walnuts and asparagus with a honey mustard dressing. "Any way, can you believe this woman next door, had the nerve to ask me if Mother was a hundred years old? Some people." Bernstein scoffed and shook his head. Bernstein was an old friend of Meg's, one she met at her husband Denny's club before he died, and she inherited his fortune, his companies, and of course, his tax problems. But Meg was a smart woman. She understood business, it was in her genes, passed down from her father. So she knew how to keep companies, that had been floundering, survivable money makers. After all, Denny was her fifth husband, his company, her seventh that she pulled out of the ashes.

* * * *

Earlier she'd been in an argument with Connie Severson over a rumor Connie had started about Denny and his secretary. Oh, that Connie was such bur in Meg's side. Of course, Meg was able to have Connie banned from the club after her little tirade last spring that resulted in several club glasses and dishes thrown at Meg. She was an old enemy from the days when Meg was with her second husband and Connie was married to that Television evangelist. The years had not soften their hatred for one another.

Meg waited patiently for more information until she couldn't take it any longer. "Well?"

Bernstein looked up at her, incredulously, with honey mustard plastered all over his top lip. "Well what?"

"Dear wipe your mouth," Meg pointed to her own lips. "Tell me about Howard King."

Bernstein used a corner of his napkin, dabbed his lips, missing most of the dressing that dripped to his chin. "There's not much to tell, Meg," Bernstein chuckled. "Denny hasn't been in his coffin more than six months…."

* * * *

"Oh, shut up." Meg laughed and waved her hand. "You are awful. What does he do?"

"Mostly drinks and brags about himself."

"What does he do for a living?"

"Meg….okay. He is into rare commodities."

"As in what? I'm afraid I don't follow you, Lew."

"Whenever he is asked what line of work, he says that and produces a card. It says just that as well." Bernstein took an ivory card made of thick paper stock and handed it her. Sure enough, it said just that, along with a cell number and a website. "Really, Meg. I can't believe you are interested in him." Bernstein jabbed his thumb over his shoulder in the direction of Howard King.

Meg turned the card over in her hand a few times. "I'm not interested. He just seems…interesting is all. Obviously everyone likes him."

"What? Are we in high school or something? I think you should lay low for a while, Meg. Give your poor heart a rest, and Denny's memory a bit of a thought."

"Yes," Meg sighed. "Perhaps, Lew. Perhaps you are right." She watched Howard rise from his chair, drain his glass, and loudly announce he had to drain the lizard.

Howard king drunkenly ambled toward Bernstein and Meg, and when he nearly fell into Bernstein's salad, he decided to sit next to them. He was completely white, as white as the table cloth on all of the tables in the club. A dead rose was pushed into the buttonhole of his very brightly colored blazer, which drooped into the pocket.

"Looks like I'm not finishing my salad," Bernstein said in a huff and threw his napkin in the plate.

Howard leaned in to Meg and said: "He gets frustrated when he's not winning, doesn't he?" This tickled Meg. She covered her mouth to stifle a laugh. Howard sighed, looked around. "It gets harder and harder to find a place to take a piss in this joint." He swayed in his chair.

"You have the mind of a poet, Howard," Bernstein rolled his eyes.

"And don't I know it!" Howard guffawed as he jerked his knee and kicked the table, nearly turning over the wine glasses. After he settled down he leaned in to Meg again. "Hey toots, if you point me in the right direction of the toilets, I'll let you hold it."

Meg was so shocked by Howard's comment, her cheeks turned a bright red. She was flabbergasted.

Bernstein whispered in Howard's ear and pointed to his left where two ivory doors clearly marked Men and Women. Howard thanked Bernstein, showed Meg a toothy grin.

"I'll catch you later, toots. Anybody ever tell you, you got sexy ears. Yeah…sexy." Howard headed to the bathrooms mumbling to himself what he would do with Meg's earlobes.

"My God, Lew. Is he like this when he's sober?" Meg fanned herself with a hand.

Bernstein thought a few seconds. "I don't know," He said. "I've never seen him sober."

* * * *

Bernstein was late. He was supposed to be at the club at three thirty. Meg looked at her watch. She'd been waiting for him for an hour and ten minute, three rum and cokes and a Cobb salad ago. Meg was furious. Meg lit another cigarette. Now her day truly was ruined.

"Well…hello toots!" Meg heard a voice from behind her. She turned and saw Howard King.

"Oh," Meg forced a smile. "Hello, Mr. King." She took a puff of her cigarette, flicked ashes into the ashtray.

"Its Howard, toots." He sat down without being asked. "I didn't catch the name?"

"No," Meg's upper lip curled slightly. "You didn't."

Howard laughed, smacked the table top with a hand. "That was funny. I like a woman with piss and vinegar."

"That sounds quite disgusting, Mr. King." Meg had a stern look in her hazel eyes. She knew her day would not go right this morning when she noticed her jar of wrinkle cream was empty. She let Dorothy have it. What kind of maid doesn't buy refills of wrinkle cream? At Meg's age, it was extremely vital, and at sixty-one, it was getting harder to find available men that were rich enough and successful enough to car for her.

"Mr. King," Meg leaned in slightly. "I'm sorry to say this. But I really would like to be alone. I don't feel like company right now."

Howard shrugged. "Yeah, yeah. I get it. That poof Bernstein didn't show and you're a little burned right now. I get it. Maybe I can lighten the mood," Howard's hand just happened to find its way to caress Meg's knee, and it just happened to rub ever so slightly, up and down.

Meg smiled. She nodded. "I see," She said, took another drag of her cigarette. Meg brought her cigarette down underneath the table and stabbed the lit end into Howard's hand. He withdrew it quickly and howled. He blew on his shaking hand. All eyes were on them now. "I'm so sorry, Mr. King. My hand slipped."

Howard smiled a toothy smile, laughed. "No problem. So did mine."

"If you will excuse me, I have somewhere to be."

"Yeah. Yeah. Me too. Uh, hey, toots. I'd like to see you again."

Meg stood, pushed her chair in. She picked up her bag, then handed Howard her cigarette. "I'm here every day, Mr. King. Perhaps you can catch me."

"Perhaps," Howard said and placed the cigarette between his chapped lips. "Perhaps, toots."

* * * *

Meg and Bernstein was leaving a show in the village when they saw Howard King leaving an apartment building. "Well." Bernstein said. "Look who it is."

Meg tapped on the back window of her limo and the driver rolled it down just enough to hear her. "Turn around, William and drive past that apartment building on Hamblin Ave. But drive slowly, please."

"Oh my God," Bernstein scoffed. "What are you doing?"

"Nothing," Meg answered in a raspy voice she used when she was frustrated. "I'm just curious."

"Meg, dear. You are simply obsessed with this man."

"Oh shut up, Lew," Her upper lip curled slightly. "You are so critical for a man. I think you are a woman trapped in a man's body."

"If you aren't obsessed with Howard King, then why do you keep telling that story of when he molested you at the club?"

"That's not obsession, Lew. It's simply a damned good story…"

The limo eased by at the pace of a turtle. There was Howard King, drunkenly trying to fit his key into his Volvo, missing the keyhole, dropping the keys—recovering them, and starting the whole process over again until a middle aged woman in a robe, trotted down the small flight of stairs. Her hair was in disarray and her makeup looked as though she'd just been jogging hundred degree weather. The woman bent down, snatched the keys from Howard and took hold of his tie. She led him back up the small flight of stairs and back into the apartment building.

Meg was dumbfounded. "That was Connie Severson" She announced. She blinked a few times before a sour look crossed her face.

"Go back around, ma'am?" The driver asked.

"No, William," Meg said in a depressed voice. "Take me home so I can drown in a bathtub of vodka."

* * * *

There was a knock at Meg's door. The night hadn't yet ended for. She was still on her sofa where she had passed out. She had dismissed her servant girl hours ago after a tirade over an empty bottle of scotch was broken. The servant girl said her good night and retired to her bedroom. The rapping was loud and echoed in her ringing ears. Groggily, Meg rose slowly, nearly falling down. She dragged herself to the door and opened it angrily. Meg found Howard King standing in the hallway, a silly grin on his face and a bottle of wine in his hands.

"You called for Dr. Love, toots?" He said. Pushing his way inside.

"I didn't call anyone," Meg said, slightly confused. "Why are you here—and you just think you can barge in here?"

"Oh you called me," He laughed, tapping the side of his forehead. "Using this. Saying you need love and a party—oh. I see you already started without me. I hope you didn't finish." He kicked two wine bottles out of his, sat on the couch heavily.

"If you don't leave, I will be forced to call the police." Meg whispered in a humble voice. Her confidence was breaking down.

"You won't do that, toots. You like me too much."

"Mr. King…"

"No." He stood, took two quick steps toward Meg. He pulled her in his embrace and dipped her. Meg gave out a slight whimper. "Call me Howard." He leaned in close and pressed his lips to hers.

* * * *

Bernstein shook his head and clucked his tongue, rifled the newspaper from page to page. He let out a gasp, then shook his head. Meg sat across from him at a corner table at the club's restaurant. She was dressed in her green sequined dress with a very revealing neckline and even more revealing slit at the knees. She wore a long feather boa that draped from her neck and laid around her shoulders. Meg was looking to get attention, most notably from Bernstein. But he kept his nose buried in that newspaper, not paying her any mind.

Meg tore the newspaper from Bernstein's hands. "That's quite enough from you, Mister." She bawled it up into a ball and tossed it over her shoulders.

Bernstein's eyes widened. His hands shook as he fumbled his words. "What do you think you are doing…?"

"I have been sitting here for ten minutes and not once…"

"…I was reading that! It's important to our circle!"

"…And you have not commented on my dress!"

"It's ridiculous," Bernstein turned away from her.

"Ohhh," Meg faked tears. "How can you say that? It hurts me so."

Immediately, Bernstein felt terrible that he had said such an awful thing to the one friend he is so close to. Even closer than his poor aging mother. He reached and took her hand in his. Bernstein smiled. "I'm so sorry, Meg," He rubbed her hand gently. "I shouldn't have said that."

"Oh, Lew," Meg bit her lower lip. "What has come over us? The past two weeks have been so strained. I'm sorry, too." Bernstein removed his hand from Meg's. He looked away. "Your dear mother, Lew…what is the matter?"

"I know that I have been behaving badly," He said. "Meg, darling, you are the best friend I have ever had, apart from mother."

"Oh, I know that," Meg patted Bernstein's hand and laughed. "Your dear mother," Meg took a cigarette out and tapped it on the table to pack the tobacco in tighter. "How is she—have you seen her today?"

"Of course," Bernstein scoffed.

"I know she had been sick for quite a while. I thought—well, maybe she took a turn for the worst is why you've been acting—strange?"

Bernstein's face twisted up like he'd just eating something sour. "The way I have been acting…? No, Meg. Four times you have called off our dinner dates in the last two weeks, showing up late here at the club. Frankly, you've been obsessing again, over Howard king."

Meg was shocked. He had went too far now. "How dare you? You should be happy for me. I have finally found a soul mate."

"Meg, darling. I would be, if it was anyone else. I have something to tell you about our Mr. Howard King. It effects our group of friends."

"Oh Pshaw, you are my only friend. Not those old fools."

"In any case, it affects us. I was just reading in the papers. An odd connection between Howard King and the women he'd been seeing this past year? Five elderly women this year have passed away mysteriously. Five years ago it was six other elderly women. Their families are calling for an investigation."

"How did they die?" Meg was now slightly concerned. She guarded her neck as if some imaginary hands were around them?

"They have died mysteriously…but the coroner's report said it was natural causes."

Meg's hand relaxed, moved it to her knee. "Oh. Had they signed over their fortunes to him?"

Bernstein sighed, his face flushed with embarrassment. "No. They have not." He thought a second. "I guess I'm being silly. Really, what concerned me was the death of Connie Severson. We just saw her two weeks ago. Very upsetting—Meg? Are you alright?"

Meg was not alright. She was taken aback by this news. Even saddened that her old rival was gone from this planet. She swallowed hard, fought back a few tears. She forced a smile. "Yes. Yes, of course I'm... alright."

* * * *

Howard sat on the side of Meg's canopy bed, grabbed his trousers. She massaged his hairy back with her foot, hoping to coax him back into her arms to make love one more time.

"Where are you going, Mr. King?" She cooed.

"I got another appointment, toots." Howard said.

Meg sat up and threw her arms around Howard. "You never explained what line of work you're in." She kissed his neck, then his ears.

"Nothing really to explain. I'm into selling rare and exotic goods."

"Such as?" Meg prodded Howard. That was one thing Meg was good at, was getting to the bottom of something if she was curious enough.

Howard turned around, smiled at her. "Rare air," He said, removed her arms from his neck.

Meg was perplexed. "What the hell does that mean?"

"You wanna know?"

"Yes," Meg replied. By now she was getting more than a little annoyed. He was being cryptic and she didn't like for people to be cryptic.

"You really wanna know?"

"Yes! Damn it!"

Howard eased Meg on her back, made sure the pillow was comfy under her head. She laughed. "Oh, Howard. What are you doing?"

He placed a finger over lips. "Shhh..." He whispered. "No talking during the demonstration."

Meg stifled a laugh. He then parted her lips with his forefinger and thumb. He bent down. Meg closed her eyes, ready to receive a kiss. Instead, she felt a horrible pain in her lungs. Her body began to tremble. She reopened her eyes and saw the color in Howard's eyes were no longer brown, but the color of brimstone. She saw mist drift from her lips and into a long vile. Meg's arms floundered as she struggled to catch her breath.

Howard king took the vile from the inside pocket of his red and green checkered blazer. Smiling, he looked at it and shrugged. "Not bad," He said. He handed the vile to Bernstein.

Bernstein adjusted himself in his chair. He grasped the vile carefully and sighed. "Really," Bernstein said. "We are going to have to find a new set of friends, Mr. King."

Howard nodded and laughed. "I think I'll have lunch at the club this afternoon. Care to join me?"

Bernstein popped the top off of the vile and leaned in to the bed where the frail skeletal naked body of his mother lay. He forced open her sunken in lips and allowed the mist to flow between her bone white chalky lips. Her black eyes fluttered and a limp hand shook slightly.

"I can't," Bernstein said. "I have to stay and take care of mother."

Necromancer's Lair
by Chad Hensley

Broad catacombs with giant spider webs
Lead to a subterranean gallery
Where a vile underground stream slowly ebbs
And ghastly, ghoulish shapes drink with hot glee.
Here, he sits and smirks on skeletal hands,
Emerald eyes glowing brightly beneath cowl.
His tattered robes crawling as he commands
The spectral dead to perform deeds most foul.

Floating maws filled with serpentine fangs twitch.
Tiny men with reptilian scales flap wings
And screech in praise as the corpse of the witch
Rises out of putrescent earth and sings

The glory of the Necromancer's reign -
Eternal loneliness his only pain.

The Children
by J.E. Álamo

"The children, save the children!" She screamed.

He detested her, it was a crimson boiling sensation; she was safe and cozy in their shelter while he was attacked. She insisted and he closed his mind to the contact, there was no time for distractions. But she was right: if he lost the children, life would be worthless.

He leaned against the rocky wall of the gorge where he had been ambushed. He had already hidden the children, who were weeping in terror, behind a huge boulder away from the assaulters. He seized the double-headed axe and braced himself for the battle.

They saw him and roared for blood. Two charged without waiting for the rest. It was simple: a swift movement to the left caught the one who was closer and he flew spreading his viscera. The second followed the fate of the first when the blade whirled back, and the corpse collapsed on the spot alas its head rolled a few feet to the right.

They decided to attack all together. The proximity of their prey after the long hunt made them reckless. They thought their strength was in their number and hoped to finish him even at the cost of severe casualties.

That was a mistake. They would not make another.

He dropped the axe.

He snapped one´s neck with a powerful kick. He gutted three more with his bare hands. They fell without uttering a sound. They were tough. He was tougher.

A sharp word from a red bearded brute made them step back and break up in two groups to take him from both sides. He decided it was time to reveal his true nature, tired of pretending what he was not. A mental command and he vanished into thin air. Silence fell as a shroud, but was immediately shattered by a thunder clap when he came back. His enemies hesitated, fear struck their hearts just as he had expected. Alas, they would recover and attack again, but those few seconds were all that he needed. He finished them in a swirl of fangs, claws and shrieks. Then he licked the blood from their bodies with delight and opened his mind to her.

"My dearest one, the children are safe. We shall not endure a harsh winter."

There were no words in response, but he felt a sudden feverish sensation. She was happy.

He opened his broad, leathery wings, took the cage with the weeping children in his claws, and flew towards the shelter.

▲

The Helm
by Chad Hensley

With big sulfur smoke puff, the imp vanished.
Two-horned barbute of jet black, glist'ning bone
Lands on my hairless head, I am banished
With shower of blue sparks, I'm all alone

On distant subterranean sea shore,
Waters begin boiling, churning dark waves,
An elephantine eye rises to soar
Thrashing with tentacles that shall enslave.

Each tendril's tip a human mouth to scream.
White laser beams shoot from my day-glow eyes.
The enormous orb melts in glist'ning steam.
The black helmet nods in heated surprise

As occult ardor fills me with power
I am pulled back towards the spine tower.

The Radiant Boy
by Kevin Wetmore

Wednesday Night

The night held no terrors for Ray. The stars were old, familiar friends. Late at night, right before bed, was his favorite time. He would take Galileo for one last walk around his Santa Monica neighborhood and enjoy the stars. The dark did not scare him; it was the only time to see the heavens as they truly were.

Ray was thinking about tomorrow's lecture for his Introduction to Astronomy class as he pulled the leash to get Galileo to move on from the garbage can he was sniffing. They had turned down the alley that marked the last leg of their late night walk. Tomorrow's class was something Ray always did right before Halloween. He was going to lecture on the Pleiades and their connection to Halloween. It was an excuse to add some fun, scary stuff to class in order to keep their attention.

As they walked past the Ridgeway's house, Ray noticed a young boy in the space between garage and wall between the houses. The boy was looking down. His face glowed in the light of what Ray assumed was a cellphone. His first thought was that it was odd that a child this young would be out this late. It was only then that he noticed the boy's clothing. It looked old fashioned.

The boy suddenly looked up at Ray. His eyes were empty, but immediately seemed to fill with sadness. Ray realized that Galileo was growling, his ears flat against his head.

"Settle down, boy!" he said, tugging on the leash and looking at the dog. "I'm sorry, you must have startled..." and when he looked up the boy was gone. Ray figured the boy had turned around and walked back to the other side of the garage. He wondered if the boy was a relative visiting the Ridgeways.

Upon reaching his garage, Ray opened the door and passed through. Coming out the other side, he let Galileo off the leash. The mutt bounded across the short yard, past all the toys, and went up the steps to the back porch, his tail beating time as he waited for Ray to follow and open the door.

Finishing his nightly routine, Ray closed and locked the door behind him, Galileo bouncing off to sleep on Robbie's bed or under Lucas's crib. Ray double checked the front door, then went to his own bedroom where Claudia was up reading.

"How'd it go out there?" she asked, looking up over the glasses she only wore when she read.

"Same old, same old. We walked, we peed, we sniffed some garbage cans."

"You peed, too?"

"Cute. There was this kid next to Ridgeway's garage, though," he began as he took off his shirt and pants.

"Mmmm?" She had already returned to the book.

"Just seemed late for someone that young to be outside texting, you know?"

"Permissive parenting, honey. Everybody's doing it except us."

"I guess so." He headed to the bathroom to brush his teeth, and only then did it occur to him that the boy's face still had that glow even when the boy put his hands down when the dog began growling. Ray realized the boy did not have a cell phone. The light was not reflecting off the boy's face—it was coming from the boy's face.

He went back to the bed. The lights went out and he was asleep a few minutes later thinking about the Pleiades.

Thursday

"The Celts noted that the Pleiades rose right at sunset on a night about halfway between the autumnal equinox and the winter solstice."

He hit a button and the next image was projected.

"That same night the Pleiades would rise to the highest point in the sky. The Celts read this to mean that this night was special, a night when the veil between the world of the living and the world of the dead was thinnest."

"Halloween, right, Professor Casey?" called a voice from the darkened amphitheater.

"That's right. The tradition of Halloween developed out of the Celts' understanding of the night sky. So this Saturday, when you kids are having fun in costumes, take a minute to look up at the stars and see what the Celts saw. Understand how your world has been shaped by the stars."

He could hear the shuffling of papers and the placing of possessions in backpacks as the end of class approached. "Extra credit for anyone who snaps a photo of the Pleiades with a cell phone Saturday night and sends it to me via email!" He did everything he could to get the community college students to invest in the subject matter more.

He hit the switch killing the projector and turning on the classroom lights. The students shuffled out, most of them already thinking about something else. Hell, most of them were probably thinking of something else during class. At least they could not text in class without him being able to see the glow from the phone as he projected images of the night sky at the front of the darkened lecture hall.

Thinking of that, he suddenly remembered the boy from last night. Very odd.

* * * *

Office hours, a committee meeting and his Introduction to Cosmology course (for students thinking about transferring to a four year school with a major in physics or astronomy) and his day was done. He got into his car and listened to NPR on the drive home.

Walking in the back door he was immediately greeted by Galileo and then entered the kitchen to see how Claudia was doing.

"Daddy!" Robbie yelled and ran over and hugged his leg. He had been drawing at the table. Claudia sat next to him, attempting (unsuccessfully it seemed) to get Lucas to eat puréed carrots.

"How's it going?" he asked everyone.

"Here," she said, the frustration obvious in her voice, "you take over with him. I'm done."

Ray slid into the seat, taking the spoon. "Long day?"

"This one," she said putting her hand on Robbie's head as he returned to his drawing, "decided to help clean today and so the diaper pail was spilled all over the floor and this one," she said nodding toward the baby, "did not want to nap, so we're all kind of cranky."

Ray smiled. "You're almost done with maternity leave. You'll be back at work next month and the boys will be in daycare and then you will treasure every second with them."

"Remind me then. Right now I just need a half hour alone in a tub."

"Go. I got them," he reassured her.

She kissed him on the forehead and slid off down the hall. A door closed and a few seconds later he heard the water start to run.

"How about you, Sport?" he asked Robbie. "What are you drawing?"

"Don't look! It's almost done. Then I'll show you." Robbie put his arm over the drawing and continued working.

"OK, Lucas. So looks like it's just you and me. You wanna tell me why you don't want to eat?"

The baby opened his mouth and grunted. Ray took advantage of the moment to put some more carrots in. They mostly just ended up on the bib.

"OK, daddy. Here it is." Robbie held up the drawing.

"Wow. That's great!"

"Daddy, you're not really looking!"

He looked over at the drawing his older son held up. There was a house with five figures in it and one outside.

"Wow. That's great. Is that us?"

"Yup. This is you and mommy and me and Lucas." Ray noticed Lucas was bigger than he was.

"And who is this?" he pointed to the fifth figure. "That Galileo?"

"No," said Robbie. "This is Galileo." He pointed to the figure outside.

"Then who's this?" Ray asked.

"Wallace." Robbie started working on another drawing.

"Who's Wallace?"

"He's my friend."

"Oh?" Ray again focused on Robbie. "Where did you meet him?"

"He used to live next door."

"Where does he live now?"

"Dunno. He was in my room last night."

"Oh. Well tell him he should show up during the day."

"OK."

After dinner, while Ray washed the dishes Claudia got the kids ready for bed. They both said goodnight to Robbie and Ray read him *Goodnight Moon*. Robbie liked it because Ray always added all this information about the actual moon, which Robbie thought was really funny. Lucas was asleep in his room the second they set him in his crib.

Claudia and Ray sat down in the living room and before she could turn on the television he said, "Why didn't you tell me Robbie has an imaginary friend?"

She looked at him. "I didn't know he had one. When did this come up?"

"While you were in the bath. He says his friend 'Wallace' came over last night."

She smiled. "Well, he's at that age. And Lucas takes up so much of my time through the day I'm sure he is looking for some attention."

Ray said, "Well, why don't I take just him out on trick or treating on Saturday? You know, some father son time?

She looked sad, "Oh, but I bought Lucas the cutest little bee outfit."

Ray put his arm around her. "And you will put it on him, take a lot of pictures to send to friends and family, go to one or two of the neighbor's houses and then bring him back here. Besides, you have to give out the candy while I take Robbie around."

"I know, it's just you get to be fun dad and I get to take care of the baby and then give candy to other people's kids."

"And that's why I'm saying, let's go out as a family before trick or treating starts in earnest and then I'll take Robbie around. You can watch something spooky while giving out candy and when we get back, Robbie goes to bed then you get your treat."

"You better mean any leftover candy."

"No, I mean…" and he tickled her a little.

She squirmed but laughed softly. "Isn't that how we got two of them in the first place?"

"Speaking of which, let me know if Robbie tells you about Wallace."

She grew serious. "It's such an odd name. I wonder where he heard it."

"He said Wallace used to live next door."

"Really? I thought the Silvermans lived there since forever."

"It's an imaginary friend, Claud, he probably has wings and now lives on the moon."

They settled down and flipped through the channels. Finding nothing exciting, they settled on *The Innocents* on a classic movie channel.

* * * *

Later that night, Ray walked Galileo. As he walked past the Ridge-way place he looked all over, expecting to see the boy again. But he wasn't there.

Back and front doors locked and double checked. He checked both children, sleeping soundly. He walked into the bedroom where Claudia was already asleep. The baby monitor crackled as Lucas shifted in his crib in his sleep. Claudia had not shut the blinds. Ray walked over and reached for the cord. He stopped because he saw a faint light in the back-yard. It was the boy from last night. He stood in the backyard, staring at the house. He was looking further down, towards where the boys slept. Ray could see that the boy, who looked about ten, wore a dirty white shirt with a collar. His arms hung down by his side. His pants were a faded brown and ended just below the knee. Darker stockings or socks came out of the pants down to tied leather shoes, all of which faintly glowed. It was the boy's face, however, that made him shudder. The boy had thin brown hair in a bowl cut which made his face and forehead seem bigger. The boy's eyes were staring at the house in a mixture of fear and sadness.

The boy turned and looked at Ray. His expression suddenly emptied. It was a blank, emotionless stare.

Ray turned and ran out of the bedroom. Somewhere in the house Galileo began barking. Ray unlocked the back door and ran into the yard, which was empty. The boy was gone. Ray heard the baby start to cry, but ran to the fence on either side of the yard. No sign of the boy.

When he walked back in the house, Claudia was comforting Lucas, trying to get him to go back to sleep. Ray checked on Robbie, who had slept through it.

"What the hell?" Claudia whispered while dancing with the infant who was still quietly fighting sleep. "Was it a prowler?"

"No, that boy from last night was in our backyard!"

"What boy?"

"The one I told you about. From the Ridgefield's. He was in our yard. He was staring at the house."

"OK. So some kid was in the yard. You have to raise holy hell getting out there?"

"Sorry, sorry. I just…It's weird, right?"

She rolled her eyes and began to walk back into Lucas's room. "C'mon. Go to sleep for mommy. Daddy's crazy."

Ray went and brushed his teeth.

Claudia came back to bed and went right to sleep without saying anything.

Ray turned out the lamp on his side of the bed and laid there thinking. Maybe tomorrow he'd ask the neighbors if they'd seen the kid.

Just as he started to drift off, he heard the baby monitor crackle. Just Lucas moving in the crib.

"Soon."

He sat bolt upright in bed. He had heard a voice coming through the baby monitor. He jumped out of bed and ran to Lucas's room. The baby was fast asleep. The window was closed and locked. He knew he had heard a voice.

He woke up Claudia. "I heard a voice in Lucas's room."

She rubbed her eyes. "What?"

"I was falling asleep and I heard a voice over the baby monitor say something."

"You sure you didn't just dream it?"

"No," he insisted. "I was still awake."

"So you think the baby is just excited for Halloween?"

"I'm not joking here. It sounded like a woman or maybe a kid."

"And you saw a kid earlier tonight, so maybe the kid is now in the bedroom?"

"Look, I know you're not taking this seriously, but I did hear it."

"I believe you," she said slowly. "But could it be that you imagined it? I mean we've both been so stressed lately. Maybe your subconscious is doing something. I mean you're a scientist. What is the more likely scenario: we are now being haunted by a boy or you are stressed and seeing things in the dark and hearing things in your sleep."

"Well, when you put it that way…"

She kissed him. "Go back to sleep. Happy Halloween."

She fell asleep immediately. It took him a long time to drift off.

Friday

It took longer than usual to get going in the morning. Ray was running late for his nine o'clock lab at the university. He stopped in the kitchen to grab an energy bar and kissed Lucas on the head in his high chair. Robbie sat at the table, yawning, playing with his cereal.

"Up late, sport?" he asked as he kissed Robbie on the head.

"Wallace woke me up to play. I told him that you said to only come in the day time."

Ray smiled. "Good job, sport. And did he let you go back to bed?"

"He said he couldn't come during the day. He said to tell you that she's coming soon. Why is he so sad, Daddy?"

"What?"

"That's what he said. Can I watch TV?"

* * * *

Ray spent his morning lab in a haze. At noon he went to the faculty club for his regular last-Friday-of-the-month lunch with his cohort. There was a group of six of them that had started working at the college at the same time and after new faculty orientation had continued to meet for lunch despite differences in disciplines.

Today he sat next to Leilani McKenzie, who taught English. She dressed every bit the part of an English professor, wearing a black dress with glasses on a chain and turquoise jewelry to tie the ensemble together.

"Good lord, Ray, you look like you're plotting the overthrow of the kingdom. Or that Hamlet's father showed up and told you to get to work."

"What? Wait, what?"

"Oh dear, you're worse than the students. Is this the level of conversation I can expect from you today? 'Wait, what?'" She smiled.

"No, no. You, uh, you just landed a little close to home."

Her smile turned a little crooked. "What do you mean?"

Perhaps because Claudia didn't seem to realize anything was wrong or because he couldn't tell other professors in the school of sciences that he thought he had seen a ghost, it all came pouring out. The boy, Robbie's pronouncements, the baby monitor—all of it.

"He sounds like a 'Radiant Boy,'" she pronounced.

"What's that?"

"Old English ghost story, Victorian, really. It's the ghost of a young boy killed by his mother. You know Victorians and childhood. If you see a Radiant Boy it's a portent of doom," she cackled.

"So the boy was probably killed by his mother?" Ray asked.

"That's how the story goes. And in his fear and terror at mommy doing him in, his little soul becomes a Radiant Boy. But don't tell me you believe it."

"But you just said he sounds like this Victorian ghost!"

"Yes, but I am an English teacher. I give the kids *Wuthering Heights*. I thought you scientists didn't go for ghosts."

He considered this for a second. "I did just tell a class that the rise of the Pleiades at sunset meant the veil between this world and the next is at its thinnest."

"Wonderful! We'll make a poet of you, yet. But seriously, are you sure it's not just neighborhood kids punking you or whatever they call it?"

"Probably. You said if I see him it's a portent of doom?"

"Not quite. A Radiant Boy is an omen that something awful will happen, but a Radiant Boy is not a danger in and of himself."

"So I don't have to worry about Robbie's imaginary friend kidnapping him or killing him?"

"Are we really having this conversation? Thanksgiving Break cannot come soon enough."

"Happy Halloween, Leilani."

"Stop worrying, Ray. Four year olds are discovering imagination. Rather than fear it, enjoy it."

* * * *

That night when he went home, he asked Robbie again about his friend.

"His name is Wallace. He's nine. I'm four, but we're friends. He comes to my room at night and tells me we could be friends forever. But his mom won't let him play with other kids."

"Is his mom mean?"

"Yeah. He says she yells a lot and hits him."

"Robbie, look at me. Is anyone hitting you? Is there someone being mean to you?"

"Sometimes mommy yells at me."

"But no one else is being mean to you?"

"You're funny, daddy."

* * * *

That night Ray walked Galileo and saw nothing. He stood at the back door looking out into the yard, but the boy never showed up. Maybe it was just Halloween fun for some jerk kid.

Saturday

The next morning ray was cutting his lawn and saw his neighbor Arthur Silverman out doing the same. He went over.

"Hi Art, how are you?"

"Not bad. Damn kids are gonna come by tonight. Little beggars looking for a handout. Damn candy gets more expensive every year."

"I know what you mean. You must have seen a lot of Halloweens. How long you been in this house, Art?"

"Jesus, I grew up in this house. My father bought this place back when the war started. That's WW 2, none of this recent bullshit."

"Wow. That's a long time. Did your father build this place?"

"Naw. Before that it was owned by a Mrs. Keinstern."

"She live here alone?"

Suddenly Art got suspicious. "Why do you want to know?"

"Just interested." Ray decided to take a gamble. "I heard she killed her kid."

Art started at that. "Where the hell you hear that? One of the neighbors?"

"I forget. I just heard that some boy was killed here."

"Jesus, I haven't thought about him in years. She had a boy who died tragically. Fell asleep and never woke up. Husband died in the war or something. That's why she moved. Wanted to leave the scene of so much tragedy and loneliness, I guess."

"So she didn't kill him?"

"Hell if I know, that was all before I was born, sometime in the late thirties. Wow, Ray, you picked the right day to ask me about the kid who died in my house. Happy Halloween." With that, he turned, went inside and slammed the door.

Ray thought it all a bit weird. If tonight was a night when the veil was thin, well, as a scientist he figured he could take reasonable precautions.

He went through the day in a haze. Then it was dinner time. Robbie was beside himself with excitement. He was going to dress up like an astronaut. The sky had turned all ash-gray and orange when Ray looked outside. Ten minutes later and he knew the Pleiades had come up, though with Santa Monica's light pollution and smog you could not see them yet.

Claudia got Lucas into the bee costume and Robbie dressed in his space suit. Ray grabbed a flashlight. They went to the Ridgeway's first, where Maryann Ridgeway cooed over Lucas and told Robbie he looked like a real astronaut and gave him a full size Milky Way. Then they went to the Silverman's. Mrs. Silverman told both boys they were darling and threw a handful of Tootsie Rolls into Robbie's sack.

"Hey, Ray, look what I got for you." Art came down the stairs with an old cardboard box. "After our conversation today, I went into my dad's stuff and found this."

He handed Ray an old faded photograph. It showed the front of Art's house before the addition and the rose bushes in front. Standing on the porch was a stern-looking woman in a black dress holding the hand of a young boy. The boy was the same one he had seen twice now. Ray flipped it over. Written on the back in faded ink was "Mother and Wallace, '38."

"I guess my father found this after Mrs. Keinstern moved away. This is the boy that died in his sleep. So sad, to lose one at such an age."

"Thanks, Art. We have to be going."

Claudia looked at him. "No need to rush, Ray, we don't have to be rude."

"No, no, lots of houses to visit tonight. Happy Halloween, Art. Happy Halloween, Irma."

Ray shuffled his family back to their house.

"Daddy, I want to trick or treat!"

"Not tonight, honey. I heard that trick or treating had been cancelled."

"No it hasn't! You're lying!" Robbie pulled away from him.

Claudia grabbed his arm. "What are you doing, Ray?"

"We're not going out and we're not answering the door tonight, OK? We're going to have family fun!"

"But I want to go trick or treating!" Robbie whined, pulling at his father's arm away from the house, towards the street.

"Well you're not! So get used to the idea! Now everyone inside!"

Robbie froze. Ray had never yelled at him like that before. Then he ran through the front door crying all the way to his room.

Claudia carried Lucas in. "I don't know what has gotten into you but that was uncalled for."

He grabbed her shoulder and turned her back to face him. "The boy in the photo, the one Art showed me? The one he said had died? That's the kid I've been seeing."

"Oh, I do not have time for this. I have two screaming children in the house right now, I do not need a third. Come on, Robbie. I'll take you out. Daddy is just in a bad mood." She glared at Ray. "I'm putting Daddy on time out and we'll go get some candy."

He glared back. Then whispered, "Fine. I will take the boy out. But only to the houses nearby. We will be back in half an hour. I don't want you opening this door tonight and he is spending the night in our room."

"Who are you?" she asked. "My husband would never allow himself to get this spooked over something stupid. Think about the example you are setting for your son! Now stop scaring him."

Ignoring her, he went to Robbie's room. "I'm sorry I yelled at you, sport. Sometimes Daddy gets a little weirded out. Come on, let's go trick or treating."

"Mean it?" Robbie asked through his tears.

"Of course. Now get your helmet and sack and let's get some candy."

After half an hour of trick or treating Ray had to admit he had over-reacted. The night was a normal Halloween. Kids in costumes were running around having fun. He allowed himself to relax and enjoy Robbie enjoying the holiday. After going through the whole block they headed home.

Robbie was thrilled with all the candy and was not disappointed when Claudia told him he could only eat two pieces before bed. Ray had relaxed, but still insisted that Robbie and Lucas sleep in their room with them. Claudia knew not to fight him on this one. He pulled the crib into their bedroom and placed it between the bed and the bathroom.

They did not speak before bed. Robbie already passed out on the bed between them before they even got in, Lucas sleeping soundly in his crib.

"Thanks for humoring me," Ray said. "I know this is all silly. But I'm freaking out that this dead boy is talking to our son and wants them to be friends forever. Tomorrow everything will be fine."

"It better be," Claudia warned.

He drifted off, feeling somewhat relieved, hearing his son's measured breathing in the bed next to him. He did not know if a few minutes or a few hours had past when something woke him.

"It's time," said a voice.

His blood ran cold. He leapt from the bed and ran to the window. It was closed. He turned back to face the room. The bedroom door was open, but he heard nothing else. On the floor in the doorway sat Lucas's blanket. The crib was empty.

Claudia's scream broke through his thoughts. "Where's the baby, Ray? Where's Lucas? What have you done?"

Then he heard his older son, now his only son's sleepy voice from the bed. "Wallace said he tried to warn you, Daddy. Now his mommy has Lucas."

"What is he talking about, Ray?" Claudia screamed as he stared at his son.

"He says his mommy wanted a new boy to raise. She will be Lucas's mommy now. Can Wallace come and live with us?"

Ray sank to the floor in horror as his wife clung to the crib and screamed. In the doorway, the Radiant Boy turned away sadly and wept silent tears.

▲

Ex Arca Sepulcrali
by Wade German

A music comes across the tombs,
A supplication, weird and low;
Above, the blood moon brightly looms,
Casting a hellish, crimson glow
On sepulchres of amethyst
Engulfed by greenish, glowing mist.

Around the ancient monuments,
Unholy song has exorcised
The sleep of those in cerements—
Shadowy apparitions rise
And glide beneath the blood-red moon
To heed a witch's eerie croon.

The Whisperer in the Woods
by Peter Schranz

Emperor Lothair I died in the November of 835 at the age of forty from a knot that had grown in his body. His four sons fitted his bald, gray head with a garland of oak leaves, yielding to that archaic tradition whose meaning they had not been taught. His four daughters were sent to a convent; the emperor's brothers had removed their noses so that they would not marry.

Ten thousand Franks attended the funeral of the emperor and they circled the catafalque for hours. His four sons divided his things and lands and the principle parts of Italy and the empire fell to Louis his eldest. Lothair II took a new place called after him Lotharingia, Charles took Provence, and Carloman the bastard of his father's mistress Doda took an oaken case of beads.

Carloman's brothers began immediately to quarrel with each other and Ermengarde the wife of his father came with ministers and gifts to his mother's bower.

"My darling and esteemed young lord," she greeted him hungrily as he paged through a fragile book in his room. He had no throne on which to greet her so he laid down his book and stood. "I did not realize you read, bright Carloman."

"I am looking at the pictures."

"Very well." Ermengarde folded her hands together. "You are not beclouded I trust about your poor brothers' plight."

"I have no brothers," Carloman said, leaning at the window recess.

The wavering fires of tallow candles lit Ermengarde's face as she came nearer to him. She placed her hand on that part of her flaxy dress under which lay her heart. "I have a gift for you, little pea."

"I don't need another gift. The beads were quite enough."

"But that was not a gift," Ermengarde said. Carloman nearly believed that he had truly confused her, that she was not still weaving an insult. "It was your birthright.

"I have a terribly fine gift for you to have, if only you'll do a thing for me and for my eldest and dearest son, who wears his spear to the shaft against Lothair and Charles."

"What thing?"

"Would you first not prefer to know what I want to give you? Such a selfless young lord is this Carloman the Pious, and so fitting a friend to the Holy Roman Emperor." He waited for her to continue, or to push him out the window. "Consider whether you would like to be the King of Burgundy."

"I will not consider it. I am not eligible. Do you think bastards are fools like the head-knocked children?"

"But you have not rebelled against the Holy Emperor, who Sergius our Father in Rome himself crowned. You and Louis are the only good sons of your father." Ermengarde drew closer, drew to the window recess, snaked her hand around Carloman's waist. "But you must bring something to my son in the north of his country.

"My ministers carry with them a great and saintly treasure from Milan, and if you would carry it the rest of the way, the defeat of Louis by his confused and foolish brothers will be impossible."

"This treasure will make it this way?"

"Come with me, Carloman the Pious."

Ermengarde led Carloman to the chambers she had taken where two stout ministers laid across a table a long item concealed in linen. "Remove it," she said, sitting where a boiled boar's leg on a silver plate steamed.

Carloman swept aside the folds of linen like curtains from a window. A crosier of oak in the shape of a cross waited under them. "Is this what your son wants?"

"Yes, darling," said Ermengarde, whose lips glistened. "The staff of Saint Ambrose which brigands took from Milan and Louis's people found again in the lairs of Lothair. Return it to its city, watch Louis with the good will of the saint rout his poor brothers, and do what you wish with Burgundy."

"And why won't you bring it there?"

"Because the woods are not safe for a woman like me."

Ermengarde had brought with her so many of her ministers that they outnumbered the few left to Carloman and his mother. He did not want to go and leave her alone with Ermengarde but she had not come to ask for but to demand his help, and she did not let him stay. He went to say goodbye to his mother but he was not allowed by Ermengarde's ministers to see her and so he said goodbye to the cook instead, who had boiled meat for the monks of Turin for so much of his life that he'd learned to read.

Carloman took his beads and he took the crosier and he went south on a hinny. Nobody in the lands of his brothers knew his face and he was once confronted by a cutpurse in the woods, who he scared off with the staff. He thought he heard the staff rattling as he brandished it above the head of the cutpurse, and he thought the same when the hinny bucked over stony paths, but the beads rattled without pause and he did not think terribly hard on the subject.

He stopped at dusk one day at an inn to fodder his hinny. Quiet and darkness had entered the inn before he came, and a smell like that of dead, wet moths drifted from it as he approached. A terrible old man lurched from the entranceway and fell at the hinny's hooves. Boils encrusted his nape.

* * * *

Carloman hurried from the inn and found nearby in the woods more who died of boils on their necks and mouths and beneath their hilly clothing.

He camped far from the bodies in the woods that night. He had never started a fire and could not do so then. He held the crosier tight to his chest as he wore out the darkness. In the direction of the inn he heard animals grunting and rooting and he heard things very close to him sliding through the underbrush. His hinny panicked and fled and Carloman never saw her again. In the morning he walked south and found another collection of little huts and little people with boils lying on the ground, chewed and bitten by hungry things no longer present.

On his knees, a second and ghastly-faced cutpurse on the road to Milan searched through the pockets and felt the breasts of a dead young woman. Carloman did not spy one boil on her flesh though the cutpurse had loosed much of her clothing, but a great long gash had opened her neck. The woods were lousy with fiends seeking to loot the dead and the alone. The cutpurse rose and flashed a long, used knife at Carloman who he mistook for a pilgrim. Carloman again conscripted the staff of Saint Ambrose this time for the purpose of striking down the ghoulish toad.

Carloman hit him in the head so cruelly that one of the arms of the cross broke off: it did not fall from the shaft altogether, but limped from it, jointed by some soft hinge.

This second cutpurse Carloman killed, his forehead flattened. He fell to his knees and from there to the dirt, unable to bear the many things he suddenly bore.

The strike had loosened not just the arm of the crosier. Two boards of oak had been joined together in the item, and they had become jostled from each other. Carloman took care not to further damage the crosier as he escaped from the dead young woman and her dead murderer.

By a hollow oak deeper in the woods he laid the crosier down and, unable to stop himself, separated the loose long boards as though opening a book. In an empty space in the intersection of the cross lay a curled and leathery hand, brown and sluggish its skin, long and thin its nails. Splayed, the thumb was in the cross's left arm, the long fingers in the top, and the short fingers in the right. Carloman clapped shut the two halves of the crosier and stuffed them up into the hollow oak.

Though now weaponless Carloman was not waylaid again before he came to Milan. With difficulty he entered the city which Louis had barricaded to prepare for Lothair, who approached from the Alps. Ten bearded sentries stopped Carloman and one of them held him by his hair before he could dangle strings of beads before them. This inspired the sentries to offer him succor, and they led Carloman under the meurtrieres and hoardings and machicolations of the walls.

Louis and the archbishop Angilbert awaited Carloman at the Basilica of Saint Ambrose before the crypt where his bones were laid.

"My city belongs to you, sweet brother," Louis said. Chain cowls held his and the archbishop's heads in place and Louis had done without his circlet. He did not see the crosier with Carloman, but curiosity did not yet darken what hope and relief made bright. "You could not have come at a more urgent moment. Lothair approaches and will be here in only days, but you have come, and you have brought the crosier of Saint Ambrose back to him."

"Emperor," Carloman said, "Listen to my sorry tale. I was left to defend myself from a vulture-feeder with the treasure that you seek: it cracked open and within I found a withered hand, a devil's tool." Louis listened, breathing deeply. "While in your brother's lands a dreadful demon must have impregnated this staff with the black heart I found inside of it. I hid it in an oak in the woods beyond your city." Carloman waited to be congratulated, but Louis did not yet speak. "I saved this place from a great evil, brother."

"Go with the archbishop now," Louis said, "Go with the ten sentries and retrieve it. If he fails, your Grace, have his throat beaten for lies."

Chain surrounded the archbishop and the sentries, but not Carloman, who at the point of spears followed him to the oak tree in which he'd hid the crosier.

"Don't you believe me?" Carloman asked when they discovered that someone had emptied the oak again. "I left it in here—but only because of the witchcraft within."

"You devil," said the archbishop Angilbert, "you left the crosier of Saint Ambrose for the brigands in these woods to take as weapons with which to waylay. Moreover you have separated the benedictory hand of Saint Ambrose forever from all Christendom. It is no surprise, Carloman, that you are a bastard." The sentries surrounded him and knelt him on the ground. One, with a string of beads entwined in his armor, removed his scabbard from his belt, while the others craned Carloman's head back by the hair.

The sentry struck him in the throat with his scabbard and Carloman shrieked. He did it again; Carloman's second cry was weaker. The sentry beat Carloman until he could no longer made noise at all, but writhed on the ground where he could no longer smell the smell of rotten wood and boil skin.

He tried to sob but could not, nor could he speak, but he heard one of the sentries cry out and point at something on the ground.

"It's the hand," he said, "the cursed hand!"

"Were you not listening to me?" the archbishop said, "That is the hand of Saint Ambrose that you insult."

"And here," another said, squatting by the oak tree, "teeth. Back teeth."

Carloman pretended to be dead; he could not be sure that they wanted him alive. The sentries found altogether fourteen teeth.

"You didn't say anything about teeth," one of the bright sentries said to the archbishop.

"They too were housed in the reliquary that now is lost. They are the molars of Saint Ambrose."

"How many molars did he have?" the sentry asked. Several others pushed their cheeks back with their fingers to count their own.

"He had fourteen of them, one for each station of the cross. We have found them all, so we will return to the city with them." The archbishop and the sentries left Carloman in the woods. He lay there on the ground, breathing hastily and trying to swallow. At each attempt his poor broken throat drafted every muscle in his neck to assist in the task, but even then he did not always succeed and his mouth filled with blood and drool that he had to drop through his lips. He feared death in Milan and in the outlying country where everyone had died by boils or murder and so he crept in the empty oak himself and wept silently and waited to die in peace.

A day passed and he hadn't died, and where before he felt as though a stone were caught in his throat, now it felt more like a cork. He tried to speak to himself but still could not, which was for the best, as two brigands passed by the oak, singing and play-fighting with the two halves of the crosier. They could have killed him with the halves, but one got the chance only to hit him in the face when they found him hiding in the tree.

"We'll take what you have," said the one with the long greasy hair and the pretty blue eyes. Carloman could not speak. If he could, he would have said that he had nothing, which was true, but not true enough to avoid a head cut. The second, the one with the clean clothing and the broken teeth, struck Carloman in the forehead. It was only half the crosier, and the brigand was far less well fed than Carloman and his strike could only do a daze.

The brigands were run down by the horsemen of Lothair as they approached the city from the dark of the woods. Hooves snapped the molested remains of the broken oaken reliquary and the skinny bodies of the brigands, and would have the body of Carloman had he not been silent and dazed in the oak hollow.

More horsemen swept by him, and men on foot, and things on wheels, but Carloman did not see because blood crept over his eyes. For the rest of the day he heard the strange sounds of the fight: the hard, alarming smacks of arrows entering bodies, the squeals; the cries of grown, bearded, German men begging not to be killed, weeping as they died, vomiting, going mad.

Few saw Carloman in the tree, and those who did thought he was dead. There were dead, hacked men at the walls of Milan who looked less dead than Carloman in the hollow.

Lothair had come not in days as Louis had explained but hours, and so was the length of the fight, rather than months. Soon he heard nothing in the direction of Milan but perhaps some final moans, or wind. Carloman rubbed blood from his eyelids and saw enough to emerge from the woods and wander toward Milan.

The ground became marshy before the walls of the city and a panicked bowman from a tower asked Carloman what his name was. His throat had swollen and he could not breathe very well, and he certainly could not talk, but he raised his hands in the air. He thought to himself that he really was no longer dazed, but had been telling himself otherwise so he wouldn't have to think. Now Carloman was thinking and could not understand where he went wrong.

They opened the gates and Carloman walked through them, imagining he'd be struck down.

The bowman, quivering, hooded in leather the color of that secret relic's skin, greeted him at the gates. "Are you Louis's or Lothair's?" Carloman shrugged and pointed at his big throat.

"You're mute," said the bowman. "You're not armed." Carloman shrugged again. "You look more like a swineherd than a fighter." Carloman didn't shrug, he pointed at the blackening slug-mucus that covered his face.

"I'll take you to the well," the bowman said, "Your head is drenched in sword-water."

The bowman led Carloman through the city, which appeared to have been neither captured nor preserved. Woodsmen had been called to strip hauberks from the dead. Lonely horses snuffed and leaned trembling against the walls of buildings. At the well Carloman slapped stinging nose-benumbing November well water onto his face and it reformed the gore back into blood. He revealed liplike swellings on his forehead between which a tongue of crust stuck. His breath was easier; he'd unplugged blood from his nose, but he still could not speak.

The bowman followed Carloman carefully as he returned to the church of Saint Ambrose, where before his crypt the archbishop knelt. "I found a mute," the bowman said, weaving about behind Carloman. A little glass reliquary stood atop the crypt and housed fourteen molars, and on the floor two shrouded, not-odorless corpses lay.

"This is Carloman, good bowman," the archbishop said, "son of Lothair the first the king of Italy and the Emperor of the Romans, and of—of his mistress Doda.

"Listen to me, Carloman," the archbishop said, shooing away the bowman, "Your brothers Louis and Lothair have died and Milan belongs to neither of them." The archbishop peeled the shrouds from the faces of the two bodies of Louis and Lothair. Carloman wished to say that he would take Milan but he could not. "And a message from your mother has come." The archbishop from the sleeve in his mail removed a page of vellum and offered it to Carloman, who shrugged.

"Can you not read?" Carloman shrugged again, this time wondering if she dictated her letter to the cook, or if not when she herself had learned to read. The archbishop read, "My dear son Carloman, by the grace of God I have lived in your absence, but your father's wife remains here with her ministers and will not leave, as she is awaiting orders from your father's son the Emperor who means to overtake and use our home for a defense of Milan which your father's son Lothair means to acquire. I suspect that she instructed you to leave here but she tells me very little and will not let me go. Please return to me at once. Your mother."

All the bones but the naked toothy skull of Saint Ambrose were clad in white waves of vestments; his hands were covered in delicate gloves of white and gold. A third hand whose fingers had been bent in the shape of a cross lay upon his pectoral cross. Carloman pointed at it.

"It is not his," Angilbert said, "His two hands are on him. That is why it did not preserve my lord. It is the hand of a criminal, no doubt. A curse upon it." Carloman wanted to explain that Saint Ambrose had three hands, one for each person of the Trinity, but his neck was too busy relearning to swallow. He wanted to explain that if it was not a relic of Saint Ambrose then it should not be in the company of his bones, but he pointed at the hand and stepped closer to the archbishop.

"Would you take it from me? Is the son of the emperor a moon-guest?" Archbishop Angilbert, Carloman surmised, meant to tell those who wanted the hand that it was worthless, and those who wanted to see the hand that seeing it was worth a very dear sum.

The archbishop had no weapon, but mail weighed him down. Carloman took the hand from atop the bones of Saint Ambrose and fled the crypt. The archbishop momentarily attempted a hopeless pursuit, despairing at the stairs.

Carloman left Milan to he who wanted it. He could not find a horse still living who had not been driven by what it had seen in battle to hate men. He walked from the fetid and barren city and into the woods, where the intermittent smell of boils replaced the pervasive smell of kill. To avoid all closeness to huts and inns was to avoid closeness to that old smell.

Once in a while Carloman felt the hand where in his tunic it was hidden.

By the time he reached the home of his mother he could speak, but only in the merest, hoarsest croak. She spun flax by her window when she saw him walk from the woods, but even though she'd dropped the spindle so carelessly that her threads unskeined she was not let from her bower to greet him.

Instead, as he for the first time since his injury pointed his chin above his throat to make himself look happy and victorious, his father's wife Ermengarde greeted him, saying "My dear and righteous boy, you must have seen such glorious battle as to return so infirm, for though your body has become dark with wounds, I see your soul through it, bright as the shining edge of a blade. Do tell me what's become of my Emperor."

She came close to him and put her arms on his shoulders and her fingers close to his throat. His hoarse whisper entered her ear: "Emperor Louis repelled his brother. In celebration he forgot to send word. We were far away from need of help."

"It so worried me that I received no news."

"I would have Burgundy."

"Your brother Charles has unfortunately claimed it," Ermengarde whispered back, though her voice had been unmolested.

"I do not have a brother," he answered quietly. "But tonight we'll feast and await your victorious son."

Ermengarde was happy to empty the larder of the bastard and his mother. The kitchen sat in the outer ward and was built on the burned remains of the old kitchen. The skinny little cook was twenty or so and had tried and failed to teach Carloman to read. While Ermengarde stayed with them he put meaty boiled bones of boar with currants on a plate in a basket and tied it to the thread of linen Doda dropped from her bower window at night.

"I have something for you," Carloman whispered to the cook, whose lips currants had dyed, "an ingredient." From his tunic he removed the bog-brown hand with the compass rose fingers.

"Not enough to last us the month, I'm afraid," the cook said. He looked wearily at the hand, hunger clouding an immediate, grotesque reaction.

"Wrong," whispered Carloman. "Stew it and feed the stew to my father's wife and her ministers, and you will see how bountiful the larder becomes. Do not remove the bones from the stew, but do not reveal them to my father's wife, and do not serve my mother tonight at all."

Carloman sought his mother, but her chambers had been locked, and Ermengarde and her ministers did not know where he could find the key, nor did they seem at all to feel any urgency on the question.

"Brave pious victor," Ermengarde's minister entreated Carloman as he sat by his mother's door, "My lady begs you come and eat with us."

"I will not eat until I see my mother," said Carloman.

"Perhaps you will find the key where you lie and weep," the minister guessed.

They had not fed her in Carloman's absence; only the cook had, and he had done so furtively. Carloman had not heard his mother but he knew someone was within her bower eating and sending down what the cook sent up.

Carloman awoke in the cold stony corridor, aching and awash with drool his neck in sleep could not manage. In the gray other-wall light of dawn Carloman found the ministers and Ermengarde still largely on their chairs in the dining hall. One minister had fallen into the lap of another at the next chair; one had submerged his face in his stew. Ermengarde had over the course of the night slid down her chair until her back was on the seat and her knees were on the floor. Carloman rifled through the folds of their clothing and found the key to his mother's bower in the pouch of the very first of Ermengarde's servants to whom he inquired about it.

Doda was spinning when Carloman greeted her. She leaped up to embrace him and threw her distaff out the window.

"I imagine we are in need of a war chest in which to bury your father's wife," Doda said as she hugged her son. He spied from the window the bowls, the cauldron, and the cook, digging.

"What is he doing?" Carloman whispered.

"He has a cauldron that is no longer fit for use," Doda said, "A cauldron, he said, and bowls."

Carloman went by horse to a carpenter and his son who built him a dozen coffins in a morning. He returned by horse and cart with a pyramidal load, where his brother Charles, sweating and white, waited with

Doda and the cook over the yawning grave into which the cook had thrown the cauldron and the bowls.

"Your mother has explained to me about what became of my mother," said Charles, who turned his crown in his hands, who was alone and without ministers of his own. "And the archbishop of Milan has written to me about my brothers and about—" Charles pointed at the cauldron, but did not explain what he was looking at. "I have never wanted quarrel with you and I mourn my mother's choice to cross you and lead you into our quarrels."

"I have certainly served my purpose though, my dear father's son," Carloman whispered. "Now you are Emperor of the Romans."

"What did my mother promise you?"

"Burgundy," said Doda.

"He deserves more than that," Charles said to her, begged. His gaze had not risen yet from the hole the cook had dug. "Would you forgive me if you were to take Lotharingia? My brother gave it that name but he is dead and you may of course call it what you wish."

"It will keep its name and I will be king of it," Carloman whispered.

In the end Carloman was the hoarse, whispering king of Lotharingia, which was larger and more populous than Burgundy, and though Charles was Emperor of the Romans he never lifted a finger against his father's son. Charles knew that under the ground that Doda's bower window overlooked was buried a cauldron, and that burnt to the bottom of the cauldron were the bones of a hand that could not be scraped or scoured loose.

▲

Sweet Oblivion
by Andrew Darlington

They'd killed him once, they'd killed him twice, they'd killed him three times. But he refused to die. This time, when they kill him, they must be certain he stays dead.

"It seems you're not being entirely truthful with us here" says the interrogating officer. "You were drinking Mr Hemming."

"A Bud. One bottle. Well within the limit." Just a suggestion of hesitation hovering between each quiet pronouncement.

He listens with such calm detachment, Dom wonder if he's listening at all. And when he does betray reaction it's a barely disguised cynicism. "But you were drinking. Something you've had problems with before. Let's say, you've not been entirely truthful with your employer, have you…?" Isn't DCI Plod supposed to say "sir"? or do they drop that courtesy for low-life's?

"Yeah, yes—OK, hands up. But none of that means anything here. What I saw, what I did, had nothing to do with any of that. You must believe this."

"There's no must about what I believe, or choose to disbelieve. Speculation doesn't enter into this. And there's a question of credibility. You were drinking. It's in your bloodstream. You've got a history of substance abuse, although you lied about that to get your license. Which, of course, is another offence. You're in deep deep shit, no two ways about that."

The DCI pauses, as if waiting for another chip to be inserted into his brain-slot, and triggered.

* * * *

One step at a time. First step is to find some kind of regular work. A discipline, a framework to structure time around, to build up from. What comes next will work its way out from that point. Not much of a plan. But a plan. A structured program. One step at a time. Mr Sharma's not too discriminating. He needs drivers. He doesn't do background checks too thoroughly. He can't be arsed to go through all that inconvenience. It's not strictly necessary to lie, not exactly, just to be a tad economical with the truth. At worst, what he pays brings in enough to keep him in booze.

Until this. He's strayed into someone else's nightmare. This derails everything. This flushes all those flimsy plans down the pan.

"Are you happy with the way your life's worked out?" says the bar-fly with the e-cig. The smell of stale liquor lingers.

"Are you suggesting something is wrong with my life?" A shrug as old as time. Social drinking turns to need. And need becomes habit. His skin itches. And beneath the skin, it itches too.

"See her, she used to work in a Florida bar." He indicates the girl behind the bar. "Says the astronauts used to call around. She once served drinks to Buzz Aldrin. He was not a heavy tipper. Can you believe that? She tells me this stuff. Why disbelieve her? Things aren't always exactly what they seem. Some things go deeper than surface appearances. I look at you, I recognize things. Me and you both, we've waded through heavy crap and come out the other side."

"I've never met a rocket-jockey. Not knowingly. I've been to some pretty strange places in inner space though. You recognized that right."

"You know something, Dom? I'll tell you. This is the golden age. The best of all possible worlds. Sure, your life's gone down the shit-ter. But you've got plastic in your wallet. You're here and now, in this comfortably upholstered bar with a comprehensive range of the exotic intoxicants of the world within reach. Enjoying the company of good companions. A snooker table. A Hi-Def TV with the sound down. Kara-oke Friday nights. The stuff of gluttons and sybarites. It could be worse. And I've got something in a wrap for you to make it even better. You interested…?"

"Every culture in the world dances. Every culture in the world uses intoxicants. It's what makes us human. You know, my wife texted me. I'm on my way to see her. I need something to help." Liquor is the soundtrack, you don't see it as a downer, instead, its the antigravity that lifts you. That enables a degree of functionality, even when you're crippled inside.

* * * *

There's a dead TV in the garden, tuned to Proxima Centauri. It's that kind of estate. The situation is awkward. This house had once been his home too. Until it all went wrong. She admits him coldly. Her face withdrawn, blonde hair combed back into a plait that hangs over one shoulder. He looks around, unsure how to react. As though he's the inter-loper, the salesman pushing solar panels, cavity-wall insulation or triple-glazing. A resented presence. There are photos on the mantelpiece. But none of him. The palms of his hands are moist. He feels the need for the wrap thrust deep in his pocket.

"Do I get coffee, Rachel? You texted me. You wanted to see me."

"Not me. Not exactly. Someone is looking for you. A Mr Matsu, to do with an incident. Something you were involved in. You know what this means? They traced you through the taxi firm. You no longer have the right to reference this address."

He nods. "I know. I had to quote a place of permanent residence. Transients don't have such a thing. But my name's still on the joint tenancy agreement. It's a small, but harmless lie." If this was a grittier more socio-realist sequence in a tele-Soap, all this dialogue would be scripted. The pauses and hesitations rehearsed for calculated effect. The director would want a shot of pathos next, a futile gesture for reconciliation. "I thought maybe you wanted me for something else. We were good together once" he manages weakly.

"We're not travelling back in time. I refuse to go back in time on this. I need more than just good. Good is not good enough. Sometimes just being there is better. Dumb boring reliability. I mean, you haven't asked. You haven't even bloody asked."

He looks guiltily at the ceiling. Their daughter is up there, in her room. Severely impaired motor skills. Unable to speak, or feed herself, due to cerebral palsy caused by oxygen starvation during the forceps-delivery birthing process. "How is she?"

"She has name. Clare is the same. She'll always be the same. She'll never grow up, she'll never leave home, she'll never be any different from the way she was five years ago when you got the hell out."

"I'm not a bad man."

"No Dom. You're just weak, easily led. This is important. But oh no, you just had to call off for liquid courage first. Didn't you? Didn't you? You think I can't stink it on you?"

"It happens."

"Sure, it happens. No matter what you imagine—somewhere, at some time, it's happened to someone. You think I care about that?" her painted nails are tipped with flame. He sees the tiredness in her eyes that belies the softness of her voice. The defensive hurt. He'd put those things there. The defiant strength is all hers. He'd never been able to match that.

"What does he want, this creep that's looking for me?"

"Listen, and listen good. He left a skype address. That's all he told me. I've delivered the message. Now it's done. Goodbye Dom."

One day you wake, and you're conscious of change. Everything you knew is broken. Nothing is intact. Like a hang-over without the pleasure of the booze the night before. You're aware of the world in which you live, but also conscious of another. Another plane of existence you can feel around you, but can't define. As though you've stepped over the event-horizon into a parallel continuum. It's almost visual, but not quite, something you glimpse from the corner of your eye, but can't focus in time. When you look, it's not there, there's nothing. Yet you still half-see it.

* * * *

Sitting cross-legged on Brighton shingle watching the endless lap of the tide, thinking of cosmic energies and thinking of Japanese poet Matsuo Bashō. Starlight roaring in your veins, starlight pulsing in your brain. While chemicals melt it all into fluctuating flux. The setting sun is a burnished drop of gold hovering just above the sill of the world. What is life but what our senses tell us? There's no way of getting outside your own head. So you sit, working your way through it all, as Basho would have done. He'd have reduced it down to three precise lines of text.

Then there's another light. Brighter than the sun. Washing ripples of fire across the shingle. It's all so highly contrasty, it's scary. Your nerves are cracking. Your hands so tight-clenched your fingernails break and puncture half-moons in the flesh of your palm. The sound of weight applied to, and settling upon loose stones. Causing a shivering trickle of pebbles. And two dark figures above you, black against the whirling sky.

"Dom Hemming. Arise." You rise, in awe of it all. They pace, one on either side of you. Their touch is ice. Their words are riddles. Their words are conundrums, denser than a Bashō haiku. You follow. The scrunch of shingle coming peripherally, as if from the pace of someone else's feet. Along the seafront people are slow-moving, elderly couples, some people walking dogs, joggers wearing iPods, families laughing and talking. How is it they can't see what's going on? How can they be so unaware? The black figures must be operating an invisibility shield, a force-field that disrupts the passage of light. Clever stuff. Advanced technology.

Their craft thrums softly at the kerbside, as though straining, eager for the off. It swallows you into its softly enveloping upholstery. It moves forward as the drive is engaged, then accelerates into smooth motion with a low hiss. It feels strange. It feels exhilarating. Even with eyes closed the images still flicker by on the inside of your retina like a high-definition movie, with full CGi embellishments. Sometimes it gets difficult to parse out what's real and what is overlaid effect. You've seen these movies, you know. It seems like no time at all that the craft ellipses in towards their station. Back on your feet, gravity seems lighter. You take big ponderous strides.

They use a swipe-card, and the metal gate slams down once you're inside. We are in a clinical white room. We sit in a close circle. Me, and the two others.

"He's totally loaded." The one sitting to my left is looking at me, but he's speaking to the one sitting to my left. "We'll get nothing. This is pointless."

"On the contrary. Because he's so out of it he's incapable of telling fiberoonies. Now's the best chance to get what we need."

"Tell us." Speaking to me now. "Tell us what you saw."

"I already told it all to the police, they didn't believe me."

"So tell us, exactly what occurred. We could prove more sympathetic. They were in your cab. You picked up two men. They are in your taxi. You were attacked. There are gunshots from an overtaking car. You took evasive action."

"I've seen it in those big dumb action-movies. The road is a white scar. You hang a sharp turn, wrong way onto a one-way strip. The bad guys aren't supposed to follow. Well, it shakes them. It certainly shakes them, but they do follow us. By then I've gained an advantage. On-coming trucks and cars are spinning this way and that way, a gravitational dance, blaring horns, yelling, giving me the finger. There's an underpass, illuminated. We're hurtling down its curve. The bad guys in hot pursuit. Traffic howling around us in a series of random and unlikely misses. But we're doing it. Once we get out the other side we can connect with the inner orbital, we can lose them... but it doesn't work out that way. An oncoming coach fails to clear, it clips us, clobbers us hard, shatters into us, stoves in the front wing, wheels spin and spark. A shock physical impact, bouncing us around like pinballs in an arcade game, as I fight the wheel in a shrieking skid. The punch hurtles the two guys behind me. Mr Matsu, and his assistant. It must have been that. It must have been. Next thing is, we're slewed up on the central reservation concrete island. In an amazing stillness, but for the pulse and hiss of the fractured radiator, the ziss-ziss-ziss of a revolving wheel. And the cops already there. Their blue light flash-flash-flashing."

"Slow now. Freeze it. What exactly are you seeing. Each detail."

"I turn around to look. Two guys in the back seat of the cab. One directly behind me. The other to the right. And the stench of burnt meat. The passenger side guy—Mt Matsu, is out cold. The one immediately behind me—the assistant, is twitching and spasming, his head is a mess, it's smashed open, as though it exploded from the inside..."

"Could it be the result of the autowreck, or maybe the shooting?"

"I've seen impact wounds. To me, these resemble no impact wound I've ever encountered."

"But you wouldn't discount the possibility?"

"Hell. What do I know? I say what I see. This is what I saw. Next thing he stops twitching. And simultaneously the other guy, Matsu, opens his eyes."

"Could be coincidence. Nothing more."

"That's not the impression I got. It was instantaneous. And the expression in the eyes, as they shock open, is pure terror."

"Naturally there'd be terror. He's been in a near-death auto-collision. The inside of his assistant's head is smeared all over the inside of the cab. C'mon, how could he not be in shock."

"Yes and yes. But no. What I got is, something transferred from one guy to the other. In the instant of death, it awoke in the other head."

They lean back. My head is clearing. The buzz working it's way out of my system. The room is not a mothership. It's just a room. The two men are not galactics. Just men. Carl and Lennie, ha-ha.

The one to the right looks at the one to the left, Carl to Lennie. "What do you think?"

"There's an indeterminacy factor. But it's pretty low. I'd hazard we've got a new transfer."

That's when it clicks. "I know who you are. You're the bad guys. It's you that started this off. It's you attacked my cab…!"

They refrain from anything resembling denial. It's good to have a physical target for rage. You can't rail against the lure of sweet oblivion. You can't hold narcotic dependency in your fist and crush the life out of it. You know it's chewing away like rats inside your head, that it was the cause of all the bad things in your life. You lose, and you lose, and you keep on losing. The marriage that ran aground. The career-structure that dissolved. But you can't hit out at that. This is something real to lash out at. But you don't. You just sit there and sweat. This is looking increasingly to be a three-bottle problem.

Dom Hemming munches Wasabi peas from a Matsu pack, and listens, as the Men in Black speculate. "Look, I've wended my way through a wilderness of chaotic metaphysics searching for answers. I know my Sci-Fi. Once I thought there's just a chance the thing could be Saturnian or Mercurian. There are fluidic silicon-based entities on Mercury, the only life-form capable of existing in such extreme temperatures. And there are tenuous gaseous things eternally hovering within gas-giant Saturn, resembling triangular bats that glide on storm-belts and atmospheric currents."

"Maybe we're wandering into the realm of fantasy here?" suggests the other one. Carl is logical, analytical. Both are dark-skinned, short black hair, dark brooding eyes. Middle-eastern origins?

Lennie shrugs dismissively. He's more given to wild theory. "There are Earth-mysteries too. We think we know stuff. We know shit. We're a mere drop in the ocean of time. During climate-change ten-thousand years ago, melting ice-age glaciers raised global sea-levels, inundating coastal cities and transfiguring the map of temperate zones. This is fact. There are city-structures submerged off the Indian coast, and on the Mediterranean seabed. The Sahara was fertile, with lakes, forests, and lost communities. This is not speculation. We now enjoy the benefits of a logical rational technological civilization. Those prediluvians were as brain-smart as us, but specialized in other directions. I'm hazarding here, free-associating if you like, but it's possible they're still here. Still with us. That they devised mental disciplines allowing them to survive death, in a kind of non-corporeal way. The mind-techniques were lost in the deluge, but the stories persist, passed down in the oral tradition of religions. Are you following me on this…?"

"I'm following you as sympathetically as I can. I admire optimism, no matter how deluded."

"So you've got alternative theories?"

"I know what I saw" insists Dom. "But I don't know what it means. What are we dealing with?"

"It's some kind of parasite. That's all we can ascertain. We, or rather the group we represent has been following it and killing it for centuries."

"Don't give me that. I've read all the Dan Brown conspiracy theories. The secret forces controlling history."

"So don't believe. Makes no difference. What does a parasite do when its host dies? If it's smart it transfers to a new host, the closest one available. That's what you saw happening. You saw a sponge absorbing souls."

"There's just one of these? How can there be just one of them?"

"That's how we calculate it can die. If it's the lost relic of a bygone age, the last remnant of its species, it must be capable of dying. If it can die, that means we can kill it. So we kill it in different ways. We've killed it once, we've killed it twice, we've killed it three times. But it refuses to die. We experiment with different methods. Most recently with an incendiary slug primed with a metallic sodium core. Somewhere in the atomic periodic table—we tried silver and potassium too, there must be something sufficiently poisonous to its nature that it will kill it, before it has time to slough off its borrowed human body. Yet each time, the host dies, but not the parasite. Next time, when we kill it, we must be certain it stays dead."

I'm supposed to be the cab-driver (license revoked), but it's me that's been taken for a ride. It's time to turn things around. "I can contact Matsu. I've got a mainline to his skype address."

The stunned silence endures for several eternities. "So how do we play it?"

"First, we find out what he wants."

* * * *

The link blinks up on the laptop.

"I'm Dom Hemming. Matsu requested I call." The onscreen face isn't the man in the cab. "Who am I speaking to?"

"I'm Mr Matsu's personal assistant. I'm authorized to speak on his behalf. This is confidential. It will be to your advantage to understand this."

"Understanding is not an issue so far."

He hesitates. "Mr Matsu values his privacy. He appreciates simplicity. With goodwill on both sides this can be arranged. You've been interviewed by the police regarding the incident in the underpass. A man died. There will be a hearing. We know your circumstances. We sympathise. We're in a position to assist you, your wife and daughter, through these hard times. All we require is some reciprocity."

"Go on, I'm listening."

"You will accept full responsibility. You'd been drinking. You made a mistake. You lost control of the vehicle, resulting in the accident. There were no other factors. If you are prepared to present this simplified version of the events at the hearing, I can assure you that your domestic financial problems are over."

"You can set this up?"

"As good as done. We've already prepared a statement on your behalf. We can pdf it to you."

"I want personal assurances. I want to hear it from him—from Mr Matsu himself, face-to-face."

It seems he's glancing off-screen for confirmation. Then, "as a favour, as a gesture of sincere goodwill, that will be possible. On neutral turf."

* * * *

Red taillights glide down the street. The pavement hard beneath his feet. As it should be. But an unreality too. As though, if you blink it away hard enough, you'll see the other hidden world more clearly. The shining city of silver towers and graceful domes, the pirouette of arches and impossible skyways, coloured torpedo-bugs in a glittering storm of dragonflies. A vision from the cover of a 1940s pulp SF magazine. Then there's the murmur of voices just below the threshold of audibility, fairy whispers and elfin chimes. You strain your ears, but you can't make out the words. The language seems teasingly familiar, as though it's echoes of speech you've heard in other lives, on other worlds of space-time. Or are the voices just loose neurons firing in your head, bam-bam-bam? Deliriums. Madness. How can you be sure? You can't.

Mr Sharma's hire-car Honda Civic is still there. License suspended, of course. Not that that's a major consideration now. Carl sits beside him. Lennie in the back as he takes off. Stay within speed limits. Observe lane discipline and signals. Don't attract unwelcome attention. He takes the route out of town, the coast road east. Something ticking away at the back of his mind. Something not quite right. He'd browsed the lap-top files they'd compiled. The pattern of what they term "transfers". According to the tree-chart they've assembled the entity had manipulated its way up the Matsu management structure by switching body-to-body. Leaving a trail of husks, suicides and accidental deaths. Maybe reusing an aspirational technique it had learned over centuries. In a time of chaos, war or revolution, it would be easy. Maybe in previous centuries it had been Hitler, Genghis Khan or Ivan the Terrible. Today it must be necessary for it to manufacture opportunities. It had been Matsu's personal assistant. Think. It was one step away from the apex. Who booked the cab from Sharma? It did. Who knew exactly where the cab would be at its most vulnerable? It did.

"I must have messed up your plans, the way I reacted when you were going in for the hit?"

Carl nods grimly. "It should have been straightforward. The police would have filed it as a mistaken gang-related drive-by shooting. But instead, you take off like it's a high-speed movie chase-sequence, wrong way down the one-way. Yes, it threw us. Now there's the hearing, no-one likes loose ends."

"Sorry. It was just instinct."

"It paid off. In a sense. Matsu's money-transfer is complete, through untraceable intermediaries into an independent account, to be released as a monthly pension to your wife in perpetuity. Nothing can change that."

A lay-by pulled in off the road some twenty miles from Brighton. And there ahead, close to the cliff-edge, a parked car. They slot in beside it, and wait. Beachy Head is close. 162-metres down to the freezing sea. Lennie sits in the back. Carl in the passenger seat. Until abruptly Lennie thrusts his arms through and around, across Dom's chest, pinioning his arms to his side. Carl reaches across simultaneously. The sharp stab of a syringe in his arm. As the two men in black get out of the car he feels the familiar narcotic ice in his veins.

The occupant of the other car has also emerged. They're pacing across to stand together beneath a close copse of trees. Dom watches, fighting the slow crawl of drugs in his body. Cross, and double-cross. Missing pieces fall into place. Both parties require closure. Neither want the hearing to go ahead. So Dom Hemming must assume the guilt, must take it all upon himself. Until he can take the self-recrimination no longer. And he suicides off the cliff into that freezing tide. He was known to be unstable, in a bad situation, a substance abuser. No need to hunt further for motive. It can take months before bodies are hauled out. Some are never found. Whatever, it's done. The enquiry will be closed.

Matsu starts walking towards him as the other two climb into the empty car and rev. The world is melting around the edges. But being a narcotics connoisseur has its advantages. He can navigate his altered state, to a degree. Matsu opens the car door and looks down at him. The bad guy always gloats over his victim. It's standard procedure. Small and rather portly, with reptilian eyes, although that might be the insight gifted him by the chemicals in his bloodstream. Yes, this is the man from the cab. He recalls Matsu, and the expression in those eyes as they opened, as they shocked open in pure terror. What he'd forgotten is that a second later the terror was replaced by smug satisfaction. The transfer complete. The parasite seated in its new host.

Dom is seeing him surrounded by a kind of luminous glow. A supernatural halo brighter than the sun. He sees the dull ancient pulse beneath the skull. The quick deadly survival instinct. He concentrates his energies and reaches out his hand to the standing man, a gesture of defeat, of inevitability. Matsu looks at the extended hand strangely, as though momentarily conflicted. Then condescends to grasp it. Dom feels the slender hand locked into his own, the smooth hairless skin, the frail bones beneath the skin.

The revving of an auto-engine behind him. Matsu's car maneuvering in tight. Then the shock of slow impact as it comes up hard against the Honda's rear, nudging it forward. As Matsu seeks to disengage his hand, Dom grips harder. For a second they strain against each other. Then Dom feels the bones splinter and crack as he crushes. The other man screams and his knees buckle. The car lurches forward, towards the cliff edge. With his free hand he reaches down and releases the handbrake.

Now he can reach out and seize around that flabby throat. Matsu falls inwards, up against the steering wheel, spluttering and gasping. Nothing else exists in the universe but to crush that windpipe. A sickening jolt, the car hangs out over space. Obscene tides of foulness engulf him. Formless black on blackness, congealed from shadow in feral pulsing horror. A vile cellular presence as ancient as time, probing its way into him. Matsu is dying, the death-rattle of trapped phlegm caught and vibrating in his ruptured trachea. The parasite within him slithering into its next host… a thing slobbering with slime and delirium spawned from nightmare.

I wasn't as strong as you, Rachel. I've never been as strong as you. I'm going to be strong now.

Carl and Lennie watch the Civic vanish over the cliff-edge and plummet down towards sweet oblivion. The thing can't be killed. But how long can it survive frozen to a corpse on the seabed? The car idles for a moment. Then reverses away from the brink, turns, and cuts back onto the Brighton road. The coast road is a white scar through the night. ▲

An Unsolicited Lucidity
by Lee Clark Zumpe

The following journal was found amidst the possessions of the late David Arthur Brown, noted nature photographer. Though undated, records obtained from William Whitley College list a D. Brown as "team archivist and publicist" in connection with the ill-fated 1961 expedition.

Day 1: Marooned

The world takes sinister pleasure at reminding people like me that the meticulous designs of meager men may be easily swept away by the folly of destiny.

What should have been a standard assignment for a veteran writer and photojournalist has disintegrated into chaos. What should have been a routine voyage to the Malagasy Republic has deteriorated into crisis. Now, instead of documenting the biodiversity of endemic lemurs, I find myself penning the first few lines of a journal that will hopefully be restricted to a few pages in length.

All five passengers and four crewmen aboard the cabin cruiser *Aurora* survived the tempest that beached our 1925 Elco flat top motor yacht on the shore of this remote island. Having endured two days of fierce squalls, incessant gales and rouge waves, I am not surprised that the captain hesitates when asked exactly where we might be and how long we might have to wait for rescuers to locate us.

In this part of the world, I wonder if authorities even bother to search for ships lost at sea.

Little more than a week ago, I was enjoying a cup of locally brewed coffee in the lobby of a hotel on Kilindini Road in Mombassa. The establishment caters to Westerners vacationing in Kenya, eager to walk the sandy beaches along the azure waters of the Indian Ocean. On the streets of the Old Harbor quarter, native Africans mingle with bearded Arab seaman dressed in turbans; European tourists barter with market square vendors trying to lose themselves in postcolonial culture; and chatty American businessmen scramble to profit from a fledgling country's doubt and indecision much like their carpetbagger ancestors did almost a century ago during the Reconstruction era.

There, where dhows set sail with cargoes of coconuts and ivory, I met with members of an expedition from William Whitley College, a small liberal arts school located in the highland town of Tahlequah, N.C. Professor Alfred P. Weating, the team leader and chair of the school's biology department, monopolized the conversation that afternoon, detailing his desire to inventory the *Strepsirrhini clade* and lauding the Malagasy Republic as "the eighth continent" because of its long ecological isolation and the distinctiveness of its fauna.

"Should fortune smile on us," I distinctly remember the professor saying, "We may even find certain species thought to be extinct."

The college commissioned me to document the expedition. More than just taking notes and snapping pictures in the jungle, they have entrusted me to authenticate their research in a professional manner and to make public their findings at the conclusion of the effort. While I do not share Weating's enthusiasm over the subject matter, I found the salary William Whitley offered quite pleasing.

As a freelancer, I contribute both copy and photographs to several scientific- and travel-related periodicals including *Modern Biologist, National Geographic, Safari Journal, Science Digest* and *Bizarre Destinations*. In those magazines, I generally work as part of an entourage and I rarely see a byline or earn a photo credit. The appeal of being the sole writer and photographer enticed me almost as much as the promise of substantial income.

Of course, it will be difficult spending that paycheck stuck here on this island.

Ironically, Weating insisted on an approach by sea so that he could investigate islands in Mozambique Channel for additional signs of biodiversity. Scheduled stops on our journey to the seaport of Majunga on Bombetoka Bay included Anjouan, Mayotte and Nosy Be. Unfortunately, the captain believes we were driven eastward on monsoon winds, deeper into the Indian Ocean and far from our intended course.

"We're among the Seychelles," the Kenyan seafarer told me this morning as we considered options for rationing provisions. His English phrasing comes slowly and deliberately, so I am not certain if the hesitation I detected in his voice stemmed from struggling with the language or some unspoken doubt. A few moments later, he conferred with his first mate about the condition of the radio, speaking then in his native Swahili. Though I did not understand what he said, I recognized both exasperation and frustration in his expression.

Tomorrow, the captain and his crew will explore the waters offshore, hoping to find the Indian Ocean brimming with fish. Weating has asked me to join him and his colleagues as they attempt to circumnavigate the island. The captain warned us both to avoid the forested interior. I see wisdom in his caution, but I have already noticed the professor staring past the palm trees that skirt the beach into the lush tropical flora that no doubt accommodates a thriving population of exotic animals and at the dark gray mountain that rises from the jungle floor and stretches skyward.

Day 2: Natural exclusion

The captain admitted this morning that the radio is beyond repair. What he refrained from mentioning until my persistent questioning embarrassed him sufficiently is that the radio never worked in the first place. The damage had been done on a previous voyage. The first mate failed to have it rebuilt or replaced on their most recent stay in port.

My own suspicions justified, I immediately regretted pressing the issue when I realized the other crewmen had also been kept in the dark. Upon discovering the oversight, they quickly turned on their former friend with murderous eyes. Only the captain's stern commands, delivered in sharply spoken Swahili, pacified them—at least for the time being.

With tempers at least temporarily moderated, I set out with Weating and his five colleagues to explore the perimeter of the island.

In front of us, the gentle surf rolled ashore—a beguilingly tranquil vision considering the stormy waves that dashed our 65-foot vessel against a coral ledge before depositing it on the coast. Behind us, the white wood hull of the *Aurora* gleamed in the midmorning sun while the Kenyan crew gathered nets and gaffs to facilitate their hunt for a meal.

The moment we were out of earshot, Weating made his concerns about the captain known.

"I've nothing against the man personally," he said, prefacing the accusations that would follow. The professor questioned his abilities the moment he came on board. He noticed navigational charts hopelessly out-of-date, shoddy housekeeping and a copious amount of rum squirreled away in nooks and niches all over the ship. Aside from these few abstract allegations, he completely disagreed about our location. "The Seychelles," he told us, "Are mostly low, raised coral atolls and granitic islands. We can all see that this island owes its existence to some ancient volcanic eruption."

Weating believes the storm drove us southeastward toward the Mascarene Islands, leaving us several hundred miles east of our destination.

His calculations, if they should prove accurate, offer little comfort. Perhaps it is my chronic cynicism that encumbers me with a flood of foreboding and dread over our predicament. Though I expect our team's benefactors at William Whitley College to mount some kind of recovery effort once our absence is observed, such a mission might take weeks or even months to organize. Among both members of the expedition and members of the crew, I seem to be the only one pessimistic enough to imagine a worst-case scenario.

While my negativity may represent one extreme, Weating personifies the antithesis.

The professor, despite all the prospective consequences of our dilemma, considers this an unparalleled opportunity for discovery. He envisions himself and his team as potentially the first scientific visitors to the island and has developed a strategy to identify and classify the endemic flora and fauna in hopes of uncovering some new species.

"It is places like this," Weating said during our survey of the beachhead this morning, "that the most exciting finds are made. An isolated environment allows for natural exclusivity and evolutionary aberration." He referenced the many creatures known only to exist in the Malagasy Republic as well as the extinct *Raphus cucullatus* of Mauritius. "On this island, we may find something that has never been seen by man before."

Tracing the edges of a lagoon, we located a small, fresh water stream within an hour's walk of the boat. Disregarding the captain's counsel, we followed the tributary beneath the tropical moist broadleaf forest along its meandering course. While Weating and his companions dutifully collected samples of the local insect population for further study, I mashed more than a few bloodsucking sandflies and other vexing bugs without a trace of remorse.

Despite initial protestations, Weating grudgingly complied when I eventually demanded we wrap up the day's exploration. By that time, the stream had led us up into a steep-sided ravine thick with lush vegetation. Trees of every shape and size and hue surrounded us, many stippled with colorful blossoms and others dangling sprays of white bell flowers with fine lacy petals. The professor rattled off a list of indigenous timber, including bois de natte, colophane, ebony, and tatamaka.

Retracing our steps, I became acutely aware of an unseen presence. Having had time to reflect on the situation, I realize now that the forest possesses a hush and stillness that is both unnatural and unsettling. While the omnipresent insects continued to plague us during our return, no other living things made themselves evident. One might expect to see a variety of birds, geckos and even small rodents on an island of this size and age.

The absence of these creatures provokes a certain sense of anxiety and uneasiness in me. Weating never spoke of it, but I suspect he feels it, too.

By the time we reached the beach, the sun had begun its listless descent, slipping out of view behind the mammoth summit of the long-dormant volcano. A deep shadow spread across the forest, its primordial darkness settling on us heavily as if it meant to snuff out our lives with the same indifferent aggravation I had exhibited toward the marauding sandflies.

A raging bonfire on the beach welcomed us back to the *Aurora.*

Day 3: The first mate disappears

It is early morning. The dawn is still an hour away.

Weating and his colleagues, exhausted from their hike, remain in their staterooms aboard the beached *Aurora,* their bellies full of fresh fish.

The captain did not see fit to allow me the consolation of a full night's sleep. He summoned me an hour ago to tell me that the first mate vanished during the course of the night. He claims that the man feels singly responsible for our troubles. The other crewmen apparently shunned him yesterday, driving him off with unremitting verbal affronts.

Though the first mate's silence at dinner substantiated a degree of despondency, I find the captain's contention that he simply wandered off less than convincing. As a detached observer and a competent judge of character, I have no difficulty in suggesting the possible involvement of the other crewmates in his disappearance. The blatant rage they displayed yesterday upon learning of his negligence provided me ample incentive to recommend at least a cursory inquiry.

The captain, however, does not agree with me and refuses to even explore that prospect. He reports that the first mate's last words to him last night were "open your eyes." The cryptic message makes no more sense to me than it did to him.

Today, I will join the captain in a search of the adjacent lowland forest while Weating leads the crewmen to the creek so that the water tanks aboard *Aurora* can be filled to capacity. The professor will probably insist upon further study of the interior, though the captain again cautioned him against it. I echoed the captain's admonition last night, advising each member of the team separately that the island may conceal as many risks as it does rarities.

Weating will not listen. Men driven by unconstrained curiosity habitually fail to notice looming threats as they clamber to accumulate knowledge.

Even with the encroaching light of dawn and the fire beside me, the skies overhead are swarming with stars. I have never seen so many lights in the heavens, so many beacons of distant galaxies. Staring up into the endless cosmos, I grapple with its breadth—all units of measure seem obsolete, all understanding of distance and duration and scope become hopelessly inadequate.

Like the deep shadow that threatened to suffocate us yesterday, the twilight anchors a singular burden in its vastness—an undeniable apathy that unknowingly mocks the greatest civilizations and ravages any cognizant being attentive enough to recognize it.

* * * *

It is not as though I have not seen death. I was 18—a willful and intractable boy with elaborate aspirations—when I covered the battle of Dien Bien Phu in north-western Vietnam when the Viet Minh captured the French fortress. A few years later, I happened to be on assignment when anti-European riots swept through Leopoldville in the Belgian Congo.

I have seen enough of the gruesomeness and grimness of death in my 25 years to dislodge all those lingering delusions preachers utilized to frame the Sunday morning sermons of my childhood. I cannot speak for the survival of the soul once the body has expired, but I can speak of the body itself. I can attest to the speed with which the semblance of life evaporates, the abrupt alteration in the skin's tone and texture, the prompt and unpleasant hollowness that supplants vitality.

Still, when the captain signaled that he had found his first mate, nothing I had witnessed could have prepared me for what I was about to see.

His remains waited for us beneath a coconut palm on the edge of the beach not far from the *Aurora*.

We buried him before the others could return, worried that seeing his mutilated corpse might lead to panic, violence or madness. Considering the scale and severity of his injuries, neither of us bothered to ponder the precise circumstances that culminated in his death. Hordes of voracious insects had already claimed ownership of his inert flesh and had to be discouraged against carrying off any more meaty morsels as we dug his grave.

More unsettling than the scavenging bugs, though, was the man's white-knuckled grasp on his own knife and the gaping and apparently self-inflicted wound beneath his chin. The gash suggested that he had not merely tried to cut his own throat: He tried to commit suicide by decapitating himself.

We agreed not to speak of the matter with the others.

* * * *

Tomorrow, I will follow Weating into the interior again. He is anxious to show me something he found in the jungle. His colleagues did not reflect his excitement regarding the day's find—in fact, they seemed sluggish and sullen this evening. Perhaps their inquisitiveness had waned. Unaccustomed to long hikes in tropical weather, they will not be joining us tomorrow. At the mention of another expedition, they swiftly volunteered to stay behind and help the captain and crew restock our supply of fish.

Day 4: An ancient shrine

It rises from the jungle floor unobtrusively, its archaic design showing no signs of deterioration though smothering vines have utterly encased it. No more than a simple pile of brick, it consists of a threefold base, a dome and a pointed top. Architecturally, it resembles the dagoba temples of Ceylon.

Weating is inspecting the inner chamber while I stand guard at the doorway to the temple. Occasionally, he blurts out a fact he deems interesting, and I make a note of it in the margin of my journal without investing much in the investigation. My interest in the archeological spectacle might be stimulated if I could distance myself from the gravity of our situation. Discovering the remnants of an ancient religious complex seems inconsequential unless the news can be conveyed to the rest of the world.

Right now, the world is distant and inaccessible. To it, we are as imperceptible as the bones of the builders of this forgotten monument.

* * * *

Weating is waiting outside having instructed me to take a series of photographs of the inner walls of the temple for the sake of documentation. Intricate murals depict various religious motifs, some of which reverberate with Hindu and Judaic influences; others appear far more pagan and prehistoric. The professor specified some of the more obscure representations he identified, including several names which held little or no meaning for me such as Beelzebub, Chepre, Nyarlathotep and Siggogul-phot.

There is some form of hieroglyph stretched across the stone that resembles no script I have ever seen. Weating claims that scholars from William Whitley have made breakthroughs in translating similar writings from other sources. He supposedly recognizes a few of the more prevalent symbols and connects them with cults that once flourished in Egypt, Aksum and India.

What he has failed to notice here I find simultaneously encouraging and disturbing. My first discovery came before I even set foot inside the shrine: Discarded cigarette butts lay scattered amidst the brown leaves on the ground just outside the doorway. While the crew of the *Aurora* smokes constantly, I have not seen the professor or any one of his colleagues light up since we set out on this voyage.

There are additional signs of recent visitation hidden in the shadows of the temple. So far, I have found an emptied bottle of cognac, modern candlesticks, alkaline batteries and a cache of 20th century literature including occult pamphlets and issues of a exploitative magazine called *Wicked Worship*, the most recent edition of which dates to February, 1960.

At this moment, I am standing in front of an altar that has not been denied fresh blood. I cannot estimate its last use, but I doubt more than a month has elapsed since the screams of a sacrifice dissolved in the dark surrounding forest.

I pride myself on being attentive and alert. It takes a sharp eye to discern captivating images through the lens of a camera—picking out details that can be captured and confined and reproduced in the glossy pages of commercial periodicals. Men like Weating have an entirely different set of parameters when it comes to perceiving the world around them. They assemble fragments, arrange pertinent data to arrive at a conclusion. They neglect those elements which do not play into their assessment.

That is why, I believe, Weating did not notice any of these things. That is why, also, he did not notice the bugs.

Admittedly, I did not detect them initially, even when I stood with the tip of my nose no more than a foot away from the wall. Now, I see them clearly—or, rather, I see how their immeasurable ranks quiver ever so slightly. I see how the glyphs on the walls ripple with life every few seconds, how the walls themselves shiver and wobble. They appear to be all-pervading, covering every surface inside the temple.

The flash from my camera agitates them. Each picture I snap momentarily dislodges them from their methodically formed mosaic, forces them retrace the delicate lines of their mural, reform the thousands of symbols that comprise their hieroglyphic composition.

They have sent sentries to encourage me to depart. I feel the pinprick bites on my ankles, feel their slow steady advance up my legs. It is time to go.

* * * *

I did not bother to explain my experience inside the temple to Weating. When I found him outside, the jungle insects had launched an attack. We both felt retreat was an immediate necessity, though I do not believe he assigned any preternatural aspect to the incident.

Short of dismissing it as a hallucination, I am uncertain what to make of it all. Crediting a swarm of miniscule bugs with the creation and continual preservation of the temple's murals and hieroglyphs seems tantamount to admitting to madness. Yet, I know what I saw in that chamber and I have never doubted my senses.

And there is more.

In our flight from that clearing in the jungle I turned once and looked over my shoulder. There, where the temple should have been, I saw nothing but an indistinct haze—a cloud of frantic insects angrily buzzing at their uninvited guests.

A few moments ago, Weating made an odd comment as he shambled off to bed. He said, "open your eyes."

Day 5: Screams in the night

I must keep my entries brief.

We are now only four. The captain, the remaining crewmen and one of Weating's associates vanished overnight. I pray it was not their screams that the forest failed to suppress sometime past midnight.

I had not noticed before this morning that the island changes its facets endlessly. The rock I placed to mark the first mate's burial plot I cannot find. The tree beneath which we recovered his corpse is no longer there. Even the *Aurora* has swung about on the beach. Tides might account for shifting sands; anyone might have picked up the grave marker. I might be mistaken about the location of the coconut palm.

I might be mistaken about a great many things. But I am not.

Weating has seen something, too. He will not speak of it, but it has clearly affected him. He stands in the surf, unwilling to set foot on shore. I do not know what he will do when fatigue finally claims him. I do not know if I can convince him to come back to the *Aurora*.

* * * *

Weating is floating on his back in the Indian Ocean beneath the stars. I am sitting at the water's edge, calling out to him every few minutes to make sure he hasn't drifted off.

Just before the last light of day faded from the sky, he said something that seems worth recording.

"At Heliopolis, they worshiped the dung-beetle," he said. "They believed it sprang from the earth without any generative process—that it created itself. I have a friend in the religious studies department back in Tahlequah. I tell him about the biology of bugs; he tells me why so many people have worshipped them throughout history. There have been cults in every corner of the globe scattered through centuries. They survive to this day."

He trailed off at the end, drowning in his own musings. I did not question him further. I understand.

The others are gone. Something lured them into that forest, into that oppressive darkness that is crawling with some imperceptible manifestation of primordial malevolence. I feel its pull, too, but I can resist it. I have at least caught a glimpse of it—enough to recognize its mercilessness; enough to see through any illusion it might employ to entice me.

Weating is no longer returning my calls.

Day 6: Alone, with company

As I walked along the shoreline this morning, I saw their silhouettes beneath the trees in the shade of the jungle.

The first mate, the captain, the crew and the team members from William Whitley beckoned me, waving their arms hysterically, determined to draw my attention. From a distance, they looked perfectly normal right down to the tone of their flesh and the fit of the clothing. To my astonishment, they called out when they realized they could not dupe me with their disciplined ruse. Their voices carried a tinny inflection that betrayed the chirp and buzz of the drones that perpetrated the counterfeit vocalizations.

Of course, they were not real. They were effigies orchestrated by those loathsome insects, impatient to add me to their list of victims.

"Don't go to them," Weating said, startling me. "They'll take you. They'll become you. They'll use your identity to do their bidding on earth. Open your eyes." His body floated in the surf face down. Something had taken a chunk out of his hip, and I backed away from the cloudy, crimson aura that tainted the water around him. He was dead, of that I am certain. Still, I heard his voice in my head, a faint whisper like a fading radio transmission. "Their influence is already too strong. Don't become another faceless entity in their collective. Don't become subordinate to the Crawling Chaos."

* * * *

Nightfall threatens to dissolve the world around me, reduce it to nothing more than shadow and fear and the reassurance of inevitable death. I scribble these last few words expecting them to fall into obscurity along with my existence, but hoping that somehow they will survive me. To anyone who finds this journal—consider it a testament to the lingering darkness that maintains foothold in the remote corners of the earth.

We can see more than we imagine.

Open your eyes.

Day 7: Rescue

Before dawn, I saw lights on one horizon; a black, blurry cloud on the opposite one.

I see it now, a boat flying an American flag.

I am on rock in the middle of the ocean.

Where is the island?

January, 1963

I am the only known survivor of the *Aurora*. My rescuers indicated that there were no islands within 50 miles of the small coral atoll where the found me. During a prolonged hospital stay, I was assured continually that the events recorded in this journal had been part of some elaborate phantasm—a delirium unconsciously contrived to keep my mind occupied while my body deteriorated.

It is the lingering unsolicited lucidity that makes me unwilling to dismiss everything I described in my journal. To this day, I see things that should not be there. In staggered glimpses, I perceive that the things that surround us and the people with whom we interact are not necessarily what science tells us they are supposed to be.

Sometimes, they are real. Sometimes, they are something else, pretending to be real.

I have done a fair amount of research in the last year and I have found references to the deities I recorded on Day 4 amidst an array of obscure but accessible esoteric literature. Though my camera was not recovered, I was able to reproduce some of the symbols I saw in the temple. I sent these to William Whitley College for examination more than six months ago, but to date have not received a response.

In fact, many of my inquiries have gone unanswered regarding the existence of bug-worshiping cultists. I have compiled as much research on the matter as I am able to stomach, and I have decided to shelve my investigation before it becomes an obsession.

I hope that I can put all this behind me some day soon, convince myself that the doctors are right—that it was all just an awful nightmare.

But if that is the case, I have to ask myself—why is it that each word I write on this page seems to flutter for an instant before settling into place?

David Arthur Brown, aged 71, was last seen at the port of Majunga in Madagascar. There, authorities report he chartered a small yacht for sightseeing and game fishing. A month after the vessel sailed from the harbor, it was found adrift some 100 miles north of Mauritius. No trace of Brown or the crew was ever found.

▲

Black Carnival
by Bobby Cranestone

Amberfield, a small town in England near the city of Derm. A Satur-
day evening.

* * * *

"Do you want the normal entry or the full program?"

Sam´s eyes gleamed. "The full program sir."

The incredible old man at the counter offered him a ticket which seemed somehow to be made of leather. Sam looked at it from all sides and found that there were imprints of ugly faces which seemed strangely alive.

The man leaned a bit over. "Stay always with your pals." Sam looked around, he was here with his class mates. They had paid and received the normal tickets which sported clowns and other more or less fun creatures.

"But how shall I stay with the others if they have to see the normal tour?"

The old man shrugged his shoulders.

Sam went through a banner decorated entrance and laying beyound, past the first few stores which sold all kinds of stuff from ancient spices, over to socks and from plastic monster figures over to candles. He had a strange liking for the painted placards which were still made like hundred years ago with a real printingpress and not a computer and a laser printer. There was a women which was said to dance like a snake and to be able to scratch herself behind the ears…something which might come handy at times, so Sam thought. There was the first tent which had a dog called cerberus, like the greek beast, and a calve which had ´only´ two heads. He knew those already…it came in tv almost weekly, not too exciting. The next stand was a wizard. The guy there was surprisingly young not like the wizards in circus. He was lean and dark haired and even wore a leather jacket. The cylinder hung upon a hook at the door. Sam wasn´t sure if he was a real wizard but he had something strange about him that promised that there was more than the eye could see. He did a card trick on a low mahogany table. He seemed to practice.

"Hello."

The man looked up. "Hello, boy."

"What can you do?"

The guy rolled with the eyes as if he had expected a question like that from a small boy like him but he chuckled and didn't seem to mind. "Almost everything."

"But don't do that coin from my ear thing...that's soo old. Even my sister can do it. Well, actually she put a penny into her ear once and we had to drive to the hospital."

The wizard laughed and Sam wondered why he told him all that.

"Well, I can do a bit more. I am a real wizard."

"Hmm?"

"You know there is more about an wizard than those tricks...that are magicians. Wizards are as old as the mankind. They know the secrets of the earth, the plans of nature and even the mind of people."

"Isn't that a bit numb? Well, I mean this is a carnival, aren't you supposed to do a show...not that I mind you talking about that kind of stuff, it's quiet interesting." Damn....Sam scratched his head and wondered again what kind of rubbish he told.

"I did not say that there isn't a show to follow up." the wizard walked past a plaque where stood "Aznagel—the wondrous wizard" and took up an old frame.

"Nice cat."

Sam looked around in surprise. Really there sat a small black kitten next to him. "it isn't mine." he said and patted it but he felt strangely touched when he saw the wise and allknowing eyes.

"It sure is yours. Every boy should have a cat."

"Doesn't the saying go, every boy should have a dog?"

Aznagel shrugged his shoulders. "How old are you Sam?"

"I'm eight."

"Well then you should like what I show you..."

"Is it scary?"

"Not too much, you're still a little boy."

Sam made a face as if he had bitten into a lemon. "I came to a carnival to become scared, not to be pampered."

"Be careful what you wish for. It could become granted. This place must be handled with care."

Sam was impressed by the serious look on his face.

"Sorry..."

Aznagel smiled only and put the frame before the boys face. "What do you see?"

"Nothing. The frame is empty. There is no picture inside."

"Well, some sure think it's empty but if I'm right you're the kind of person to see through that."

Sam starred at the frame for some time. At once he thought that he saw some fine lines. They became brighter, pulsating in some strange rythmus...faster and faster. It took some time until Sam found that it was in the rythm of his heart beat. There were the outlines of a tree and dark clouds that moved slowly over a velvet sky. A stroke of thunder went over the picture. Once, twice, three times... at last it hit the tree. All vanished in a wild dance of forms and shapes.

"There was a tree. But unlike any tree I ever saw...more like a bended man."

"It was a picture of your soul."

"What? What does a tree have in common with me?"

"The old indian cultures believed that every human has something in nature that resembles it's true self. It's a tree in your case."

The cat mewed as if in agreement.

"hmm", was Sam's not very intelligent answer. "That sure was an trick, wasn't it?"

Aznagel gave the frame to Sam to check it for some hidded electronic parts.

"You can keep it if you want to."

"No, thanks." He returned it to the wizard. It was too heavy to carry around anyway.

A cold, chill wind tore at the tents and brushed Sam's cheek.

"It seems to get stormy." Guessed the man after a testifying look. "Don't stay too long and if you loose track of time don't forget the way back or what I told you."

A flash of lighting struck over the sky. Sam had turned his head to watch it when he looked around to answer Aznagel he found that he was gone.

Sam wasn't sure what kind of trick this was but he didn't quiet like the feeling that crept up inside him. He had wanted to be scared, right. But he wanted to have that funny feeling that you have watching a horror film and when it's over you laugh because you behaved so foolish, knowing all along that it was only a film. But this felt real. Somehow.

Sam passed on. He saw an exhibition held by an women who reminded him of his aunt, who showed pictures of elves around and from some meeting place of theirs. There was also a small golden cup which she said was once the belonging of an elve given to her. The next attraction was a fortune teller which looked at a glass ball and the smoke that seemed to issue from it's inner. When Sam looked around he saw that the small black kitten still followed him. After a while he wondered where his classmates had all gone to. There was no stoppage which kept him from the normal tour and he had not entered a special area so they should actually be somewhere around..but they were all gone. Even of other visitors there were few. Sam looked at his watch and found that it was after eight..late but a carnival was only fun when it turned dark outsite. He had to hurry to see the other attractions he longed for. He didn't quiet like the men working at the carnival, they all seemed to be sinister chaps fit for a news message. It wasn't the first time that he went to a carnival but these guys were even for a place like this, which attracted many strange people, unusually sinister. Their looks were very grim. Next thing Sam went to was a creature show. There was a big ugly toad on display. Unusually big and with a skin so white that one could see the arteries in a sickish pink where the blood floaded through the creatures body. Sam was dismayed.

He came at last to a wooden constructure which looked like an old mill lacking it's windmill sails. On a crumpled paper tacked to it's walls stood that a strange golden object was inside. An eye of some sort. Sam wanted to enter but one of the workers there pressed the door shut again. "Show is over" he grunted.

"But I've got a full program ticket. No limitations" he added.

The man laughed nastily. "It's better you go home if you still re-member the way."

Sam felt cold at once. Still he was nosey what kind of object was held therein. He opened the door again and saw on a platform a fun-nily shaped thing made of metall. It was of no real geometric origin it seemed more as if several shapes melted one into another, a mad tangle of forms…as if only half remembered from a world so very different from ours.

There was something at his leg. Sam looked down and found that his well known fellow the black kitten was tearing at the stuff of his trouser as if to hold him back. This time he did follow the advice.

"Ok, let's go home. You wanna come with me?" The cat pourred as if in an answer.

He took the way back he had come, past the women with the elves and the fortuneteller. He passed Aznagel the wizard too and left the dog cerberus also behind. Then Sam stood awestruck. There was another tent and another. In the far back stood a labyrinth of mirrors. "Wasn't this the way back?" He thought. "Yes, I came there. But why, where is the way out?" He went past the tents and the cat followed him. The tents didn't go on eternally but after a time he came to a high fence made of wooden beams. "Maybe it was the other way round." He knew it was not but he had to try. The cat followed him. He tried different ways but all lead ei-ther to the building with the golden "eye" or ended at the fence. Visiting the shows he had before seen in an effort to get behind the secret he even went to the calve with the two heads and screened the ground for any signs that the tents had been mysteriously moved. When he came again to the fence he saw a hole and looked through it. All he saw of the world outsite was a strange greyish mist as if all the world outsite had vanished and there was only the sinister carnival left. Sam sat down at last. The kitten jumped into his lap and mewed sadly. "What shall I do now?" He felt all blue and miserably close to crying even if he was a big boy.

He tried to talk to the people of the carnival, all visitors had vanished in the meanwhile, but it was no use. Either they pretented not to listen or they only smiled strangely. But what startled him most was the fact that every time he went around again there appeared less people to be there and the place seemed to turn even more sinister. The narrow lane between the tents was quiet and the shadows unusually long. A cold chill wind used to come up then and again but funnily it did not move the stuff of the tents but mysteriously seemed to follow him wherever he went. This was no good. Once when he tried a new turn he thought he saw a very dark shadow, or maybe it wasn't a shadow, move fantastically and creeping fast over ther hull of the tents. Sam followed the kitten which jumped away in a haste.

It felt like hours had been passing but when he checked his watch it claimed that it was 7 o'clock in the evening. "can't be. It was already 8… hours ago." When he checked again the hands pointed at 6 PM. "As if time turns backwards." He looked at the sky but it was still dark.

He held again at the strange wooden building. "Last thing I can try." The cat mewed again but he wasn't sure if it was in agreement or otherwise. Sam pushed the door open. Suddenly he stood in the labyrinth with the mirrors. "What the.." A strange unearthly sound made him falter. He felt that something was there. He turned slowly around and saw million times the reflections of a terrorfying face so unlike anything he had ever before beheld. He screamed but the sound was lost. The thing moved. But where was it? Was it close to him? Was he moving away or was he getting closer to it? Sam tried to find some kind of door, some halfway natural explanation how he got here. There was a doorknob and his hand reached over to it. The cat jumped away rushing into a different direction. Sam hesitated. Should he try the door? Or follow the cat? This place was strange..everything seemed to change all the time. Maybe the cat knew more. He remembered the things he had learned in school about the way the egyptians had cherished cats, bastet the cat goddess…maybe they really knew more. He turned and followed the pouring fellow.

Three more tangles and he went through an archway all made of mirrors. There was suddenly a space, a small hill rising and a tree lighted by a mysterious pale orb. He walked to the tree and stopped. There grew heads out of the bark at least did those knobs look like heads and faces that grinned sinnister or looked in anguish.

The cat went up in a big leap, up the tree and then placed itself on a twig looking at him with big eyes full of expectation.

"I shall climb that tree?" Sam shook his head. "I want to get out of here, not to get up that tree." There was this strange sound like something brushing the walls very softly. Sam cursed and started climbing up. He remembered what Aznagel the wizard had said. "My soul is a tree, maybe it isn´t such a bad idea to cling to it then" he thought. The tree was bigger then he had thought.

He reached a certain branch beside the cat..

Suddenly he saw from above all kinds of places and times and things that had been, were or maybe would be one day. Strange dimensions and pictures he had seen in dream when he had dared to dream so fantastically. He remembered stories he had heard about faceless creatures that were nightcrawlers called, that a mexican lady once had mentioned when they were in hollydays. The strange winds in Australia of whom he had seen a low budget documentary filmed by some enthusiastic american, winds that set up and went when there was no wind and who seemed to have some kind of conscousness or to follow a certain plan that only they knew. He thought about the wind he had felt, about the shadow that had lurked everywhere along the tents. The strange trapezohedron of which his teacher had once told him, that his brother had found on some antiquarian trip, before he went on that long journey and never came back. Also did he remember the strange thing that went with the gipsies, as it was whispered of by the bigger boys who laughed afterwards but preffered to shut their windows at night anyway.

He had to think at all those. Maybe they were all true.

The wizard, why had he known his name? He had not told him.

The tree seemed to whirl about, more pictures and more scenes… some fantastic others terrifying and scary. He closed his eyes but the feline pawed his back, nudged him into the side. He looked down, he thought he saw himself way down there waiting in anguish before the ticket stub, waiting to be let in and to be scared so he would feel his heart beat…and feel alive. "Remember the way back home", he mumbled. A thought came to his mind. Maybe it was a bad idea, maybe he would crush himself but on the other side this place was nothing much like reality…

He jumped down. At first it felt like cold ice water poured into his face. Then he felt that it was the night wind. But no unearthly wind, one that had reason and belonged to nature, that made the trees bow and whip and the leaves rustle at their twigs. He opened his eyes.

Sam stood again before the ticket stub.

"What do you want boy? Full tour or the normal roundabout?" Asked the very old man.

Sam shook his head. "None thanks."

The man smiled at him grimly.

Something mewed next to him on the ground. He turned at the cat.

"You're still with me then. I nearly forgot I don't even know your name." He knelt down and for the first time he saw that the cat wore a brass plate.

And there stood in golden letters one word: Aznagel.

The Laughter of Ghouls
by K. A. Opperman

I have heard it of midnights, the laughter of ghouls,
On the winds that have strayed through my dreaming
As I nap in my armchair upholstered in gules,
By the window where shadows are teeming.

What a high, awful sound is the laughter I hear—
So exultant beneath the moon's crescent!
How I long through the forest autumnal and sere—
Neath Aldebaran's beacon rubescent—

To go roam with the ghouls, to partake of their ways,
And to share in their hideous laughter!—
Would to God I could howl with the ghouls in the haze
Of the graveyard a charnel feast after…!

I have heard it of midnights, the laughter of ghouls,
And the night is not long in the coming
When my dream-driven body that gibbers and drools
Will go join them, to madness succumbing.

The Howard Family Tradition

P. R. O'Leary

Every time my dad went into a hotel room he would look in the closet, in the shower stall, under the beds, and then finally he would slam down on the mattresses with whatever was handy. A pillow, a suitcase, his hands. Thumping down on them, pressing with his palms, checking for signs that only he understood.

He always did it with a smile on his face. And he always told us it was a tradition. A Howard family tradition done to bless the room and clear it of evil spirits. As kids, we loved it. After he gave the all-clear we would run into the room and start to jump on the beds. A trio of boys, pounding the evil spirits out of those terrible mattresses.

The hotels we saw him do this in were the ones we stayed at during family vacations. The jersey shore, upstate New York, even once and a while on the beaches of North Carolina. Two or three times a year we went, since as far back as I could remember, and over the course of my childhood I started to realize something was off about my father's strange activity. Maybe it was because I was the oldest, or maybe I was just more observant than my brothers, but they didn't seem to notice the same things that I had.

First, it was the behaviour of my mother. She was normally very involved, *too* involved in our lives, but always at these times she found something else to do. Maybe it was asking questions at the front desk, or putzing around with our luggage outside, or straightening up the mess we always left in the family car. If it was a Howard Family tradition, why did my mother leave my father alone to do it? Us kids, we just watched from outside the room, never setting a foot inside until our father was done. But our mother was never even there and only made an appearance well after the whole ritual was complete.

Second, it was the general unease of our father when we were arriving at a hotel. Us kids, we were excited. Bouncing up and down on the back seat of the car with pent up energy, ready to explode out of it like flying worms from a can. But he always took his time getting us there, like he was gathering himself for something. I was starting to see it in how slowly he pulled the car into the parking lot. How he let it idle in the parking space a few seconds too long before turning it off. How he took longer than usual to stretch his legs before making it to the front desk to check-in.

And third was the forced smile on his face while he went about conducting the Howard family tradition. This took a while for me to notice and it marked a maturity on my part to do so. Because it wasn't obvious. My father, like most middle-aged men, was good at hiding his feelings.

Maybe it was because I was already suspicious, but while he pounded the mattress I could see that the set in his jaw was too tight. His eyes were moving too quickly. The muscles of his arms and back were too tense for the easy smile he was trying to project.

So one time, well into one of these vacations, I decided to ask him what was going on. I remember we were on the beach in Nags Head. A day so hot that the sun shining off the water was blinding your eyes and the sand was too painful to walk on. I don't know exactly how old I was at the time, but I wasn't yet a teenager. I was just starting to get those strange feelings when girls walked by in their bikinis.

"Dad," I said, plopping down besides his beach chair. "Why do you do that thing to the hotel rooms?"

My Mom wasn't around, having gone for a walk or something, and my brothers were playing in the surf. My Dad was just sitting there, watching the water, a cool beer in his hand, the bottle sweating. I held my palm under it to catch the cold drops of water while I waited for his answer.

He didn't speak at first, his expression hard to read behind sunglasses and a hat. I was about to ask again when he answered. And it wasn't what he said that made me drop the subject. It was how he said it. There was a choke in his voice. Like something from deep down in him was trying to come out. It didn't sound like him. It sounded scared.

"It's a Howard Family tradition." was all he said, and then paused. When he next spoke he was my dad again. His voice calm, firm and friendly. "I'll explain it to you when you're older."

That glimpse into something bigger was too much for my young self to understand at the time. So I got up and ran back to the ocean, forgetting for the moment anything more important than tackling one of my brothers into a wave.

The years went on from there. Vacations came and went and the Howard family tradition continued on unchanging. Then, my junior year of high school rolled around. My buddies and I were talking about taking a trip down to Florida for spring break. Sharing a hotel room together for the week and just having a good time away from parental supervision.

Knowing I was old enough to be mostly responsible, my parents agreed that as long as I kept my grades up and was able to pay for the trip myself, then it would be fine with them. Doing my part in that bargain wasn't a problem, and my friends and I had the plans finalized a week or two before we had to leave.

I briefly wondered if I would keep up the Howard family Tradition when I was on my own. It almost felt that being given that option was like crossing over into adulthood. It had always been my father doing it. Now I had a chance to do something reserved only for him. It was a nice thought, but what would my friends think? It wasn't something I contemplated long. There were more important logistics of our trip to think about: How to meet girls, and specifically, what to do with them once we met them.

A few days before I was to leave my father pulled me aside. No one else was home. My brothers and my mother were out doing something or other so my dad and I had a good two hours by ourselves. We sat down in the kitchen, my dad grabbed himself a beer and, hesitating, pulled one out for me.

"Son, you are going on a trip by yourself soon and I want to tell you a story."

My mind immediately thought he was going to give me the "Be Responsible" talk, or the "Don't Talk to Strangers" talk, or god-forbid, the "Safe Sex" talk, but no. It turned out to be something very different.

"I want to tell you about our tradition. Why I do what I do every time we get a hotel room."

"The Howard family tradition" I said, taking small sips of the beer. I didn't know which was more odd: drinking with my Dad, or hearing that vulnerability creeping into his voice again.

"The Howard family tradition" he continued, nodding his head. Sighing. Pausing. He took a big sip of his beer and started talking.

1972.

Your Mom and I aren't married yet. In fact, this was so long ago we haven't even met. I was nineteen. In my second year of college. I had plans to spend a semester off with some friends out in Colorado. So, I packed up my old Buick and headed west. It was an almost thirty hour trip. So, young as I was, I figured I could drive the whole thing by myself in two days.

And I probably could have. I was making good time, had made it to the edge of Tennessee before I had to take a nap. Some time near midnight. Unfortunately, it was winter, and I was up in the Smoky

Mountains, and it was damn cold. Too cold to sleep in the car like I had initially planned. So I drove half-asleep until I saw a sign for a motel.

Good thing, too.I was in the middle of nowhere. The road was surrounded by dense forest, and twisted and turned up and down the mountains. In the state I was in, I was lucky not to run the car right off the road. But then I saw the motel, nestled in the side of the mountain, almost hidden behind giant trees. I remember what it was called, thought the name was clever: The Waterfall Inn. It's no longer around, but at the time I was glad it was there. I pulled in and without even grabbing my bags I went looking for the front desk.

The place was actually nice. The building was small, looked very well taken care of, and pretty clean. If I wasn't so tired and cold I probably would have appreciated its seclusion and atmosphere. But right then all I wanted was a bed.

I did take exception with the owners calling it an Inn, though. It was definitely a motel. Each room had its own entrance along the front of the building. Not many of them, just six on the front, maybe more in the back. There was a door marked "Office" and I made a beeline for that. Inside was a simple undecorated front desk. No one was around but ringing the bell caused an old woman to emerge from the back room. She was wearing a nightdress and yawning. She made her way over and placed a ledger on the counter for me to sign, never looking up or greeting me. Just yawning.

Well, her yawning made me yawn and vice versa so I was eager to get through check-in and into a room. I gave her the fee (a Motel price, not an Inn price, which was good) and she gave me a key and shuffled away.

I had room number three. I went outside, walked three doors down, opened it and flicked on the lights to give it a once over. The room was small but nice. Smelled a little stale but seemed clean. It had its own bathroom at the back, a small dresser, no TV, not back then, but there was a phone. The bed was a queen, really thick and looked soft and comfortable. The room was warm which, compared to the chill of the air outside, made me even more tired.

So right then all I wanted to do was get in that bed. There was no Howard family tradition at the time so I turned off the lights, walked right over to it and, without even changing clothes or getting under the blanket, collapsed and fell instantly asleep.

* * * *

It was at that point in telling his story that my Dad paused. He had finished his beer and was working on a second. He leaned back, closed his eyes, and took one giant sip from the bottle.

"You know, I told your mother this story but she never believed it."

He said that as if he was talking to the world and not just to me. I didn't respond.

"She refuses to talk to me about it anymore. Like it's a part of me she's ashamed of."

He put the beer bottle on the table, a little harder than he normally would have. The knock of the glass on the wood seemed to jolt him back to reality. His eyes focused back on me.

"But we aren't talking about your mother here. I'm just telling you what happened that night."

* * * *

It was the kind of sleep so deep that an alarm clock would need to ring for twenty minutes before I even heard it. The mattress had been soft and inviting and I sunk into it and didn't remember a thing until I started waking up. And for a minute I didn't even know where I was. It was dark still, and the room was unfamiliar. Finally I remembered. But why was it still dark out? And why was I waking up?

The mattress was moving. Undulating beneath me. I shifted, rolled over, looked about, trying to let my eyes adjust to the darkness. It looked like something was moving at the foot of the bed. And I still felt movement underneath me.

Then I heard it, too. The shuffle of something moving on the carpet, moving away from the foot of the bed, coming around it towards me. Adrenaline shot through my body, waking me up and chilling me down deep. I rolled off the bed in the other direction, which happened to be away from the front door, towards the bathroom. My eyes were starting to adjust and there was definitely something there. Something in the room. I backed up to the bathroom door, fumbled against the frame, my hand frantically sliding across the wall, feeling for the lightswitch.

The thing by the bed stopped moving. It was a human, short enough to be a child. It turned towards me and started to move closer on its stubby legs. Then, from the foot of the bed, something else appeared out of nowhere. A black shape in the darkness, it looked like it was coming out of the mattress. That was impossible, right? But in the shadows that's what it looked like. The thing sloughed onto the ground, disgorged from the gullet of the bed, and rose up on two legs. Another child-shaped thing. This one also starting to move towards me.

Both of my arms were feeling for the lightswitch now as I backed further into the bathroom. My head hit something, and I screamed. A thin chain hanging from the ceiling. The light! The things in front of me momentarily stopped moving when I made the sound. I reached up and grabbed the chain, and pulled it just as something else poked out of the mattress.

The bathroom light flared on, and for a second I couldn't see a thing, blinded. But I recovered quickly and the light was now illuminating the other room enough for me to see what was in there. When I did, my fist tightened on the chain, my whole arm shaking. I had to will myself to let it go so I didn't accidentally turn off the light.

They were children. Two small naked boys, no more than toddlers. Both looked exactly the same, like twins. Thin and emaciated, their skin pale as milk. Chests sunken. Their hair wild and dirty, long like it hadn't been cut. Their nails as well, long, some cracked and broken. Mouths open, breathing heavy, teeth a smudgy brown. Their eyes almost completely black, pupils the size of nickels, were aimed straight at me.

The thing behind them was sticking out of a hole in the foot of the mattress. A jagged slash in the white fabric. It was a woman's head, two shoulders, one arm out, the other emerging as she looked at me. Her hair was black with streaks of grey, her skin also dead-white. Her eyes like black buttons on her skull. Her teeth crooked and rotting, mouth open.

She was making a sound. A high-pitched keen almost like a tea-kettle letting out air. The children turned their attention away from me and back to her. I had backed away as far as I could. The bathroom window was behind me. I tried to open it, but it was stuck or locked and I didn't want to turn my back on those things to figure it out.

By now the woman was half out of the bed, she was naked as well, her breasts small and thin, hanging down like deflated balloons. Her hands were reaching out towards the children, arms and fingers just skin around bone, bird-like. The children got within her reach and she snatched them up, her eyes darting back and forth between them and me, and then she started sliding back into the mattress, pulling them with her.

Her face disappeared into the bed, her arms still out guiding first one child in after her and then the other. The children helped part the slash in the mattress with their tiny hands and then each slid in head first. The last I saw of them was one of the child's little feet kicking, its long nails like talons, as it disappeared inside the mattress.

One of the hardest things I ever had to do was run past that mattress to the front door, right past that slash in the side of it. But I did it. The fear of staying in that room overcame the fear of a pale white arm reaching out and grabbing for me as I ran by.

I ran, and nothing reached out to grab me. At least, I don't think so, I never turned to check. I fumbled with that door knob for what felt like minutes but was probably a second, and ran out, slamming it behind me.

* * * *

My father seemed to deflate a little at that point. Recalling the story had taken a toll on him. Me too. I had been listening, rapt, and didn't even realize my mouth was completely dry. I went to take another sip of the beer, but it was empty.

"After that, I debated just getting in my car and leaving. But instead I went back to the front desk and woke up the old lady."

He stood, went to the refrigerator and took out two more beers. He handed one to me and took one for himself. I drank from it eagerly.

"What did you tell her?" I asked.

He wiped some of the perspiration off of the beer bottle with his hand and ran it across his face, his bald pate, the back of his neck.

"I'm not sure to be honest." he said. "I was in shock, babbling incoherently probably. But whatever I said eventually got her to call the police. And within the hour two officers were there and I was explaining the story to everyone."

"Did they believe you?"

My Dad laughed. "Nope! But they did check the room anyway. And the slash in the mattress was there, just like I told them it was."

"And that…family?" I asked.

He shook his head. "Nothing. The mattress was empty. They even had one of them pry it open, and the other stuck his head inside with a flashlight. Nothing. They said it was just an old mattress with a slash cut in it and some stuffing missing."

"So then what happened?" I asked.

He was staring off into space, my question seemed to have startled him.

"Then? Well, nothing. That was it. The cops said they would write it up and then just left."

He shrugged. "And I wasn't going to stay. I got in my car and drove straight through to Colorado. But that was only after checking the trunk and hitting each seat with the crowbar a couple of times."

That was when my father looked me in the eyes for the first time since he started telling the story. I wasn't sure what to think, but I knew I owed him enough to at least hold his gaze.

He looked at me and said "I don't know who those people were, or where they came from or why they were there. And sometimes I even wonder if it really happened. But then I remember their big black eyes, and the sound that woman made, and the feeling of them moving beneath me while I laid on the bed. That's why I do what I do when we go to a hotel room. And that's why I want you to do the same thing when I'm not around."

I imagined being in that hotel room. In the dark. I nodded.

"Promise me." he said, his eyes never leaving mine.

"I promise." I said. And I meant it.

"Good!" and just like that he was my dad again. The dad I know. No fear. No dark secrets. Just jovial and easy-going and carefree.

Together we downed the last of our drinks and threw out the bottles. By the time my mom got home we were in the living room watching a game. But I wasn't really paying attention. I was thinking about what my friends would say when they saw the Howard family tradition, or what my future kids would think when I someday passed it on to them. But mostly I thought about those things in the hotel room. I wondered if they now had their own tradition. One where they thumped on the inside of the mattress before climbing out. ▲

Ode to Ashtoreth

by K.A. Opperman

For David Park Barnitz

O Ashtoreth, O perfect corpse-wan queen,
O Goddess gowned in glimmers of the moon,
O shining eyes half-shut in silver swoon,
I set your crown with what white gems men glean
From out the stars; I send you perfumed praise
Upon a golden censer's breath, so soon
Extinguishèd.... I fain would die between
Your deathly breasts, thereon to end my days.

For I have seen you in my love's fair face—
She who lies cold beneath the moon's blue rays!
And I have kissed on her corrupt pale lips
Your poppied lips; in hers, known your embrace.
O Ashtoreth, pray pity him who sips
From out your down-tipped opalled cup—I chase
Upon my love's cold breast the last eclipse.

Hell in a Boxcar
by Scott A. Cupp

Rising from the floor of the boxcar, Bob was reminded of just how hot it was. The Rising Star Bank, a few blocks away, had proudly proclaimed the temperature to be 103° an hour or so ago when he and his friends had arrived a scant hour ago. He also vowed to kill Dave Lee when this was over.

Dave had brought a smudged handbill back from Ft. Worth. He had a friend working at the Hotel Texas who was able to procure most anything. When he mentioned a friend who was a good boxer, "Dolly" Jim Thompson had searched his files and produced an advertising flyer. Dave said "Dolly" was working an occasional boxing match with $100 prize for anyone who could go three rounds with the Champion. "Dolly" Thompson said that he wanted to be a writer himself someday and had written a few profiles of some oil field workers that he was trying to sell. He found it exciting that a writer would be a boxer. He wanted to meet Bob at some point. So Dave had convinced Bob and Clyde to check out the fight. A couple of beers on a hot day and they were more than willing to go.

That was how Bob found himself, bruised, stripped to the waist, boxing—not for the prize anymore but for his very life against this hellish being.

The boxcar had once been a refrigerated car. The car was now abandoned on a small rail spur. There was a crowd of people standing around the edges, cheering him on. Their cries echoed off the steel walls and were amplified in his ears. At least he hoped it was him they were cheering on.

The sound was powerful, but the smell was worse. The smell of long gone meat and blood. The smell of men inflamed into a blood lust. Bob's own sweat was tremendous. Even though he had fought just one three minute round, he felt like he had lost a couple of pounds. Rivers of sweat poured over his chest, making little mud pies in the dirt as it fell to the floor. The sweat offered no cooling in the heat as no wind hastened its evaporation.

Bob looked at Clyde who was trying to loosen him up. "God Almighty, Bob! How do you fight a thing like that?" His eyes widened with fear. "Let's just get the Hell out of here!"

Bob stared at Clyde in disbelief. "Are you deaf, man? Did you not hear the man say that once we started we go until three rounds have passed or until one of us could go no more? There's no throwin' in the towel. This is bare knuckles boxing as it's always been done."

Bob looked over in the corner at the fight promoter. The strange man was of no ethnic origin that Bob could identify. He might be part Egyptian or something worse.

It had been so easy. Bob and the boys had found the crowd gathered near the boxcar just as the flyer had indicated. The gnomish wizened figure in the ornate purple robe might have had gray skin. It certainly was not white, black, brown, yellow, or tanned. The skin was stretched tightly across a bald head, resembling nothing as much as a skull.

He certainly had an accent. He introduced himself as Todd Amen, or, at least that is how Bob had heard it. The old man's voice was quiet and hard to discern against the background noise from within the boxcar.

The boxcar had maybe 25 people crowded inside. They looked like a typical mixed bag of workers—some from the oil fields, some from the farms, others were just the ramblers that passed on through from somewhere headed to somewhere else.

Bob had pointed inside the car. "Them yahoos gonna fight your boy, too?'

The old man shook his head. "No, sirrah. They have not the courage, strength, will, nor the heart to do such a thing. The Tulsa Doom—my boy, as you call him—is well known among their crowd. I offer the $100 to entice folks to come and I never have to pay. He is unbeatable. At least, up to now. Do you have those qualities, sirrah? Is the $100 enough to make you try?"

"Where is he?" said Bob, "I need to size up the competition before I beat the tar out of him." He punched Dave on the shoulder and began to take off his shirt. Bob was a big strong man—6 feet tall and 200 pounds. He was a born fighter. His fists were large, positioned at the end of powerfully muscled arms. But he was neither a bully nor a rowdy. He was writer of tales filled with action and adventure.

His heroes were larger than life—strong men of undeniable strength, courage and honor. To learn about them and to write realistic tales about them, Bob had learned to box. He may have been an amateur but he was good.

The old man continued. "The Doom—he does not come out until we are ready to begin." Bob could not place the promoter's age—he could be 60, 70, maybe older. The voice had a gleeful, almost sinister cackle to it.

"OK, then, "said Bob, "where's the gloves?" His shirt off, he extended his hands, ready to receive the leather gauntlets.

"We use no gloves. Things can be hidden there, sirrah. This is no frills, bare knuckle boxing, just as our ancestors fought. Bone and sinew, strength and stamina, brutal and honest."

Bob was taken aback by this. But he had come too far. The beer he had had earlier gave him some courage. Besides, he was good and his father, the good doctor, could help him out if he got bruised or cut up a little.

Someone gave him a push. "Come on, Bob. You can do it! You can lick any man. Show them who is King of the Ring and King of the Pulps."

Bob glared at the old promoter. "Let's see the color of your cash before we get going. You say you've never had to pay. Let's see that you can pay."

The old man bowed slightly. "Your fear shows you to be a prudent man, effendi. Here is the color of my money." He pulled a roll of bills from within his purple robe. It was large. "Now, let's see the color of your courage. Step inside and meet the Doom."

They entered the boxcar and a cheer went up. Clyde and Dave began making a few side bets with other spectators. Bob stood in the center of the car. Only one way in. The door let in a little light. He surveyed the crowd, looking for his opponent.

It was damn hot. If it was 103° outside, it must be 120° or more inside. Damn Texas summers. At least the humidity was low. But 120° is hot no matter what. Sweat beads began appearing on his chest.

The promoter moved to the center of the boxcar, next to Bob. "Gentlemen," he yelled. "We have a challenger! Someone brave enough to face his Doom—my Doom—the Tulsa Doom! Your name, please."

"I'm Bob Howard of Cross Plains. I'm big as a bear and twice as mean. I will send you Doom back to Tulsa!" A broad smile filled his face. He flexed his muscles and posed for the crowd.

The crowd gave a lackluster cheer. They seemed jaded. But, plenty of men were willing to take bets from Clyde and Dave.

"Mr. Howard, this is three rounds of bare knuckles boxing. Each round is three minutes. Time will be kept by Mr. James "Dolly" Thompson, formerly of the Texas Hotel in Ft. Worth." A dapper young man raised his hand and a big stopwatch. Bob reached over and shook his hand.

"Keep good time," Bob said. Thompson nodded and sat down.

"You will box until the bell rings or until you cannot continue. There is no quitting once the round starts. The Doom—he fights from bell to bell. If you are still standing at the end of the three rounds, you win $100 in US American cash money!" He displayed the roll of bills again, fanning it out to show various denominations. "If you should somehow knock out my fighter," he reached in another pocket for another wad of bills, "you win twice the prize!"

The crowd cheered wildly at the sight of so much money. Larcenous thoughts were almost tangible across their faces. Amen pointed to the corner. "Deputy Stark of the local police is here to hold the money and ensure that we have a fair fight. Show them your gun, Clay." The deputy produced a huge Colt revolver.

"No one better have no thoughts about this here money," he said. He put the money into his uniform pocket. He kept the pistol out.

Amen worked his way through the rough crowd, now beginning to smell with the heat and sweat in the confined area. In a dark corner he approached a stained canvas covering. With a flourish he pulled the cover away revealing a corpse-like figure. The figure was a dusky Negroid fully six and one half feet tall.

Amen approached the figure and whispered into its ear. Instantly the eyes of the figure opened widely. The eyes may have been open but there did not appear to be a spark of awareness behind them or anywhere on the face. "Behold!" shouted Amen. "I give you the Tulsa Doom!" He whispered in the ear again.

The large body began to move, stiffly at first. It began to flex atrophied muscles. But the fighter made no sound.

Behind Bob, Dave punched his shoulders. "He may be big, but the bigger they are...eh, Bob?" Bob eyed the figure, seeing the heavily muscled arms and chest.

The fighter remained mute, not that anyone could hear over the din of excited voices increasing by the second. The fighter moved slowly into the light.

He was built solidly. When he turned to face Bob, the writer could see the catgut stitching his lips together. One word flashed into his mind—Zombie!

Bob had thought them to be figures of imagination. Boogies to frighten children and week minded individuals. But here was the proof before him.

Still, Bob was not that worried. Well, not much. He was young, strong, and possessed of a powerful mind. Zombies were, by nature, rather slow moving and without conscious thought or free will. Bob looked at the boxcar entrance. The deputy stood there, pistol drawn, blocking the way.

Amen finished whispering in the creature's ear. It approached the center of the boxcar. Spectators backed away, hugging the sides, never taking their eyes off of this amazing being.

Amen looked at Bob. "Well, Mr. Howard, let's see your stuff. Thompson!" The sharp sound of a bell echoed from the walls. The creature advanced slowly, raising hands the size of two pound flour bags, but nowhere nearly as soft. Bob drove a powerful right jab into the solar plexus. The creature did not try to block it. It did not flinch. Bob's left fist hit the ribcage. A rib cracked loudly.

The zombie moved forward swinging at and hitting Bob's head. The blow should have shattered granite. Bob found himself staggering back as the zombie advanced forward.

Another flurry of punches resulted in more broken ribs for the zombie. They knocked the being back a few feet. Bob stared at his opponent. The creature was not breathing hard. It may not have been breathing at all. It was like punching a brick wall.

Bob backed away, trying to assess his situation. The creature was strong, impervious to pain, and closing on him. A big black left arm came crashing toward him but Bob avoided it, backing away to a chorus of "Boo's!" from the bloodthirsty crowd.

"Pure brawn will not win this match," thought Bob. Clearly he had been tricked into fighting an opponent who would be very, very tough to beat.

The zombie punched his face again, bringing Bob to the floor of the boxcar. Bob wiped dirt, sweat and blood off. Sweat kept pouring into his eyes, the salt stinging and blurring his vision.

Somewhere he heard the distant sound of a sharp bell toll and Clyde and Dave were at his side lifting him off the floor while Amen pushed the zombie back into a corner. "Jesus, Bob, how do you beat a thing like that? Is it even alive?"

Bob shook his head hoping to clear his thoughts. That was a mistake. His vision was already blurry and his head felt like an anvil blown skyward on a Fourth of July celebration. But this was no celebration.

"Hell, no, Dave! This thing aint alive. That's a zombie, you moron! The living walking dead! Big and powerful, but slow. I've got to figure out how to beat it. But I can't beat it with my fists. Damn thing doesn't feel pain. I've got to beat it with my brains, what few I have left."

Somewhere that damned bell tolled again and Bob found himself doing a boxcar two-step with a monster. "Zombie! Zombie! Zombie!" he screamed mentally. "What do I know about Zombies? I know I've read stories about them. How do I go about beating one? Thing doesn't feel pain or weariness or compassion."

A punch aimed at his head missed but the shoulder it clipped hurt like the devil. "Bob and weave! Bob and weave! Keep moving. To stand still is to get punched into next Wednesday."

Bob saw the gnomish promoter cackling in the corner, moving his fingers in a weird rhythmic pattern. Was he controlling the zombie's movements? Bob did not know but he had a way of finding out. Bob and weave! Bob and weave! He moved around the boxcar letting the monster follow him.

Soon he was directly in front of Amen. The little man kept his fingers twitching. Bob slowed and dropped his guard. The zombie aimed a punch at the knockout button at the end of Bob's chin. At the last second, Bob lunged to the right and the punch caught the unwary promoter full in the face. He dropped like a stunned ox. The zombie stopped for a moment. Bob struck hard at the chest of the beast but with little effect.

The stunned promoter regained his wits faster than Bob would have liked and began moving his arms and hands in a number of arcane motions. The zombie rushed at Bob with the subtlety of a freight train. Blow by blow landed, and if the earlier punches had been hard, these were devastating. Blood poured freely from multiple cuts and gouges. Somewhere a bell rang again. Two rounds down but Bob knew he would not survive another one. Amen was pissed and was going to have his surrogate take it out on Bob.

In the far corner, Bob huddled with his friends. He had trouble standing and fell down to his knees. His bloody hands hit a small piece of salt, a remnant of the old occupants of this refrigerator car.

The salt stung his hands worse than the cuts of his face. Bob drew his hands back and then stopped. "Sure," he thought, "that's the trick! Zombies don't know they're dead. When they taste salt, they realize their status and they die. All I have to do is make him taste the salt!"

"Boys, put as much salt as you can find on my knuckles, right now. Do it fast before the bell rings and we lose the chance. Pile it on!" Clyde and Dave did what he asked; never questioning the request, fearing that if they didn't, Bob would die here. Bob winced as they did it; his hands were burning weapons of death.

"Got you now, you bastard!" The bell rang.

Jack Dempsey and Joe Louis would have fled at the sight of the madman with salted bleeding fists who attacked the monster. Blow after blow went at the zombie's catgut sealed mouth. He had to get that mouth open.

And the zombie did not just let Bob attack him. Amen's fingers were twitching furiously. This was the money round. For each blow that Bob landed, the zombie returned one to Bob's ribs or shoulder or back or arms. Bob's hands were on fire.

The zombie seemed unphased by the pummeling. It just kept coming and hitting and being hit. Bob caught a hard left to the jaw, something he had been desperately avoiding, and went down to his knees. As he tried to rise, he saw a small stone, with a sharp edge.

His salt encrusted fist grabbed the stone. He held it between two fingers where, hopefully, Amen would not see it. The sharp end just barely protruded. He slashed at the zombie's face and a small gash appeared on the cheek. Another slash. A larger gash. Teeth inside the zombie's mouth became visible.

More blows landed on Bob. He ignored them. Adrenaline was pumping into his blood as fast as it could go. Another quick jab and there was a visible gap. With all his might, he pushed a salted fist into the wound. It didn't go far in but it must have been enough.

The zombie's eyes seemed to register something—fear, hatred, knowledge of his doom. He tried to bite Bob but his mouth was still sewn up. Salt mixed with Bob's blood and sweat went into the zombie's maw. The monster made a horrifying noise, stiffened and fell prone to the floor. The glorious bell rang and echoed throughout the stunned boxcar.

The Tulsa Doom was lying there, fully dead. The promoter had collapsed onto the floor also and was unconscious. Drunken men milled around the boxcar, not quite sure what had happened. The deputy and the money seemed to have disappeared.

Friendly hands lifted Bob from the floor and got him into the open air. Clyde and Dave tried to collect on their bets, but the unruly and surly crowd made that seem not worth the trouble.

"Let's get the hell out of here," someone suggested and they all agreed that it might be a good idea.

Within minutes Bob was laughing and roaring in the car. "I damned sure as Hell beat that demon but no one will ever believe me. I beat the hell out of a zombie. Even old Grandpa Theobold won't believe this one."

"Hell, Bob," said Clyde, "it sounds like one of your Weird Tales stories, except there aint no nekkid women in it. How's Brundage going to do a cover that will sell more copies if you don't have a helpless woman?" Dave laughed along with Clyde. "C'mon, Bob! You got to do this."

Bob thought for a minute. "Might be a way to make a story out of this and get some of the money back, though. Maybe I'll change Dave into a woman for it. Pay him back for this beating." He winked at the man and feigned a kiss. "Margaret will do you right. Make you look better than you ever did or ever will." They all laughed the whole way back home. ▲

Jorōgumo
by Kelda Crich

The windscreen wipers ticked like metronomes, pushing the snow to the edges of the windscreen to melt in crystalline deliquescence. Skerritt edged the truck through another switchback. He'd been driving for eighteen hours, without a break. His hand reached for the bottle of pine-resin spirit. He took a swallow. He laughed as he threw the empty bottle out of the Jeep window. The snow outside was like his mind: cold and clean and blank.

Swirling snow, feather flakes of cold spun-silk falling on the pristine quiet ice, covering the hard rock. The Goddess Mountains the locals called them. They were a people with a lot of gods and goddesses. That would change.

Skerritt had no destination in mind. All he knew was that he needed to be away from the city below; away from Vinnie and Karram, the last two members of his squad; away from his swarming brothers-in-arms, the men of the Weatherman's army, drunk on victory, euphoric after half a decade of war.

* * * *

Soliders camped in a conquered land, waiting for the sergeant to issue leave, watching their comrades returning in the cold dawn from a night in the foreign city. Except that it wasn't foreign anymore. It was the Weatherman's city since the surrender.

"When's it going to be our turn?" asked Karram. He was young, impatient.

Vinnie looked up from cleaning his lucky knife. "Better be soon, or the city might run out of beer or women."

"It's not right," said Karram. "We should be next. What do you think, Skerritt?"

Skerritt shrugged. War had curbed his impatience. He was used to the endless days of waiting. He looked at the white mountains in the distance. Snow in August? He shook his head, slowly. "It'll be our turn soon enough."

* * * *

The sergeant issued them their pay and their leave, a week later. "Don't spend it all at once, lads," He said with a wink, handing over an envelope of Weatherman notes.

"About time," said Karram.

"What was that?" The sergeant was a man with a changeable temper.

"Ack," said Vinnie. "He didn't mean anything. Just impatient. You know what the young ones are like."

"Virgin, is he?" said the sergeant, grinning.

"I'm no virgin," said Karram, angrily.

"Oh, no, Sergeant. He's had more women than any man I've ever met— if his stories are to be believed," said Vinnie with a wink at the sergeant. "Have you got any advice for us? You been out there?"

The sergeant nodded. "They're friendly enough in the tenderloin district. There's been some fighting in the temple district, depends what you're looking for."

"Thanks," said Vinnie.

* * * *

They set off for the tenderloin district. They knew well enough where to find it, that information had passed from man to man, wildfire through the camp.

* * * *

Skerritt took a long swallow from his drink. The local spirit was a fierce alcohol distilled from the pinewood resin. He drank methodically, longing for summer tasting beer, ripe with sun. He watched the women dancing to the foreign music. It was too soon for the musicians to have learnt decent tunes. The musicians plucked out their peculiar melodies on funny shaped guitars, grinning encouragingly. The madam stood by the cash register, trying to maintain her composure, but revealing her nervousness in a compulsive twitch jumping at the corner of her mouth. From time to time a woman would take a soldier into a back room, leading him through a doorway lined with heavy red silks.

Vinnie returned from the back rooms. He took a seat on a black lacquered chair next to Skerritt and he stretched out of his arms. "Well?" he said.

"Well what?"

"Aren't you going to try the locals?"

"I am," said Karram. He stared at the dancing women. His face was an agony of indecision. "I just can't choose."

"Doesn't take much choosing. They're all much of a muchness," said Vinnie.

Skerritt refilled his glass from the bottle of pungent spirit.

"And you, Skerritt? Aren't you going to take a woman? It's been a while hasn't it? Last time I recall was when that group of camp followers found us on the plains." Vinnie sighed. "Been a long time."

"Maybe later." Skerritt took a long drink. He glanced at his reflection in the table's black glass. That had been a good time. That had been before. Truth was, he was scared: scared that a woman, even a whore, would look on him with revulsion. How could she not, when he could barely manage to look at his own face.

"Aye. They're not much cop here," said Vinnie. "Drink up, lads."

"But I haven't…" said Karram.

Vinnie laughed. "Don't worry, son. You'll get yours." He stood, and made his way over to the stage. "But these women are no good." His voice carried over the sounds of the music.

The madam took a couple of nervous steps forward, gesturing to a couple of local men, sitting at a table in the shadows.

Skerritt said, "You're right, Vinnie. You've always had a good eye for the women." That was true enough. Vinnie took full use of the Weatherman's indulgences. He had three wives waiting for him at home.

"Let's find some real woman," said Karram.

The madam nodded to Skerritt as he passed. Grateful that he had averted trouble. Skerritt scowled at her. He hadn't done it for her sake, he'd done it for Vinnie.

They left the bar. They made their way into the moon-glazed night, heavy with the promise of more snow. They wandered through the small and twisting streets, until they found the temple.

* * * *

Through the windscreen, beyond the haze of snow, Skerritt saw a dark slender shape ahead. He slowed the Jeep to a crawl alongside. It was a woman, her head was veiled, but he caught the glimpse of her pale face. She carried a bundle in her arms. She would freeze to death out here unless he stopped. He pulled up a few yards ahead, but left the engine ticking over. It would be a devil of thing to try to get it restarted with the snow coming down.

Skerritt opened the passenger door as she approached. "Hey. Where are you going?"

When she looked at him, Skerritt looked away, not because she was beautiful, (as beautiful as the woman they'd found in the temple) but because she looked at him directly, and, though he was watching for it, he didn't see her flinch.

"Get in you'll freeze out here," said Skerritt, recovering his composure.

She hesitated for a moment, still staring into his face with her ice-blue eyes. Skerritt liked that; it was unusual; most of the locals had brown eyes.

"Come in I say. Get in," said Skerritt, wondering if he was being foolish. Perhaps a woman wouldn't take a lift from the soldier. She glanced at the bundle in her arms, and touched it tenderly. Why would she bring a child into this freezing weather?

When she climbed into the Jeep, she bought the cold with her.

Skerritt grunted. He felt conscious of the stink of alcohol in the Jeep. The woman sat quietly with her head bowed. The women here, well, they weren't like the women at home. They were amenable...pliable. And this woman was so lovely. Maybe...maybe if she was as amenable as she looked, he could take her to the camp. Maybe even take her back home when the time came. It happened all the time Weatherman soldiers bringing back exotic wives. Then everyone would know that he wasn't someone who had to be pitied.

"What's your name?" he asked.

She said nothing. That pleased him; she was modest. But from time to time she would glance at him with her elusive blue, multifaceted eyes—and that pleased him, too.

* * * *

At first, the streets were full of soldiers laughing shouting, smashing things. Some had found women. Skerritt heard their sounds down the dark corridors.

"It's not like home, is it?" said Karram, staring at the sloping bamboo roofs, the sway of coloured paper lanterns.

"That's right, son," said Vinnie. "It's something out of the ordinary, all right. Something to tell the girls back home. Take a good look, because all this will all change in the next few years, now that it's part of the Weatherman's empire. A pity, somehow."

"I don't think we're heading in the right direction," complained Karram. "I don't think that we're going to find any women down here."

It was true that there were less lights, and they hadn't seen another soul for the last half hour.

"You'll get yours, don't you worry, son," said Vinnie. To the younger boys of the squad, Vinnie had been something of a father figure. He looked out for them, on the battle field and off it. To Skerritt, who was closer to Vinnie's age, he was a brother. Closer than a brother. It'd been Vinnie who'd dragged him Skerritt off the battlefield, carrying him, dragging him, with the right side of his face sliced off. And in the medic tent, when he'd begged for Vinnie for a clean cut, to end it. Vinnie had looked at him with so much contempt that he'd been ashamed. "You'll live," he'd hissed. "By the Weatherman you'll live. You'll not be like my brother. You will live. Or it's all been for nothing."

Yes. Skerritt owed Vinnie his life. For better or for worse.

"It's like a nest, this place," complained Karram.

Into the silence came the slang of a metal-throated bell. Karram sprinted round the corner. "I've found something," he shouted.

The temple stood in a courtyard, rising high above the surrounding building, with eight floor of descending breadth, a simple timber building with a shingle roof, the only decoration being two ancient metal spiders, larger than a man at flanking the open gateway.

"It's a spider temple," said Karram.

"You don't say," said Vinnie.

Light shone from the temple's windows. The voice of the temple bell was like an invitation into the cold night.

"Who would worship spiders?" asked Skerritt.

"Let's go inside and see," suggested Vinnie.

A stone-grey spider idol, crouched in the back of the room. Tall as ten men. Its outstretched legs touched the walls. Its head was studded with gemstones the size of skulls which gleamed in the light, from the lanterns decorated with eight-legged characters, strung on wires, hung low. The spider's face was a disquieting merging of the human and the arachnoid.

"Savages," said Vinnie. "Mixing beasts, even insects, with people and calling them gods."

"There is only the Weatherman," said Karram piously.

"You got that right."

A woman emerged from the stone spider. She placed her palms together and inclined her head. "Welcome, my friends. How can I serve you?" Skerritt stepped back into the shadows.

"Who are you, miss?" said Vinnie.

"I am Ash-lan, servant of the spider," replied the woman. She was very beautiful, dressed in a loose fitting black robe that to Skerritt was more alluring than the scanty costume of the dancing girls. Her hair hung like silk over one shoulder.

"We want to see the spider," said Vinnie. He laughed as if he'd made a witty reply.

The priestess nodded. "She will help you. Which one of you is suffering?"

"Say what now?" Vinnie flicked a paper lantern and set the string of lights swaying.

"Which one of you is suffering from a skin ailment caused by the spider's children. I will draw water from the spider well and give you the holy ash." The priestess squinted slightly as she looked towards Skerritt. "I see, now." She smiled. "Come. Don't be afraid. She will heal you."

Vinnie laughed. "His scars weren't caused by a spider bite, miss. I think you misunderstood what we want from you."

Where do loyalties lie? How far can they be stretched? In a moment of premonition, Skerritt knew that this night would be the woman's last. He'd seen that look of hatred on Vinnie's face before: when Vinnie held the body of his dead brother in his arms, cut to ribbons by an enemy blade. Vinnie had screamed a vow of revenge to the Weatherman, with that same look of hatred. Skerritt had never thought of himself as a coward. He'd known fear. What soldier hadn't? But he'd always done the right thing. But in the spider temple of swaying shadows and monstrous stone idols his soul seemed to shrivel as he realised that he was not the man he thought he was.

Skerritt watched as Vinnie and Karram advanced towards the priestess.

"No!" she said, finally discerning their intentions. "This is a holy place."

Vinnie back-handed her, and she fell to the floor. "I told you that you'd get yours," he said to Karram with a wink.

"Stop." Another figure emerged from the stone spider. A young man. His elaborate uniform was partially unlaced, revealing his chest.

"Hey. Now I see someone was here before us," said Vinnie with a laugh. "Back off, son."

The priestess glanced at the man and shook her head.

Ignoring her, the man charged towards them, his long sword held high above his head.

It only took a moment for Vinnie to shoot him through the throat.

The priestess screamed. She crawled across the floor to the dead man's body. She gathered him in her arms, started singing a low, amusical sound of mourning.

"C'mon," said Skerritt. "Let's get out of here."

"We haven't got one we came for," said Vinnie, taking a step towards the priestess.

She grabbed the man's sword and scrambled to her feet half running half falling she stood below the stone spider, swinging the sword from hand to hand.

"I'll say this for them, they're fighters," said Vinnie. He raised his gun. "Put the knife down, girl."

"No." She grasped the sword with both hands and slid it across her throat. Skerritt watch her skin opening like the unfolding of a petal, before the explosion of arterial blood. The priestess fell to her knees then fell face-forward onto the floor. Her blood forming a pool running to the feet on the stone spider.

"What the?" said Vinnie.

"We only wanted to..." whispered Karram.

* * * *

A causality of war that was all. She wasn't the first, and she wouldn't be the last. It was a pity really. A waste.

"I'll take you to the village," said Skerritt to the woman. He was a good man He'd saved her and her child from death. He was a good man.

She bent to the bundle in her arms and crooned a song to her baby.

Her silence was beginning to irritate Skerritt. It was as if he was nothing. "Didn't you hear what I said?" he asked roughly.

The sound of her song changed. Her voice was a screech.

"Stop that," said Skerritt.

She raised her face towards him. Her multifaceted eyes. Insistent. Breaking Skerritt out of the lies.

"My temple." Her arms were wires emerging from the silk of her dress.

"We didn't kill her," said Skerritt. The Jeep was small, and she was so large, so old, her legs, her eyes, her fangs. Outside the snow, the cold blank snow, a half-eye on the road, Skerritt saw another loop in the track.

"My daughter."

Her multifaceted eyes: insistent. Her face drawing close. The venom dripping from her fangs.

* * * *

"Look at the blood," said Karram.

The blood that had pooled at the statue's feet was absorbing into the stone. The leg of the spider was covered with a red web, like the capillaries of a living body. It spread quickly. They heard a cracking noise, like the breaking of stone.

"Let's go," shouted Vinnie.

Skerritt reached the door first. He fumbled at the handle. "It's locked."

"Shoot off the damn lock," said Vinnie.

Skerritt took out his pistol. He glanced behind him. Flakes of stone were falling off the statue, revealing something black, organic, moving.

"Shoot the damn lock," screamed Vinnie.

The bullet ricocheted off the metal.

"Try again."

Stone fragments exploded. They coughed as the powder filled their lung. The temple was full of chittering sound: the rubbing of its mandibles.

"Try again," shouted Karram.

From the corner of his eye, Skerrit saw the whip-fast hook of a leg. A scream.

Skerritt shot the lock open.

* * * *

And you're running through the snow. Running. Running. Leaving Vinnie and Karram behind. Listening to the click of the legs skittling over the roofs. Running to the encampment. Grabbing the Jeep and plunging into the snow storm. Getting far, far away from that thing, from that spider thing, from the things that it did to Vinnie and Karram. Pretend it didn't happen. Seal your mind, cold and clean and blank, or go crazy.

Crazy. You're in the Spider Goddess Mountains, running from her.

* * * *

"My children" she says.

Her dress falls open. Her legs unwind. Her bundle is a mess of eggs. Skerritt screams, and the Jeep spins out of control. He's falling, falling, and the spider wraps her legs around him: thin, spindle-haired, grotesque.

* * * *

In the gully. Immobile in the web. Outside the broken window, the snow is cold and pristine and blank. Quiet, so very, very quiet. Skerritt wonders if the cold will get to him first, but then he hears the tiny sound of the eggs tearing open, and feels the first, tentative movements of the spiderlings.

▲

Clay Baby
by Jack Lee Taylor

She set her tiny baby down on the kitchen table. Her baby still had no face, so she gently pushed in two slits into its clay, purple head with her fingernail until she saw the vestige of a smile. She added two more curved slits above the smile for eyes that appeared shut tight, full of glee.

She moved her baby onto a spot on the table where fading sunlight shone so she could study her work. It didn't exactly look like a baby; its shape was amorphous, a purple ghost-like thing perched above two crude flattened slabs of clay as a kind of pedestal. Her creation certainly wasn't anything comparable to the remarkable clay creatures her husband made in his studio down in the basement.

But it's cute, she thought. *And it's my first work. My first child.*

She picked up her baby from the table and then headed down the hallway until she came to a door splotched ornately with intricate designs made of clay. Above the door was a bulbous light bulb protruding out like a threatening fist. Seeing that it did not glow angry red, she opened the door and descended down creaking, boarded steps, cradling her baby in her arms. Her husband's cursing grew louder with each step down into the cold, dusty basement.

"I did not call for you," her husband said, not turning from his latest work to look at her. He hunched over a menagerie of several clay animals set across a large flat board full of realistic jungle terrain. Were it not for the pair of spotlights set upon the small animals, they would all blend with the countless clay things scattered around the concrete-bricked room, all of these creatures made from her husband's previous claymation films.

"I have something to show you," she said, stepping closer behind him. She held out her baby, cupping it in her hands. Her husband raised a finger, his back to her.

"I'm busy," he said. "You know this." She frowned, pulling her baby toward her.

"The light was not on," she said.

Her husband ignored her. Instead, he stood up and headed over to a camcorder perched on a tripod next to a blazing spotlight. He pushed a button on the camcorder and then crossed his arms, eyeing his miniature stage, his white hair and glasses gleaming next to the spotlight.

The clay animals all sprung simultaneously to life: a lion chasing a gazelle, an elephant herd tromping through the ground, exotic birds flying through the air, giraffes grazing in the distance and many more animals in their own activities. It all looked so random, unorganized. And that's what made it all look so real.

"Bah," her husband grumbled. His animals stopped moving, his birds plopping back onto the board.

"That was wonderful," she said.

"No," he said. "They are clumsy." He removed his glasses and pushed a palm into his eyes. He let out an exhausted sigh and said, "I am getting too weak. Too old for this."

"No dear," she said, coming closer to him and placing a hand on his shoulder. "You mustn't say that. You are an amazing man! A brilliant artist!"

He scowled at her, putting his glasses back on. He pointed an accusing finger at her, "You would know this. All that I've done for you. You know this well!"

He paused, calming himself. "What are you holding?" he asked with annoyance.

She showed her baby to her husband, bringing the purple child just under the spotlights so he could see her first work.

"What is that?"

"It's our baby."

Her husband chortled and then laughed hard, his chest heaving.

"That?" he said in between laughs. "You made that?"

She stepped back, confused. She waited for his laughter to die and then said, "I know I could never be as good as you. But… it's my first work. Our first baby. Would you make our baby move like you do the animals?"

Her husband frowned, shaking his head. "No. Don't you realize how hard it is to control?" he said.

"Yes," she said. They stared at each other in silence for a moment, and then her husband turned back to his work.

She moved away back toward the stairs and looked down at her baby's face. Its smile was still there. *I am forbidden to use*, she thought. *But maybe this one time…*

She pulled at the familiar vibration from her husband, the stirring power she could always feel linking him to her. She pushed the vibrations from within her down into her child. The smiling divot on her baby's mouth began to move.

"Mom-ma," her baby said. The room began to shake, clay figures falling from shelves.

"NO!" her husband cried. "Stop using!"

"I..." she began and then felt the vibration grow stronger—uncontrollable. She couldn't stop this. Her husband screamed, staggering toward her, his palms to the sides of his head. *"YOU MUST STOP!"* Her baby began to lose its shape. *NO! MY BABY!*

Something suddenly shifted inside of her and then she felt herself... what? Shrink? *He's taking it away from me!*

"I warned you," her husband said, panting. "You must never use my power."

Her arms drew into her body, her torso expanding and ripping the buttons from her dress.

"I should never have created you," he said. "You... you use up too much of the energy."

She tried to reach out to her husband, but her arms were now just nubs of clay. Her head tucked down into her neck; her legs puddled boneless to the ground.

Darkness formed around her vision, but she spotted her baby, malformed and still on the ground next to her. With a last pull from her husband's energy, she reached out with a snaking piece of her and bonded with her baby, reeling her child toward her. Into her.

For the moment just before she was unmade, she felt a sense of joy and wonder.

She was a mother.

A mother with child.

▲

The Corpse and the Rat: A Story of Friendship

by Joshua L Hood

A corpse slid into the river. Rain plipped off its milky white eyes, its blue and splotchy lips, its porcelain skin. Mud diluted into brown water and sank away from it, down to the bottom of the river. More mud from the gentle slope trailed behind its feet, in no hurry to get anywhere, marking the languid progress of the corpse's last journey.

. This corpse was miles from anyone or anywhere it used to call important. This corpse had made a good run when it was still alive, and so it lived a little longer, albeit alone—as alone as it was now, not enjoying a gentle float down a gentle river on a not sunny day.

The heat made the corpse sweat, in a way. Despite the dark red sky, there was no respite from the sticky warmth. It radiated from everything, but the water brought a little coolness, which would have been nice.

A rusty culvert glided by overhead. Where once it gushed, now it dripped. What was once runoff water, some industrial slurry, was now a vestigial trickle of sludge, rust stained red like the sky. It traced a stuttering path along the body like Jackson Pollack's first dribble onto canvas. The red slid down the arch of the nose and rimmed the milky white eyes.

Suddenly the whole body shuddered and bobbed in the current. At the last minute, sensing an opportunity slipping away, a rat the size of yesterday's housecat lunged from the drooling pipe and lit on the corpse's swollen belly. It growled a sound like gravel grinding in a clenched fist. Triumph. It squinted into the orange-tinted distance where the white glass riverbank reflected the dull sky too brightly for eyes that had been used to the drain pipes and crawlspaces of the crumbling factory. They saw, the first eyes to see, what remained of the world, and if it had known well enough the rat would have shook its head and gone back to its dark corridors.

Instead, it studied the scene like an astronaut first arriving on a desert planet—its beauty only perceptible because its cruelty had no comparison. All the same, if a rat could assume, and maybe this one could, it would have assumed that the world had always been this way, and wondered what the big fuss was all about. It was pretty though.

As the corpse floated along it began to pass familiar things. A boat dock that had been spared the fires by its convenient location. A parking lot where the cars had been realigned from neatly ordered rows into a jumble of confusion that would have rationalized itself into an outward spiral, radiating from a smoldering crater, if it could have been seen from above. It slowly began to pass other corpses, those slightly slower than it had been, who'd died a few moments sooner. They were up higher on the river bank, too far to be washed down into the flow by the burning rain.

A current took the corpse's arm and swept it outward as though reaching out to touch its fellows, falling short by just a few dozen yards. The rat flinched to see its raft move so. It scrutinized the vacant face and maybe realized, by the two eyes and mouth and nose, that this thing had once been a living thing like itself. It may have understood the concept of comradery, but if it did, didn't linger on the thought. Instead, it was distracted by a sudden compulsion. It realized then that it was standing on meat—edible meat—and rent a chunk of flesh from directly beneath where it stood. It chewed dreamily.

Concrete boulders with a few right angles and many jagged edges stretched into the distance as the parts of a city that had only partly collapsed drifted away behind them. The rat curled into the nape of the corpse's neck, nuzzling its chin with its head, letting the water lap against its grubby toes. It didn't sleep, but watched with a danger-wary eye that had become a genetic necessity amongst its kind. A fish leapt not far off. The rat didn't move, but followed the ripples with its gaze as they broke over the bent rim of a bicycle lodged part way into the muddy bank. Glassy crystals burned into the mud sparkled with the disturbance, then went back to their dull gleams. The fish jumped again—as though following the corpse.

The rat's eyes popped open. It sensed something amiss. Another fish jumped and the rat knew it and its corpse were not alone. Suddenly protective of its vessel and food, it peered into the water with a shrewd eye. Small silver glimmers darted in and out, back and amongst each other. They bounced their snub noses off the corpse, taking small bits of the tattered flesh with them. The rat growled a sound that turned to bubbles as it lashed its sharp snout into the water and snatched a writhing silver thing. With a gulp it swallowed the thing and lashed at another. The fish were gone then, fleeing with the same instinct that had preserved them through the nightmare that turned the sky red.

The rat relished the taste of victory and flesh, and only then noticed that the bank was littered with shiny silver things like the one it'd just eaten, blistered and shriveled, but bigger. But they were too far away, and its appetite had just been piqued, so it took another chunk of flesh from the corpse and resumed its dreamy daze.

The night did not bring cold. Whatever had once been normal of heat and cold was no more. The rain persisted, a slow burning drizzle. The sharp edges of concrete and delicate details of antiquity's marble memories had already begun to soften, melt away in the strange rain. The horizon was pocked with spots of light, like many suns that would take ten thousand years to set.

The rat once again looked into the face of the corpse, peered deep into its eyes. It smelled the mouth, nuzzled aside the lips with its snout. Its ears pricked at the smell of sweet meat. With its almost human hand, the rat scratched at the porcelain teeth until the jaw pried open. It creaked with rictus, and spoke to the rat, a long low moan. The rat didn't notice the corpse sink a little lower into the water as it chewed away the swollen tongue. If it understood gratitude it would have thanked the corpse, and the corpse would have nodded and smiled ever so slightly as it did in life, always embarrassed by a compliment.

Suddenly, the river began to flow faster, more chaotic. Froth churned from the jagged edges of boulders. The banks became smooth concrete, narrowing, constricting the path through a flow gate, burst open in the nightmare. Waves bustled and pushed past each other to get through the broken dam like Christmas shoppers used to. The corpse was caught by one of these waves and pushed along with it. The rat dug its claws into the flesh as speed increased, for the first time afraid of something it couldn't quite define. Death, perhaps. It hunkered down and braced against the crashing waves, too chaotic to even leap across when the banks neared.

With sturdy arms outstretched like pontoons, the corpse braved the rapids and fought its way through the center of the channel. A strip of pink tore away from its left arm against gnarled rebar, but it otherwise remained afloat and undamaged until it was spewed out the other side of the break and down a steep, rippled gradient of concrete. Here it caught on the grade's textured latice that agitated the water into a wide canal, and the rat was thrown into the froth, scrabbling, panicking against gravity and current.

Several of the little silvery fish flopped down the grade as well, and the rat snapped at one despite itself. It missed, and was plunged into a deep, swirling eddy at the diversion's base. Several drowned rats swirled with it. The threat of what that meant was lost on its panicking mind as it floundered.

A larger splash sent a gush of water that pushed the rat and several of its dead kind back into the current and it began to drift down the canal again. The source of the splash, its savior, followed after it, milky white eyes now looking towards the distant horizon as it listed in the water. Its sturdy pontoons had broken and were dragging behind it like a trail of tin cans tied to the bumper of a newlywed couple's car. The rat swam towards it.

Partially submerged, but still swollen enough in the middle to provide a comfortable place to rest and dry off, the corpse continued its final journey. The rat climbed aboard and quickly went about forgetting its cruel tumble down the dam. Buildings began to rise again, in fractured bits and pieces, then fell away to become erstwhile farmland, now fields of skeletal crops. The heat faded a little, a cooler breeze drifted from the distant mountains that still had the ability to get dark at night. No one had lived there, and so they survived. The rat looked into those distant mountains, scenting the breeze that wasn't quite fresh, but as close as breeze would ever get to being called fresh again. It climbed to the head of the corpse. Little waves rippling outward from the body as it did. Something unknown but familiar drifted in on that breeze.

Night came again, and the rat chased off the fish before its one eyed sleep. It was unable to eat any, so had some cheek meat instead. It woke some time later with a jostle. The canal had begun twisting in earnest through the countryside, like something that used to be a snake. The corpse bounced off the banks, but refused to be snagged by them. What were once trees and bramble had become brittle and black, unable to find purchase against the sodden flesh without crumbing into dust.

The rat got up. The familiar scent had returned, stronger. With a sense keened by a lifetime of darkness, it honed in on the direction of the scent in an instant. It hadn't smelled anything like this for a long time, but knew exactly what it was. Another rat—and still alive.

Two reflective eyes glinted across the canal, watching the corpse and its rider. The rat became agitated with excitement, but was wary of swimming across the tepid water. The corpse continued on, leaving the eyes in the darkness. If the rat had not known loss before that point, it would have learned it then. It nestled close to the face of the corpse and took solace in it.

Morning brought hunger. Rats are always hungry, and it had been a long time since it ate. By some new, or perhaps very old, instinct the rat knew not to eat the corpse while it floated on the water. If mankind's evolution had developed sentimentality to prevent the destruction of needed things, then this rat's genetics taken that fortunate leap forward in understanding. However, as the day wore on, and no more fish were forthcoming, the hunger grew. As with all living things, old instincts run the deepest, hunger precedes prudence, just as it had for those whose hunger for destruction had preceded the nightmare. The rat grew impatient and resentful towards its own better judgment. Compulsion always wins against learning in the end, and so the rat acted against its own good and began chewing again on the soft flesh of the corpse.

The silence of the end of the world was breached by a sucking pop, followed by the slow hissing of gas from the sodden gut. This time the rat did notice the corpse sinking, but it was too late. As it found itself floundering again in the current of the canal, swimming for the far side, its nascent sense of sentimentality felt sorry for betraying the corpse. If it had been alive, the corpse would have forgiven the rat—it always forgave if it could.

The corpse disappeared beneath the current, finding neutral buoyancy just a few inches under the surface . It continued drifting, now staring at the red sky through a shallow lens of murky water. The corpse would have felt like it was floating in a womb, if it could have.

It was once more alone. Long ago it had left the other corpses behind and had reentered solitary country. Every few miles a car could be seen overturned on the banks with maybe the black silhouette or white bones of someone else who'd made an admirable attempt to get away. But those corpses were too far away, to alien to the river corpse to offer any companionship that the corpse wouldn't feel, but may have, once.

Many lonely days passed. More dams were breached, more flesh was lost. Once the corpse snagged on the debris of what used to be a recognizable thing, but it broke free eventually. Fish made good work of its back and legs, soon nibbled down to yellow bone. One night after the left hip had lost too much of itself, it drifted free of the corpse, like a ship cutting lose a dragging life boat, and sank into the black. The corpse bobbed back above the surface ever so slightly, and would have breathed deeply with a wide smile if it could have.

All around the canal were glowing remains of things. The rain had turned black with ash. Some of the ash managed to dodge all the raindrops and stuck wetly to the tarnished paint of once bright things. A black patina struggled to cling to the shattered world between rivulets of burning rain.

The breadth of the canal became much wider. It quickly turned into a large pool that flooded over the streets of what was once a country town. Eddies and currents pushed the corpse on a scenic journey between cars and lamp posts, mail boxes and old, brittle shrubs. It was a quaint stroll through a small piece of human nostalgia. Still, the corpse went on drifting until it came to the cause of the flood. It was another dam, but this one wasn't built by mankind. It was, instead, built of mankind. Sometime ago, during the nightmare, a narrow spot in the canal's path had become obstructed by something. What that thing was couldn't be told, because it had soon been joined by another something, then another, until there was a dam of debris, including not a few of the bodies of the people who'd preceded the corpse on this journey. Many white faces of many former people piled up against all of the things they once held dear. The corpse drifted through the reservoir, languidly taking one last meandering diversion before finally joining everyone else. If it could still have felt, it would have been glad to be home, it would have wondered why it had ever run from its people to begin with.

From far away, two sets of glimmering eyes watched the corpse return to its people. They stared for no longer than they had to, then, with a nascent sense of satisfaction, headed toward the dark mountains where no one had ever lived.

▲

Getting Thin
by DJ Tyrer

It was the same worry that seemed to afflict everyone: was she fat?

If Ellie was honest, then the answer to that niggling thought had to be 'yes'. She wasn't morbidly obese, nor even as fat as a lot of people seemed to be, but she certainly had some flab.

"Am I fat?" she asked her boyfriend.

Jack winced. "Darling…"

"Well?"

Taking a deep breath, he said, "I suppose you could stand to lose a pound or two." He glanced away and hunched slightly as if expecting an outburst.

She sighed. "Yes…"

"I mean, we all could," he said hastily, reaching down to pat his stomach. "See, a couple of pounds more than I need." He gave her a hopeful grin. "It's the modern way of life: too much snacking and not enough exercise. Not that you're bad or anything. You're barely fat at all."

She nodded. "I know. But, still…" She felt her own stomach. "What should I do?"

"Take up jogging?"

She shook her head. "No. I don't do running."

"Um… aerobics?"

"Also too sweaty."

Jack opened his mouth as if to speak, then closed it again. Then, he said, "You could always join one of those diet clubs. You know, count calories and stuff."

"Hmm." She chewed her lip and mulled it over. "Yes, that would work. I could do that, and I might make some new friends."

"Yeah, it could be good."

She nodded. "Yes. I think I'll go online and look for one, right now."

He let out a sigh of relief. "Good idea."

* * * *

It had been easy to find a club. In fact, there had been plenty to choose from. In the end, Ellie took the obvious course and chose the one that was nearest to her home.

"No sense having to walk further than I need to," she told Jack, who refrained from saying anything.

Flabbattle met three times a week, so Ellie didn't have to wait long to join up. She'd already signed-up online.

"Hi," said a woman several dress sizes larger than Ellie as she entered the hall, "I'm Ange and you must be Ellie."

"Yes. How—?"

"Did I know your name? Simone told me. Simone runs the club," she quickly added, then smiled widely and said, "Welcome aboard."

"I want to lose a few pounds," Ellie said, pointlessly.

"Don't we all, dearie?" called a voice that flowed and cloyed like treacle.

Ellie turned to see an enormous woman. The newcomer wasn't just fat; she was immense. Yet, despite her girth, she moved with a peculiar grace.

"Hello," she said, her voice as heavy and agile as her body, "my name is Simone."

"Oh, hi. Ange just mentioned you."

"All bad, I trust," she tittered. "As she said, welcome aboard. It's always good to see some fresh meat." She burped, a deep and unpleasantly wet sound. "'Scusee!"

Other members of Flabbattle were beginning to arrive and Simone moved to greet them.

"No Henrietta?" Simone asked when everyone was assembled. "Dear, dear, what a shame—I do hope she hasn't fallen off the wagon." She cast her gaze over the assembled ladies. "Remember, overeating is an addiction, fatness is a disease, and dieting is a battle to overcome your demons and restore the real you."

Then came the weighings and the rejoicing at weight lost and grief at weight stubbornly clinging or even gained, followed by confessions of bad habits and barriers to weight loss, or tips for success. Finally, Simone stood before them and lectured them for a while. Ellie wasn't too keen on her haranguing style, but the fact that no chairs were provided and they all had to stand like acolytes surely burnt a lot of calories.

"I'll see you all in a couple of days," called Simone as they filed out. "Oh, Ange, a quick word, if I may."

Ellie waved goodbye to Ange and followed the others out.

* * * *

"How did it go, darling?" Jack asked when Ellie arrived home. There was a cup of tea waiting for her.

"Well, to be honest, I'm in two minds," she said. She took a sip, considering. "Simone, who runs it, is a bit too much, but I think I got a couple of decent tips out of it, and it's motivation, so it's probably worth it."

She took another sip, then said, "Hey, how about some biscuits?"

* * * *

The next session went much as Ellie's first had, although there was no sign of Ange. Spotting Simone, she thought the woman seemed even larger than ever.

"What a shame," Simone said, multiple chins wobbling, "I do hope she isn't ill—or back on the biscuits."

Ellie forgot all about Ange in her annoyance at finding she'd gained half-a-pound in just two days.

"Never mind dearie," Simone cooed, "time will tell."

"Well, I did have a couple of biscuits with my tea," Ellie admitted when it came to the confessions. The others commiserated her for her weakness in the face of temptation, except Simone who tutted at her. Ellie listened intently to the tips, in the hope of learning something useful.

Then came the lecture, slightly marred when Simone belched in midflow. "'Scusee," she chuckled, then went on.

Concluding, she called, "I'll see you all on Friday," as they began to shuffle away.

Catching Ellie's eye, Simone waved and said, "A quick word, if I may?"

Allowing the others to leave without her, Ellie walked over to her. "Yes?"

Simone smiled, glutinously, and said, "I like to tailor our assistance to each individual member's specific needs."

"Oh, that would be useful."

"Well," Simone continued, "I don't have time now, but maybe you could come in an hour early on Friday."

"Sure. That'd be great."

"Right, I'll see you then." She burped loudly, chins wobbling. "Oops! 'Scusee!"

* * * *

"Biscuit?" Jack asked, holding out the packet.

Ellie started to reach for one, then retracted her hand. "Uh, no thanks."

"Oh, okay."

"I'm watching my weight," she told him, firmly.

* * * *

"Hello?" Ellie called. The hall was empty. She glanced at her watch; she was well over an hour early. Maybe Simone wasn't in yet.

Then, she noticed the dress, lying in the corner of the room. It was a ghastly floral tent that she remembered one of the other women wearing. She racked the brain. Mary, she thought the woman was called. Why she would be here so early and wandering about without a dress on, she had no idea.

"Mary? Simone?" she called, bemused, wondering what she might have stumbled upon.

Ellie was just about to turn and leave when she heard a great rumbling belch, one that actually made the windows rattle in their frames. It had come from somewhere in the back of the community building.

Ellie laughed nervously at the noise. She wondered what to do, whether to stay or go. Curiosity got the better of her and she crossed to the rear door of the hall and she eased it open.

"Hello?" she called, but softly, uncertain if she wanted a response. The doorway opened into a wide hallway with flaking beige paint and damp patches on the walls. There was a wet smear along the cracked and scratched lino that she immediately thought must be blood; but it wasn't, she realised; it was something else, dark and viscous, like grease or bile.

She followed the smear along the corridor, ignoring the various doors, save for that at the end, which she threw open.

The door led into an office which, under normal circumstances, was probably quite spacious, but which, today, was extremely crowded. The reason it was crowded was because Simone was in it and she practically filled the entire room. The rolls of flab that surrounded her and which rippled as she craned her neck to look at Ellie were far more than any person had any right to possess. Her skin was glossy with the greasy liquid. The effect was monstrous.

"Oh, hello," Simon purred, her voice thicker than ever with the reverberation of so many chins. "I don't—" She paused to belch, a horrendous, vibrating sound. "'Scusee! Where was I? Oh, yes, I don't think I'll be needing you, after all. You see, Mary was foolish enough to come here early, for some reason, I didn't bother asking why; she was a substitute for you." She belched again. "More flesh on her bones, of course, but not, I'm sure, nearly as tasty."

"You... ate her?"

She belched again, as if in answer.

Suddenly, Simone's head and arms retracted within the blubbery mound of her body. Ellie watched in horrified fascination as it shivered and shook like a vast, greasy, quivering blancmange.

Ellie felt vomit rising in her throat. It was a disgusting sight.

Then, just as suddenly, the mound of flesh gave one final shudder, then split and seemed to peel back like the skin of an overripe banana, liquid fat sluicing out from within, splashing across the floor and soaking Ellie's feet, causing her to shriek and stumble back in revulsion.

Revealed in the midst of the scene, slick with the greasy liquid, was the slender figure of a woman who spoke with a voice a little like that of Simone, only without its timbre.

"Well," she told Ellie, "you know what they say: inside every fat person there's a thin person trying to break free. Ah, it feels good to get out of all that."

She smiled and Ellie turned and ran headlong from the building, screaming.

▲

Maybe Next Door
by Richard LaPore

Summer of '73 was just fine. A college friend had invited me to stay at his Granddad's place in rural southeastern Oregon, and the break from UW and Seattle's big city bustle was right up my alley.

One day Jackie and I were working up a good sweat, cleaning up brush and so forth, when the old man came out with glasses and a jug of his outstanding fresh lemonade a-jingle with ice. "Boys, that's first rate. Time to cool off." His warm smile flashed.

As we lounged in the shade by the creek, Jackie asked, "Grandee, what was up with that guy who pulled in earlier? Looked like he wasn't sure what planet he was on."

Grandee chuckled. "Yes indeed. He was a door-to-door salesman from Bend who decided to try his luck out here, Lord only knows why. He struck out and got lost, and was just happy to get pointed back to civilization. Hm." His eyes flickered into elsewhere.

"Grandee?" Jackie pointed like a hound scenting quail. I was just as keen; his Granddad—Sadler James by name—told amazing tales and by now I knew that "way back when" look.

"Well," said the old man, "after the Great War…"

* * *

After the Great War, door-to-door or traveling salesmen—what we used to call 'drummers'—frequently came through the Wyqumish Watershed. One year a couple of well-known ones, good fellows with first class merchandise, were selling cookware, cutlery, gewgaws and frippery in the area, but mutterings had begun about another no one had actually seen.

The story went that, on three widely separated occasions, heavy footsteps had preceded a knock at the front door. Someone was heard to answer… then came dead silence. Upon investigation, the door was found standing wide open but no one was there and whoever had answered the knocking was never seen again. So far, one husband, one wife and one stepbrother had gone missing. Kinfolk were distressed and general unease grew apace.

Notwithstanding, one fine October morning I went over to Pa and Ma Kelner's place about dawn to help Pa with some roofing. He was getting old and feeble and couldn't carry his own weight anymore—so he claimed, despite Ma's derisive snorts. That meant he worked only five tens and one six-hour day per week instead of seven fifteens like he had for fifty years. Now he liked to spend Sundays in his chair on the front porch listening to the church bells, whittling on a stick, and howdying the passersby.

With me to support his doddering efforts Pa re-roofed the house in one day. Of course Ma said she'd take it hard if I didn't stay to supper. I didn't say no; not only is roofing hungry work but Ma, a blue ribbon cook, had already stuffed me with breakfast and dinner fit for royalty. As expected, supper was ambrosial: chicken and dumplings, fried green tomatoes with okra, dandelion salad, and peach cobbler with hand-cranked vanilla ice cream that still makes my mouth water. Afterwards, as it had gotten a bit too nippy of evenings to sit on the front porch, we sat in the front parlor drinking the best coffee between Baja and the Arctic Circle, jawing about the doings around the township. Of course we discussed the phantom drummer but came to no conclusions.

Now Ma and Pa had a cat named Hatchet, one of the scariest beasts I've ever seen. Folks suggested the outlandish critter might be part bobcat, alligator, or werewolf, but finally allowed his Daddy was likely a circular saw. His shaggy pelt was like barbed wire, his eyes made you think of a drill press headed for your face, and his teeth looked like broken axe blades; but he was the goods. He was hell on rats and varmints in general and Ma even saw him sort out a black bear that wandered into the yard one day looking for chickens. Hatchet diced that bear like fruit salad and you could still hear the poor critter bawling after the cat had run him a good quarter-mile down the road.

Hatchet also kept a guard-dog eye on Ma and Pa and, if he seemed to be losing patience, visitors would scurry off thinking horrid things about drill presses. In truth, mayhem wasn't his rule but he once carved deep slices into the bottom of one drummer who was persistent to the point of menace. When folks heard this fellow was such a rube Hatchet actually cut him, his sales dwindled away and he left the Watershed for good.

However, we got along fine. He'd sniff me over and bash me on the leg with his head (kind of like getting clubbed by a tractor piston), I'd scritch his ears and we'd be good. Boy, I've known some interesting cats. Just last summer, this little girl from California visited Sailor's Halt, and her cat was the most…no, that'll keep.

Anyway, Hatchet had a funny habit. There was a peephole set in Kelner's front door a few inches under six feet from the floor and every time someone knocked, Hatchet would run over, leap straight up four-footed to hover level with that peephole and take a good look. Then he'd land with a thud and wait for Ma or Pa to answer the door so he could greet company or repel boarders.

Now, like I said, we were talking in the front parlor, the cat snoozing on the hearth, when heavy footsteps came in at the front gate, slogged up the walk and stumped up the steps onto the porch. Then came a knock on the door, a real ponderous, dull kind of knock. Hatchet came off the hearth, streaked over to the door, shot straight up and hovered then thudded back down.

But this time was different.

The cat lit in his usual crouch but didn't straighten to attention. He huddled for a moment then jerked up and reeled out of the room; stiff, staggering, lurching like a rickety sawhorse. We followed.

When he got to the kitchen, Hatchet jumped up onto the counter. There, he proceeded to rip and chew right through the back wall then crushed his way out through the jagged hole, leaving us pop-eyed as his terrified shrieks faded at bullet speed. Word gradually trickled back that lots of folks that night heard something that could have been a cat as it shot like an artillery shell across the next three counties and beyond, but no one ever heard a cat scream like that before.

We were still staring, dumb, when that heavy knock came again... at the back door. We all looked at each other then Pa said, "Well, Ma, whoever's knockin', whatever they's sellin', we don't want none. Sadler, I'd be obliged if you'd bar the doors while I board over that hole. Of course you'll stay the night. Ma will make up the couch for you."

I said thank you kindly, I will. Whatever they were selling, I didn't want none either. ▲

Containment Protocol
by Leeman Kessler

It's almost two o'clock so I should probably start getting ready to leave but I'm finding it harder to do that these days. Staring into the vat gives me a calm that I don't find anywhere else, certainly not at home. All that's waiting for me there is an empty apartment with a cat who occasionally takes the time to acknowledge me. The vat, however... the vat contains infinities and in those infinities, I find a sense of peace. I know I'm not supposed to think like that; it's the height of unprofessional conduct, and it's the quickest way to get a transfer to another department far away from my vat. Still, I can't help but feel more at home here.

It's all about the protocol. For most of the units at this facility, electronic monitoring, motion sensors, temperature regulators, and the like are all sufficient but protocol is different for the vat. The vat needs someone to actually watch it with their own two eyes, not through a lens or a monitor. I don't know why; it's just the rules, the protocol. In a few minutes, Eriksen will be here and we'll swap. He'll take my seat and keep his eyes on the vat and I'll be able to go home. Only I really don't want to.

Mind you, it's not the vat itself. That's just a simple, 33cm thick, transparent container sitting behind a 20cm plexiglass window. Even then, most of the content of the vat is seawater or at least as close as you can get to it this far inland. I don't monitor the salinity or pH or anything like that. I just have to watch. I watch and see just what the vat's occupant spends its hours doing: sleeping.

It must sound boring to just sit and watch something sleep and I'll confess that when I first got this posting, I felt like I was being punished—sitting and watching for hours on end without so much as a bathroom break. You can't read, you can't check your phone, you can't look away for more than a few seconds at a time, just enough to check the clock or to blink. There's no noise but the blood in your ears. Those first few weeks were a nightmare worse than brig duty or perimeter detail. I couldn't wait for two o'clock and Eriksen to arrive. The weird dance we'd have to do where we both kept our eyes on the vat and swap places before I could look away, my own eyes dry and itchy. It was an absolute relief to be able to go back to that empty apartment and read or watch

TV or do anything that wasn't staring into that clear water and watching it sleep.

Things change, though, and before long, I found that I wasn't checking the clock so often. I wasn't letting out a sigh of relief when Eriksen came in. One day I noticed that the urge to pee had even subsided. I discovered something serene and beautiful about sitting and watching the vat and its sole occupant.

You're not supposed to discuss your duties with anyone except immediate superiors but one time early on, when we were doing our little shuffle, I asked Eriksen if he'd ever seen it move, even to breathe. Eriksen thought for a moment and then shrugged (at least from the corner of my eye it looked like a shrug) before saying, "I don't think so. Maybe one time but I don't really know," which was pure Eriksen. He's never struck me as a man with much of an imagination from our few brief exchanges. I can't imagine what goes through his head during the shifts. Probably does his taxes or something equally stimulating. Santiago, whose shift I relieve is a touch chattier but not much more.

I tried to find ways to occupy myself at first, thinking of songs or movie lines or anything that popped into my head. Sooner or later, however, I'd begin playing the Did It Move game. My eyes would focus and unfocus, almost like it was one of those Magic Eye paintings. It didn't take long to memorize the textures of its skin, the folds where its limbs pinched together as I looked and waited for any change, even the slightest variation. Was that spot always so close to that wrinkle? Was that a vibration or just a slightly cloudier part of the water? Even when I got frustrated and told myself I was done playing the game, before long my eyes would begin probing and searching, eager to catch it giving itself away.

At one point, the game went from being a diversion to being the entirety of my duty. I'd come in and nod at the side of Santiago's face and receive a minor twitch in acknowledgement and then, as he stood up and I shuffled over, I'd give my eyes one last big close, turn around and open them to take in the vat and its sole occupant. For the next several hours, this was my existence, my life. I stopped noticing Santiago's departure or half-muttered remark. All I had now was the game.

In all the months since, I haven't noticed a single change—nothing so much as a ripple across the yards of visible flesh but I don't mind. It's not about trying to prove anything or one-up the occupant or even to make the time go that much faster any more. By watching and waiting, I lose myself and in so doing, I find something far greater. In that tranquil silence with just me, the water, the glass, and it, I have discovered who I truly am.

As I think about leaving, my eyes look over the most textured portion of its skin where there is a clear line that cuts through the mottled flesh for almost a meter. If there's going to be movement anywhere, I'm convinced that's where it will start. Of all of this thing's subtle geographies and puckered topographic details, that is the most likely candidate and so my eyes are never too far from it.

Watching today and preparing to move, my limbs no longer stiff as they once might have been from so much stillness, I suddenly sense something from that straight cut across its hide. Not movement, nothing so earth-shattering or all-consuming as that but nevertheless I feel it—like standing on a precipice. An invisible rush that promises the coming of…something.

The door swings open and I sense Eriksen's presence; I feel his warmth and hear his breath even as my eyes never leave the vat and in that moment, I know. I stand up and Eriksen mutters his barely audible greeting but I'm not listening. I'm not looking at him. Both eyes on it, I move towards Eriksen, meeting him directly, not shuffling around him and he pauses, this break in protocol—this change in format startling him. He opens his mouth to say something but I don't hear it, my ears rushing with the sound of their own blood. Reaching out, eyes still on the vat, my thumbs find his eyes and press in, a new, louder sound now resounding in our room but it's still drowned out by the pouring, oceanic roar in my ears. It is only then that I close my own eyes—the image of the vat's occupant still burned in my vision—only as my eyes close and I hear over the roaring surf the sound of glass breaking do I see movement. Even with my eyes closed, I see it and I know that the game is over and my heart breaks in joy. I'm finally going home.

▲

Under a Rock
by Lori R. Lopez

Immense and rugged, a mottled blend of grays, the boulder appeared at the precise center of town. There had been no concussion that any could recall. No dent or crater, no sign of an impact was visible. One day the spot was empty...the next day it was occupied by an enormous bump that towered like a zit on the forehead of a fashion model.

"How lucky none of us were killed!" marveled more than a few as word spread and the residents gathered to view an anomaly.

"It's just plain weird. We should have felt the ground shake if this thing landed. How did it get here? Roll down the street?" Mayor Bax Grumwald owned two restaurants and a chrome company cited thirteen times by county inspectors for health and safety violations. The florid-complexioned fat cat won elections by being the life of annual parties he hosted.

Baxter swiveled toward the crowd in bewilderment. He was afraid to touch the rock. Everyone was.

Except for a woman named Zelda Twillamung, the new librarian. She had recently moved to Triple Creeks, taking over when the elderly former librarian passed away in bed clutching an open book.

"Must have been a good book," neighbors joked.

The guide to flowering shrubs didn't kill her. A five-cigar-a-day smoking habit probably did, and being almost as sedentary as stone. People had legs and were meant to use them, yet she had ceased taking walks long before her demise, thinking she was too old to exercise by age fifty according to the assistant librarian, a quiet girl who helped check out books in her spare time from school. It was nearly all the teenager had uttered thus far to Zelda. That and "Miss Cully sure loved to read."

Miss Twillamung's legs propelled her to approach a massive incongruity from the rear of the gawkers. Pale pinkish-orange aspects divided to stare at her as if she were equally out of place. It was a tightly wound and knit community. The locals distrusted strangers. Especially a woman with skin like a cup of cocoa and thick coils of brunette hair. They considered themselves White, although none of them matched or were actually that hue. Peach was closer to the truth, which might work for crayons but you couldn't label an entire race of people after a fruit. So terms like Black and White were used, as if that clarified everything. It seemed to emphasize the difference.

Zelda drifted to the rock, a spoon to a magnet. Not brave, oh no; she was confused, a bit curious, inexplicably drawn. She clapped a hand to the rough surface, or it smacked her palm. The woman blinked. *What an odd thought. It couldn't have,* she dismissed. Her eyes scoured the texture and contours. An avid rockhound, she was at a loss to identify this particular mineral. Pages flipped in her brain. A mental orb scrutinized photographs and terms. It didn't match. It was unknown, a U.L.O. (Unidentified Lying Object). Zelda smirked at the discovery. Perhaps she could name it.

A tingle shot through her…initially warmth in the fingertips contacting the boulder, then zipping up her arm to her chest. The woman staggered, jolted by pure energy. *What the heck was that?*

Attempting to remove her hand and break the connection yielded further surprise. Her flesh was firmly plastered to the uneven facade by an invisible attraction. "It won't let me—" Her voice faltered, windpipe constricting. She struggled to be heard. A throttling pressure on her neck abated. Zelda gasped. Was it alive?

The mayor had retreated in dread. Trumpeting harrumphantly, Grumwald endeavored to restore his authority and reputation as he hurried to seize her arm. "Stay back, Miss Twill—" His gruff tone stumbled. A vapid mug blinked at her, owlish. He knew it was some foreign name. The guy released her and coughed in embarrassment. "Everybody keep back. This thing could be radioactive. I'm establishing a perimeter until the sheriff arrives. I called his office and left a message to meet me here. Has anyone seen him?" He scanned visages. "All right, well, he should be along soon. Just step away, miss."

"Uh-uh. I can't." Zelda's hand remained on the boulder. A delicate oval face reflected turmoil.

Baxter rolled his eyes. "Oh dear." He squinted to assess the rebel. "I'm not asking you. That was an order."

"Understood. But I cannot do it."

"Yes you can. It's quite simple." He demonstrated.

"No, not for me."

"And why is that?"

Zelda shrugged. "It won't let me."

"Don't be ridiculous." Baxter's eyebrows lowered, bunching together. *A troublemaker. As suspected.* He had voted against hiring her. She was inexperienced. The council insisted. There were no other applicants. "In case you aren't aware, civil disobedience is punishable by law."

"I am sorry. I truly am. I cannot obey." The young woman's countenance crinkled with dismay. "I'm unable to explain this."

Grumwald pivoted to his audience and heaved a theatrical sigh. "Then I'm afraid there's no choice but to have you taken into custody once Sheriff Aberdeen gets here," he announced, wearing a mystified expression. If this event became ugly, the man would need a scapegoat to divert attention, feed the lynch-squad's wrath. Any gathering could turn, yank out daggers or pitchforks in a heartbeat. She had practically volunteered for the role.

He adjusted a tacky blue tie adorned with yellow baby ducks, pulling at the knot jammed below his throat. The tie had been a gift from his mother, rest her soul, and now it was choking him. He hoped she was happy. Bax scowled at an overcast sky. The man was not religious, yet he did believe in ghosts and pompously assumed she was watching him every minute. He searched the features of the crowd for a withered ghoul, a shimmering apparition.

Behind him the librarian trembled. Her body stiffened. Eyeballs went white, the irises scrolling upward. Neck angled, noggin tilted, Zelda shouted to the clouds: "What fools!"

Baxter's jaw tensed. He trudged to her and growled, "Did you call me a fool?"

Zelda meekly confronted him. "Not you. The entire town."

Mayor Grumwald leaned nose to nose, his frown boring into her eyes. "That isn't better. It's worse."

"My apologies."

"I can lock you up and throw away the key." The man grabbed her free wrist. "Got it?"

She winced as he squeezed. The female nodded. He flung her arm. Zelda's mouth twisted in contempt. He was like every bully she had the displeasure to cross paths with—a very small person inside. Her wrist burned. Then the boulder talked, and the woman absorbed its statement. Her spine arched. Head tipped to regard the heavens, she gurgled incoherent. The sounds halted. Words frothed out of her lips. "I have observed while you populated to conquer then decimate this planet. In addition to warring and slaughtering, ruling and enslaving each other over diversity. Fools. That is what you are!"

Zelda straightened abruptly. Flushed and defiant, she declared that the rock had spoken.

Mayor Grumwald wheezed. He barked like a hound. Cackles and guffaws echoed him. The townsfolk chortled with amusement.

"Are you trying to tell us the rock is intelligent?" Baxter cracked up in a subsequent round of levity.

"I'm telling you what it said."

The mayor howled, bright pink with mirth, inspiring members of the community to share a good laugh at her expense. "Stop! Stop! You're killing me!" The man clasped his stomach in mock agony.

"I am not making this up," claimed Zelda. Their attitude exasperated her. Even more vexing, she continued to be attached to the thing. Why had she gone over to it? She was the biggest fool. Did the rock summon her? Was she chosen? Or was she merely the village idiot? The only person dumb enough to go up and give it five!

Hands on knees, bent forward, Baxter caught his breath. He grimaced, envisioning a public-relations fiasco involving rioters waving civil-rights banners versus gun-toting civilians, lawmen and soldiers swinging clubs, if anything happened to her. The streets would be rivers of blood. How would that look on the Five-O-Clock news? "Okay. There's no need to make a legal issue of this. Let's just step back and wait for the sheriff. He'll sort this out, and then we can return to our lives."

Zelda shook her head as if declining the appeal. It was really a gesture of impatience because no one would listen—either to her or the rock!

"I'm offering you a second chance. I strongly suggest you accept it." The mayor glowered at her. He didn't appreciate being refused, especially by an outsider, a vocal black woman from Timbuktu or wherever she was born.

"Mayor, you are asking the impossible."

"Is my English too difficult? Or our customs? In America we do things a certain way. We pay attention to the mayor of a municipality."

"I'm as American as you are, sir. I was born in this land."

"Well then, Miss Twillabug, I guess we have a problem."

"It's Twillamung, and I suppose we do."

They were trapped in an impasse, each compelled to play their part, unable to withdraw from their position.

A town raptly spectated, enjoying the drama.

Zelda spasmed violently, eyeballs white. Her fit ended. Panting, she translated a stony assurance, head bowed in reverence or fatigue: "This is not about borders and nations. It is about the world. This Earth your feet are planted upon. You will die if you fail to acknowledge the situation."

Grumwald's demeanor toughened. "Miss Twillamong, is that a threat?"

"No, Mayor, it's a promise." She regretted the words immediately and pleaded, "You must heed the warning. A rock has no sense of humor. This is not a hoax. It is of grave importance."

"Now I've heard everything." The mayor boosted his volume. "A rock has no sense of humor? A rock has no sense, period! A rock cannot communicate! Forget the sheriff. I think we need to phone the men in white jackets." The man's pitch decreased to snarls. "Let's get one thing clear, little lady. I'm in charge. Not this rock, and not some wet-behind-the-ears librarian. You should stick to shelving books and leave the politics to me."

Zelda lifted her head high and responded with dignity, "I wish I could. I would like nothing else. The rock won't let me."

Mindful of a broader public opinion beyond the city limits, easily stirred like a nest of hornets, Baxter's mood softened to mild sarcasm. "You're being stubborn. I sympathize with how you must feel. You're new here, trying to fill the shoes of a beloved denizen. No friends or family. I'm ashamed to admit, we didn't exactly give you a red-carpet welcome. We're a small town, which has its charms. We also have our flaws. And I wonder, Miss Twillamong, what was your reason for choosing this job? In a community where you were bound to be as conspicuous as…a sore thumb?" He wanted to say a raisin in a bowl of rice, but that might be construed as racist. He didn't need a journalist quoting him out of context, and a casual remark circling an incensed globe. The town might demand his resignation over the negative outcry.

"If you're implying I must be crazy to come here, I may be willing to agree." Zelda stood proudly—humble and exposed before a hamlet that was not, after all, a home.

"I'm not implying anything. You don't belong. You're not one of us. Rather than wag your tongue and spout nonsense, I recommend you go shove your nose in a book or pack your bags and skedaddle. This is a town matter. It isn't your concern."

Zelda met the scorn and rejection with a level gaze. It always amazed her there were such people, judging her by color or gender. Sometimes both. What century was it? Human nature hadn't evolved that much to still have these silly conflicts. The rock had a point.

A burst of electricity stunned her, transmitting a bulletin.

"You need guidance. Unity. Objective leadership. You have to find a middle ground," she conveyed. "You cannot see the trees for the forest."

"No, no, no. You've got it backwards." Grumwald corrected her in a condescending manner. "You can't see the forest for the trees. That's how it goes."

"I said what it wanted me to say. There are too many extremes. People see only the group and not the individual. We are all of us guilty." The reverse parable rang a chord. Though she was private, Zelda morosely divulged her story. "My parents were from Australia, my mother

White and my father an Aborigine. Her family opposed the marriage, so they went to live on an outback parcel of land that was left to my mum by her grandmother. They built a dwelling, a farmhouse. Her family wouldn't let them live in peace, burning their camp, running them off the property. Father died from a stray bullet intended to scare them. I was born in America where my mother—a white woman—raised me in a black community, hoping I could be accepted. I was different, of mixed blood, and not the same culture. Most let us be. There are those in every quarter who won't. Two hoods, thieves with knives, attacked Mum as she walked from her waitress job one night. She only had tips! My mom bled to death sprawled in an alley. I was an orphan at age twelve. I didn't fit in with people who looked like me, so I thought all Blacks were like that. I came to this place where there were none. Just me. To answer your question, that is why I'm here. I have been rolling like a stone, hunting for my niche. Librarian seemed safe. Books were my friends. The memorable ones possess their own voice and personality. But I was wrong. Being a good person has nothing to do with color. It is under the skin, on the inside. That is where a person's humanity is found."

Grumwald folded his arms. "Spare us the sappy lectures. We're good people. You're the one who's creating a disturbance. Are you going to be nice and exit the vicinity, or do I need to make you?"

"Insult me, exclude me, it doesn't change the fact that I am linked to this presence for the moment. You will have to cut off my arm to separate me from it." A bold declaration. Inwardly the woman cringed. Oh no, why did she mention that? He might do it!

Baxter did indeed ponder the notion, but he wouldn't risk a possibility of fallout. His companies could be shut down, with or without a scandal. As mayor he relied on votes, and there could be serious repercussions. A slew of nutcases might show up and set fire to the town!

He chuckled, a dry rattle. "Don't tempt me. That is an option. However, there's no need for drastic measures. I am confident you'll realize it is in your best interest to cooperate."

"Of course." Zelda gave a derisive snort. Then jerked like she was being fried by a dose of current. The contorting diminished to shivers and she sagged, braced against stone, a limp form.

The mayor huffed, elevating splayed fingers. "What? Another decree?" His hands drooped. "I don't care if God is using you for a handpuppet, lady. I don't want to hear another word from that overgrown pebble." The fingers balled at his flanks. "I want you to march yourself home and stay out of this." He glanced at the spectators, receiving murmurs of approval.

Zelda ignored him, eyelids sealed.

"Miss?" Grumwald tapped her shoulder. A surge of power knocked him a dozen feet, slamming the guy on his keister.

Zelda's head snapped up. Her eyes flashed. "I don't have a home. That was your final warning."

The mayor rose, face and ears flaming. "I must've slipped," he grumbled. "She pushed me. You saw her. I tried to be fair. I didn't start this, and I won't hesitate to end it."

Zelda's orbs glittered like dark gems as she also addressed the throng. "Nobody thinks of stone as a force. They overlook it, but it is conscious deep down, beneath the surface."

Harsh stares. Belligerence. She perceived no trace of comprehension or compassion.

"All right. That's it. You've had your fun. I'm not listening to any more of this hogwash. You're under citizen's arrest, Miss Twillamong." Baxter's announcement dripped with satisfaction. "I'll escort you downtown. The courthouse has a detainment cell for criminals, and I have a key."

"You mean your office?"

The pair beheld each other with flared nostrils.

"You won't feel so clever when you're behind bars."

"Good luck with that," Zelda hissed.

Grumwald strode forth and gripped the wrist of her hand fixed to the boulder. He strained to peel it loose without success. "She glued it," he complained. "Or it's some kind of trick." He jabbed a forefinger in her direction. "Some voodoo hocus-pocus!"

The accused replied, "I don't know what it is. I am not responsible. We all are."

Jeers were audible.

"Shut up, witch."

"How dare you!"

"We didn't do anything."

"You brought this!"

They were on his side. Hoisting a fist as a symbol of solidarity, the mayor grinned victorious and paraded in front of the boulder and his flock.

Zelda convulsed.

"Drop the act," commanded Grumwald. He reached to grasp her elbow, then clawed at air and reeled his arm in, reluctant to be shocked.

The woman's quivering subsided. "You are not the masters," she intoned with an obsidian glare. "We endure. We are everywhere and can wipe you out, grind you to dust. We are capable of moving faster. None of you are safe...on the land, in the oceans, on mountains, in caves. Even in the sky. We helped shape this planet and brought it life. We are ancient. Your existence is fleeting."

The mob gaped at her, incredulous.

Grumwald scoffed, "She's insane, preaching mythological sci-fi mumbo-jumbo. She wants you to buy into her lame fantasy that we're at the mercy of rocks. It's the stupidest thing I ever heard!"

"I don't want this!" cried Zelda. "I'm being used! I am as vulnerable as any of you. And I do not have to justify or explain myself. I told you who I am."

"Yeah. A wacko. I bet she escaped from a psychiatric ward!"

"What has made you so bitter?"

"Hey, I'm not the one on a soapbox spewing drivel about gloom and doom."

"Maybe you should be. You need to wake up."

"Why? Is this a dream? Are we in your nightmare? Or are you delusional?"

"It's very real."

Through gritted teeth, Baxter professed, "Reality is waking up to an empty house. My wife left me years ago. She went off with a bearded vagabond, an itinerant teeshirt designer who drove a van! I've been miserable ever since. Business and politics became my bedfellows. This is my city." The potbellied hothead swallowed then seethed, "If you think we're going to live under a rock, quaking in fear of a stone, you are sadly mistaken. I am in control. Not you, and not a hunk of gravel."

Turbulence rippled.

The tremor caused Mayor Grumwald to lurch. "What was that?"

Zelda hooted and beamed at her palm. It was free!

In horror, she slapped it to her lips as she witnessed the boulder shift toward Grumwald. Lethal weight trundled. His yelp was swiftly flattened. The librarian muffled her shriek, clamping her mouth. She had just been conversing with him!

Everyone froze, aghast and alarmed. Zelda was the first to react, hastening to budge a monstrosity in vain. Others joined her effort. The obstruction wouldn't give an inch, lodged securely. Zelda bleated, noticing the squashed remnants of a man in uniform. The rock had been squatting on top of Sheriff Aberdeen.

Volunteers melted to the sea of faces. The librarian wrestled alone, grappling, exerting, then sought to abandon a futile task. Both hands adhered to the boulder, widely distributed. She was its prisoner. At any instant, the rock might decide to crush her.

"No," Zelda whimpered, hunched abjectly.

With a stab of animus, her own juice this time, the woman's posture aligned...then she thrashed in a wild dance of dissent and revolt, a protest of oppression, striving to extricate herself from bondage. The mystery ore clung to her, staunch, impervious.

When her sentiments had drained, she embraced the block of stone like a weary boxer hugs an opponent: not in surrender, but a mutual state of respect. The boulder reciprocated, tickling fibers and nerves with heat, a subliminal pulse. The woman felt numb. Throbbing intensified. It was torture. Braincells hurt. Fingers stung. Ears and lips ached.

The vibrations suspended. Thrusting away, as far as circumstances would permit, she discerned an eerie bass hum like a sub-woofer. The dull roar infused her, provoking shudders that grew to paroxysms. An urgent missive was dispatched. Then the rock unhanded her, and the librarian collapsed to palms and knees, as if groveling. Or praying.

She picked herself up and swayed, unsteady, burdened by a cumbrous obligation. They would hate the message and the messenger.

A mass of strangers studied her. She couldn't recognize them and began to picture the multitude as a beast with many heads. A legion of extremists; left or right, they were the same. Incapable of compromise, of empathy. Zelda's throat clenched with emotion. They would hate her. They already did. And they didn't even know her! Tears spilled from brown eyes. She surveyed the people, clinching her left wrist in her right hand. "I'm sorry. This isn't my fault. Please remember that."

She imparted the stone's mandates, her voice congested, on the verge of sobs. "Too long have you neglected to care for this planet. You selfishly disdained the warnings of the Elements. We rocks cannot bear the Earth's pain, cannot abide her throes nor tolerate her suffering. In punishment for your actions, and inactions, all families will sacrifice their youngest child. Those without offspring will sacrifice one of their smallest fingers. As proof of your allegiance, and evidence of my passage, the city must be renamed to an appropriate title honoring our kind. Let it be a reminder, you are not above natural laws and order."

The mob was struck speechless, mouths round, features gawping in sheer astonishment. Then outrage poured through veins. A collective spirit assembled, swelling in their midst.

"What about you?" a man called.

The librarian slouched on display, a statue of jelly, a wretched cemetery angel worn smooth.

"What will you lose?" yelled a female.

"Whose side are you on?" someone else grilled.

She could only peer at them, her visage blank. She had no side.

An argument developed whether it was Zelda or the rock. Each theory required a stretch of the imagination. For one, she was an instrument or accomplice of the boulder. For the opposite, she could manipulate the stone with magic or mind.

Zelda stood there, between a rock and a hard place, a solitary figure, brooding, detached, while they discussed her like she was absent. She had been taught it was rude, but she was often treated that way. A number. A name on a list. People would decide things for her. About her.

The majority determined she had to be wielding the stone. It seemed a tad more plausible. At which a debate ensued over Zelda being a sorceress or a psychic.

"I swear that I am neither," the young woman asserted. "If any of you are interested." Shaking her head at the silence and obstinance. "I didn't think so."

"What should we do? The mayor's dead. The sheriff too."

"Because of that conjurer."

"It's her doing."

"She's to blame."

"Whatever she is, we're not safe while she's here."

The horde agitated to a lather. Raucous bellows churned a virulent frightful atmosphere into a frenzy. Zelda viewed the tempest, eyes damp, her mouth and chin crumpled.

"Sacrifice our kids? Cut off our fingers?"

"She's a witch. Let's burn her!"

"Kill the hag before she casts a spell!"

"She has to be stopped!"

"She wants our firstborn!"

"We need to defend the town."

"Quick or she'll enchant the rock!"

"The witch must die!"

A boy snatched rubble from the ground and tossed it at Zelda. The piece of brick tumbled harmless, short of the target. His mom stooped for a cobblestone. A wealth of debris littered the old town square. Mayor Grumwald frequently vowed to refurbish the spot, repave its floor and rebuild a ruined fountain. It was one of his various unkept promises. The child's mother hurled her stone and hit the mark.

Miss Twillamung squealed. Blood seeped through fingers that covered a gash on her forehead. Her voice was hoarse. "Don't do this. You are individuals, not this anger. You are not a gang! You are special. Do not forget who you are, who you can be. Think for yourselves. Feel what is in your hearts. Do not be lost in the crowd."

A hail of stones and brick pelted her as rabble-rousers and followers alike condemned the librarian to death. It would be the last public execution of a witch in centuries, at least in the Western World. Dying, Zelda crawled a brief distance to one side then succumbed.

A large marble careened, mashing a swath of mayhem, blazing its trail on a screaming populace.

The rock departed, and the square was promptly renovated by survivors, a monument to the fallen. Bronze replicas of the mayor and the new librarian were erected, greeting visitors beside a wishing fountain.

The name of the town would be changed to protect the innocent… something similar to Boulder, Little Rock, Stone City, Rock Springs, Rockford, Rockville, Stone Mountain, Rockwell, Rockingham, Rockdale, Stone Lake, Rockport, Castle Rock, Chimney Rock, Stone Town …

You get the idea.

How many towns were there? Plenty. But there were even more rocks.   ▲

The Necro-Conjuring Sorceress

by Ashley Dioses

The necro-conjurer, a sorceress of zeal,
Could feel the chill of night that crept throughout her lair.
So intricate her make, as cold as hard steel,
That even the cadaver, well preserved with care,
Was not more icy than her sinister embrace.
Her silken skin delivered forth the final touch
To his last memories that soon she must erase.
With kisses, he again was in her deadly clutch;
She killed her lover out of great and envious rage.
His cloudy eyes wide opened, first beholding her.
Her scent, desirable, intoxicating sage,
Awoke a distant vision—it was but a blur.
With runic ritual, and ancient spoken spell,
She overtook his body and his weakened mind.
With hunger now for humans, he was bound for Hell,

And a new target came, to rip and have confined.
The jealous Sorceress had found his love untrue,
For he was found to have a mistress of wyrding-skilled.
The mistress proved too hard to easily subdue,
So uttered she a spell with so cruel and darkly willed.
She turned to face her shameful love who begged and knelt,
But she could feel no pity for dishonored trust.
To kill him was a simple justice to be dealt;
He knew his end would come by unrestrainèd lust.
With magick-powered strength, she dragged his cold remains
Into her lonely tower in the haunted wood.
Preserved and prepped to soon arise upon this plane,
He would perforce obey her, and he understood.
The Sorceress caressed his pallid chest with sharp
And blackened fingertips one final time ere she
Became ensanguined, plucking tendons like a harp.
She stilled his heart to silence for all time his plea.

Malicious feelings set his dull, dim mind aflame,
Not only for the taste of luscious human flesh,
But to appease the Sorceress in her vile game,
And feel the life drain out of someone still so fresh.
His mistress was the single craving that he sought
With such a teasing image pictured in his head—
He wanted nothing but to watch her slowly rot,
Then feast upon her entrails till her corpse lay dead.

The Sorceress just stood and watched her precious pet,
Just like the proudest mother watches children grow.
He rose frustrate by stiffness, but he shuffling set
Toward his pulsing prey through the harsh wind and snow.
He left her high witch-tower and she closed her eyes
Awaiting the most savage of unearthly cues;
The silence shattered at the mistress' last cries;
The Sorceress grinned widely, knowing she was through.

The Children Must Be Hungry

by L.F. Falconer

The children must be hungry. Every morning, the thought seeded Maggie's mind, urging her into wakefulness. In the late morning sunlight, the white walls of her bedroom were speckled with dancing shadows. Several flies floated in the water of the glass upon the bedside table, the water within appearing brown from the reflection of the empty prescription bottle beside it. The day's heat had already begun to settle in, adding weight to the stagnant air.

Maggie forced her legs to move, easing them over the edge of the bed. Weary arms pushed her body upwards in a sluggish crawl and the bedsprings groaned along with her bones. How she longed to remain in bed, her body craving rest. The task of rising proved to be more daunting than the morning prior, yet Maggie forced herself to rise. For the sake of the children.

Her children. Too young to care for themselves, they needed her. So no matter how much her body resisted, every morning, Maggie arose.

* * * *

Rhonda Hawthorne lounged upon the plush sofa, sipping a mocha latte as she watched her favorite talk show host spout her scripted opinions upon the new 60 inch flat screen TV. The gentle purr of the air conditioner caused her to up the volume a bit. The doorbell rang and she turned and glared at the foyer. Who would be so rude as to stop by without calling first? With a disgusted sigh, she set the remote and her cup aside and pushed her small frame off the sofa. Slippered feet padded across the Berber carpet in a whisper and on tiptoe, she squinted through the front door peephole. No one was in sight. Taking her gaze downward, her lip curled into a scowl.

It was that Kendall brat again. She would've preferred a Jehovah's Witness, then she wouldn't feel guilty for ignoring it.

After losing her inner debate on whether to answer the door, she eased it open just enough to stare down at the elfin-eyed eight-year-old girl in desperate need of some grooming. Her dirty blonde hair was in tangles and Rhonda hoped it was a smear of dried gravy that was stuck to her left cheek.

Rosy was polite as ever. "Good morning, Mrs. Hawthorne. I'm sorry to bother you again, but my momma wants to know if she can borrow a little cooking oil. We ran out."

Rhonda's eyeballs glanced upward for a moment. "She's still sick, huh?"

Rosy nodded. "She can't make it to the store yet."

"Sure, kid. Wait here a sec." Rhonda closed the door and retrieved a half-filled bottle of olive oil from the kitchen cupboard. Was the woman really too sick, or just too broke, or too lazy? Returning to the door, she opened it wide, the cool indoor air wafting out. "Here you go. Hope your momma gets better soon." So she can quit begging from me.

"Thank you Mrs. Hawthorne." Rosy turned and hurried down the flagstone walkway that curved through the manicured lawn. Rhonda stood at the threshold and watched the child, clad in a grubby red tee shirt and once-white shorts, disappear behind the tall hedge that blocked the neighboring house from view.

Just my luck, to be stuck living beside a single mom who can't keep up with things. Little Rosy might be kind of cute if she took a shower and put on some clean clothes.

Rhonda returned to the overstuffed sofa, her attention drawn back to the television, though now it was simply noise in the background. It'd been close to a week that Rosy had been coming by, begging something or other for Maggie. Could the woman truly be that sick? Anything was possible. What a rat that Matt Kendall had been to up and leave her like that, with no job and four small brats to feed.

Brats. One of Paul's words. "I hate it when I use that expression." Rhonda snatched up her empty coffee cup and strode to the kitchen. Would she ever understand her husband's dislike of children? It might have been nice to have been a mom. But a cruel twist of fate had forced her to have a hysterectomy at age twenty-three. Too young to be left barren. She'd had no choice but to accept it, and then she'd married a man who had no desire to ever push her into motherhood, so that door was closed and padlocked.

She washed the empty cup and returned it to the cupboard. She had to admit, she was somewhat grateful. Motherhood was a never-ending job, and it would be all too easy to end up in the same predicament as Maggie Kendall.

Rhonda sank back into the cushions of the sofa. One television talk show eased into another as the cool air conditioned breeze tousled a few loose dark hairs over her shoulder. The topic of this current show was

"Easy Make-overs for the Everyday Woman." Rhonda smiled. Maggie could use a make-over. The woman had probably been fairly pretty at one time. Now she was life-worn from housework and kids. Big and robust, she was always full of smiles for her children, but she could certainly benefit from the use of some make-up and an updated hairstyle. A little weight-loss and some fashionable clothes and she might be able to find a new husband. Then she'd have someone else to help her out and she could quit sending her kid around to beg from the neighbors.

A moment of epiphany caused Rhonda to shoot to her feet. "Can't force her into a make-over or find her a husband." She quickly exchanged her slippers for shoes and grabbed her purse. "But I might be able to cut down on the begging."

* * * *

At the grocery store, she filled the shopping cart with staples of flour, eggs, oil, butter, and bread. She topped that off with what she assumed were a few child-friendly foods: chicken bites, Spaghetti-O's, hot dogs, peanut butter, and macaroni and cheese, then supplemented that with some healthier choices of soups, vegetables, fruits, and milk.

On the drive home she nearly glowed and when she finally pulled the Lexus to the curb in front of Maggie's house, she gave herself a hefty mental pat on the back. After all, if the woman was as sick as Rosy claimed, this was the neighborly thing to do, right? If Maggie couldn't get to the store—the store could come to Maggie.

With her hands full of grocery bags, Rhonda strode up the walk that cut through a crisp, thirsty lawn littered with broken bike parts, an overturned red wagon, a few weathered cardboard boxes, and miscellaneous doll parts. A sour odor laced the air and Rhonda crinkled her nose.

"What a mess." When she reached the front door, she tapped against it with her foot.

After several long moments, the door crept open a crack. A bloated bleary-eyed, sallow face peered out.

The stench contained within the house belched out through the crack and Rhonda gasped, taking a sharp step back. In a swift offer without ceremony, she thrust the plastic bags forth. "I thought you could use this." Her voice began to fail her as she took in the sight of the woman in the doorway. "Since…since you've been so sick and all."

Rhonda could hardly believe her eyes. How quickly the once hale woman had deteriorated! Lusterless eyes sat like black hollows above blotchy, puffed cheeks. The buttons on her blue gingham housecoat bulged, ready to pop. The air was alive with flies.

Maggie smiled. Thick, dappled hands opened the door wide, her frame nearly blocking the view. Her four-year-old son idly tossed marbles at the baby in the walker. On the floor, amid a clutter of toys and dirty dishes, Rosy and her six-year-old sister were glued to the cartoons playing on the TV. Like fallen monuments, two bags of overflowing trash spilled onto the floor near a kitchen island stacked with empty cans and cereal boxes.

"Oh my gracious." Maggie's voice wasn't much more than a cracked whisper and she took the bags from Rhonda's hands. The weight seemed to threaten to drop her to the floor. "How very thoughtful. Thank you so much. Please, won't you come in?"

Rhonda screamed inside. The mess and odor was appalling. "I...I really can't stay." She longed to get far away. "I do have more in the car, if...you can send Rosy out for it."

Once back in the sanctuary of her own home, Rhonda worked her way to the bottom of her second daiquiri while pacing the patio alongside the backyard pool. How sick was that woman? It was hard to recall how long it had been since she'd last seen her. Was it only two weeks ago? Yes. Definitely two weeks ago, at the post office. The woman had to have packed on 50 pounds since then. She certainly didn't look healthy and probably needed to be in the hospital. Did she even have insurance?

She took another drink. "She can't take care of herself, let alone take care of those kids."

Rhonda finished off the daiquiri, plopped into the chaise lounge, and allowed the afternoon sunshine to drive away the chill she felt inside.

"It's not your problem." Paul shuffled through the daily mail that evening after she'd recounted her experience. "But if it'll make you feel better, call Child Protection Services. They'll take care of it."

In the morning, Rhonda made the call.

* * * *

The children must be hungry. Maggie's body refused to budge from the bed. Her bones pleaded for rest, unwilling muscles dead tired. The children were up—she could hear them playing in the front room. It wasn't right to leave them unattended while she slept. They needed her.

Again, she tried to will herself to rise to face another day.

* * * *

"It's pretty bad, Mr. Yates." Rhonda met the CPS agent at the gateway to Maggie's yard. "The house reeks to high heaven, so breathe deep while you can."

"You do not need to accompany me, Mrs. Hawthorne. Your anonymity will be protected."

"It's all right. She's sure to know who called." Rhonda followed him into the yard. "And I don't really care. But something needs to be done."

Yates was firm. "Please, stay back. You've done your part."

Rhonda snorted in disbelief, but held her place near the gateway as Mr. Yates progressed through the cluttered yard. Three sharp, staccato raps upon the door brought a grimy-faced girl in dirty pajamas to answer.

"Good morning." Yates tried not to reel back from the malodorous assault. "Is your mother at home?"

Rosy looked him over before gazing beyond to the gate. She smiled and waved. "Hi Mrs. Hawthorne." As if that were her cue, Rhonda began to stride forth.

Mr. Yates spoke again. "Please, I need to speak with your mother. May I come inside?"

Rosy kept the door partially closed and glared at him. "She's still sleeping and I'm not supposed to let strangers in."

Deciding to use Mrs. Hawthorne to his advantage, Yates knelt to look Rosy level in the eye. "But Mrs. Hawthorne isn't a stranger now, is she?"

Rosy shook her head.

"I know your mother has been very sick. I want to help her get better." Yates swallowed back the rising gorge in his throat. "Can you let us in to see her?"

Rhonda reached Yates' side, her hand unconsciously covering her nose and mouth against the stench emanating from the interior. "It's all right, Rosy. We're just here to help."

After a moment's consideration, Rosy opened the door. "My momma's room is over there." She pointed the way.

As they made their way across the room, Rhonda kept close to Mr. Yates' heels, carefully dodging the obstacles of toys and books. She glanced in the direction of the open kitchen, counters mounded with soured baby bottles, empty cans, and dirty dishes. The sink overflowed with various utensils cemented with moldy remains of food and piles of dirty diapers peeked out from a white trash bag against the wall. Everything was crawling with flies.

Yates sniffed the air curiously, and then knocked upon the bedroom door. "Mrs. Kendall? Maggie, are you awake?"

There was no response. He tried again, then turned back to Rhonda. "Please, keep the children back." He opened the bedroom door just enough to slip inside, closing it behind him.

The urgency in his tone made Rhonda's heart race. Her stomach churned as she fought to keep her breakfast down. Except for the wail of the baby, still in its crib, the house became shrouded in silence and her flesh burned beneath the curious eyes of the three older children. She should have stayed out of this as Yates had insisted.

His face the color of ash, Mr. Yates quickly slipped back out of Maggie's bedroom, pulling his phone from his pocket. "It's just as I feared."

"What? What is it?"

"Please, can you try to get the children gathered together?" His voice dropped to a whisper. "And for God's sake, keep them away from their mother's room."

"Why?"

"Mrs. Kendall is dead."

Rhonda stiffened.

Yates swiftly dialed his phone. "From all appearances, she's been dead for several days."

Rhonda's face drained as she tried not to stumble. "But I just saw…" She looked toward the front door. "…her yesterday."

But Yates was no longer listening as he spoke quietly into the phone. Rhonda stared over at the trio of grubby faces that returned her stare in stoic silence. An unearthly chill embraced her then, for within the pause of the baby's cries, from behind the closed bedroom door Rhonda heard the distinct creak of bedsprings.

* * * *

The children must be hungry. Maggie opened her eyes. With all her effort, she pulled the sheet off her face and forced her body to MOVE.

▲

The Road to Hell
by Kevin L. O'Brien

The oldster looked up as a small, thin, bedraggled man appeared at the edge of the firelight. He tensed, and tightened his grip on the forty-four magnum revolver in his lap, then realized the stranger meant him no harm. He had the look of an absent-minded professor, complete with balding, disheveled gray hair, thick-lensed glasses, and a filthy lab coat.

"May I join you?" he asked, in a fine, educated voice. "My name is Marley."

"I'm Casper." He gestured across the small fire. "Please, I'd enjoy the company."

Marley sat cross-legged. "I wasn't sure if I should at first. I mean, I had no way of knowing if you were dangerous. That is—"

"That's quite alright, I wondered the same about you, until I got a good look at you."

Marley flashed an embarrassed smile as he shrugged. "Well, anyway, your fire stood out as a bit of light and warmth in the darkness, so I decided to take a chance."

"I understand. I'd have done the same."

Marley stared into the flames. "Besides, when it comes right down to it, I find I don't want to die alone."

"I know exactly how you feel. Have you made provisions yet?"

"I was going to prepare some cyanide capsules, but I ran out of time, and all the drug stores around here have been cleaned out of sleeping pills."

Casper lifted his pistol. "I can take care of you, if you don't mind."

Marley looked up and nodded. "I would appreciate it."

The conversation lapsed as both men stared into the fire. Beyond the tiny sphere of light caste by the flames, Casper could see nothing, but he heard a faint, steady murmur, almost like a low hum.

Marley chuckled. "You know, only a month ago we'd be insane to sit outside like this; now it doesn't matter."

"Yah, things were pretty messed up for awhile. Say, would you like a snort?"

Marley looked up in surprise as Casper pulled a bottle from a rucksack, and he grinned as soon as he saw it. "I'd love one, thank you."

Casper passed the bottle to him and watched as he read the label. He almost laughed when the professor's eyes grew big around and his jaw dropped open.

"My God! This is twenty-five year old single malt Scotch! Wherever did you find it, man?"

"I've had it for a number of years; been saving it for a special occasion."

Marley pulled the stopper and hefted the bottle in salute. "May you be in Heaven an hour before the Devil knows you're dead." He then took a swig. He nearly chocked, but he managed to swallow.

"God, that's smooth," he said in a horse voice. He offered the bottle back.

Casper waved him off. "Keep it for now, I'll get my share later." Then he studied him for a few minutes.

"You look familiar somehow." He cocked his head. When the other didn't reply, he muttered, "Marley...Marley—"

Suddenly the light dawned. "Land o' Goshen, you wouldn't be him, would you?"

Marley saluted with the bottle. "Afraid so." Then he took another sip.

"Well, butter my biscuits, Momma, I'm honored to make your acquaintance!"

For once Marley looked shocked. "You really mean that?"

"Damn right! It's not every day you get to share a drink with the Savior of Humanity!"

Marley barked a laugh, but it contained no humor. "Some savior I turned out to be."

"Now, you shouldn't be so hard on yourself. I mean, it really wasn't your fault."

Marley cradled the bottle against his chest like a baby. "No, it wasn't my fault at all." He spoke in a subdued voice and took a swig.

"I mean, you had the best of intentions."

Marley eyed him with a mischievous smile. "You know what they say: the road to hell is paved with good intentions."

"Still, you had to take the chance. I mean, it was a good idea. How were you to know things would turn out the way they did?"

Marley stared into the fire again. "Katherine knew. Or at least she suspected."

"Who?"

Marley grimaced, as if the memory of her carried a secret pain he had borne for some time. "My wife. She was my research partner as well as my life partner." He took another swig as if to wash it away. "She warned me that once out in the world, they might evolve. They were engineered to breed very quickly, and they were being introduced into a niche where they would have no competitors or predators. Both are conducive to rapid evolution."

"How likely did she think it might happen?"

Marley shrugged, and raised the bottle to his lips, but paused and stared at it. He grimaced again, but from distaste, and passed it back. "Maybe forty percent."

Casper took a drink. "And what were our chances of survival if you hadn't released the swarm?"

Marley looked up at him across the fire. "Practically nill."

"So you gambled, and lost." Casper took another drink. "I'd have done the same."

The conversation lagged again, and he noted the hum had gotten louder.

"By the way, did anyone ever figure out what caused the plague in the first place?"

Marley shook his head. "No."

"I heard it was some kind of man-made virus, a bioweapon released by accident, or by a terrorist mole in the military somewhere."

Marley snorted in derision. "Ridiculous! Viruses can't raise the dead."

"Then, what do you think happened?"

"Personally? I believe it was a fungus of some kind. That at least has some credibility, but it's outside my area of expertise, and I have no proof." He sighed and shook his head. "It doesn't matter now anyways. The zombies may be gone, but we're all just as good as dead, what's left of us."

"Oh, I don't know." Casper took a swig. "It was worth a try in any event. Think of how it was back then. It started off with only a few, in isolated pockets around the world, but then they became dozens, then hundreds, thousands, millions! All within a few months. And nothing we did could stop them. Oh sure, we could shot them in the head, burn them, even nuke them, but we couldn't *stop* them." He then paused and pointed at Marley. "You found a way."

Marley made no reply; he just sighed and cocked his head to listen to the hum, now louder still.

Casper took another drink. "Yes, sir, you had a stroke of genius. Maggots, you said. They eat dead tissue, devour it like candy, but they don't touch living tissue. All you had to do was change a few genes in the common housefly, add one here, take out one there, mutate a few others, and presto: you had a weapon that would destroy every zombie throughout the world in a matter of weeks."

He paused and shook his head. "Too bad once the zombies were gone, they had acquired a taste for human flesh, and came after us next."

Marley sighed again. "Yeah, too bad."

"Just one thing I don't understand."

Marley lifted his head. "What?"

"Well, I know the flies swarm all over people, and each can lay dozens of eggs, and that they hatch after only a few minutes. But why can't you just wash them off?"

Marley flashed a weak smile. "That was part of the 'genius'. It wouldn't work if a good rain storm or a dunking in a river could remove the eggs, so we engineered the flies to use a stinging ovipositor. The eggs were injected into the skin, through the outer epidermis into the underlying dermal layer."

Casper nodded. "Okay, I get you. Of course, that means you'd have to just about skin a man to remove all the eggs."

"Yes, but the sting is virtually painless. A single fly could infect you and you'd never know it until the maggots hatched. Once they get into the muscle there's nothing that can be done. They'd still kill you; it would just take longer."

"Unless you got stung in the arm or leg; those can be amputated."

Marley shrugged in a listless manner. "Where there's one fly, there's more. Chances are good you'll be stung multiple times."

"Yeah. Any chance some people might survive?"

"I don't know. They might, if they live in extremely cold climes, or can seal their habitat off completely. But the flies can get in almost anywhere; they can drift on the wind or be carried inside containers. If they do get in, they can breed prodigiously. And like I said, it only takes one sting."

"Yeah."

The conversation lapsed yet again. The hum had grown loud enough to make talking difficult.

"How much time we got left?" Casper asked.

Marley checked his watch. "The swarm should be here momentarily."

Casper nodded. He put the bottle aside and picked up the revolver. He held it in his lap for a moment, then lifted it and shot Marley through the head.

"Damn shame, really, it was such a good idea." He raised the barrel to his chin. Beyond the fire, the hum rose to a crescendo as the first flies came into view. ▲

Maggot Coffee
by Roy C. Booth and Axel Kohagen

I upended the Styrofoam cup of coffee and felt something wriggle to the back of my throat. It lodged up behind the rough of my mouth and stayed there, no matter how hard I gagged to dislodge it.

Two maggots squirmed in the bottom of my cup. After the gorge settled, I stalked about the funeral home, looking for someone to sue. All I saw were empty folding chairs and pews in the other rooms. My family, small as it was, stayed clumped together in the smallest viewing room. Tact dictated I couldn't bother them at the viewing, so I made my apologies to my great-aunt and went home.

The maggot in the back of my mouth squirmed the whole ride home. Not continuously, but regularly. It would lie dormant for just long enough for me to feel it had, perhaps, slipped out of where it was lodged. Then it would writhe again, with a new found ferocity.

Once home, I dove onto my knees in front of my toilet and retched until I thought I had nothing at all left inside me, but the damn worm still squirmed. I dug my index finger back until the webbing between my fingers tore a bit, but nothing. I even got out a coat hanger and worked at it, jabbing bloody, coppery tasting gashes into my throat. The worm hung on and did not go away.

At least, not until the next morning. I felt silly about the whole thing, especially considering the tenderness of my throat. I went to work as if nothing had happened.

The first vision hit me about mid-day. I envisioned a corpse clawing at a wall of dirt. Oddly, the dirt gave way far too quickly. It felt so real, I had to check my fingernails for dirt and grime.

I blinked a few times, then I ignored it and went about my day, doing the usual things. I did feel a little scummier as the day wore on, like I was desperately in need of a shower. When I got home, I took one right away. It didn't help any.

I took a sick day from work and went to the doctor. He didn't find anything. Oh, sure, he saw where I had immolated myself and all, but the maggot? Somehow it eluded him. I thought about getting a second opinion but realized if I got the same result I might find myself in a 72 hour hold, "for my own protection."

After that, things became a blur.

Blah days passed me by. Food lost its flavor. Days and nights, they seemed all the same. I still made it to work, but it became tougher each day to do so. My co-workers commented that I lost weight and asked if I were ill or having personal problems.

Heh. If they only knew.

The visions were the worst. Sometimes I saw just one corpse, sometimes I saw many. Always they were digging, and they were getting closer to something each time.

The corpses were a ragged bunch, dead for a very long time. They looked nothing like the movies. They hissed as they dug, like cats in a spat. Maggots flaked off of them like dandruff. Maggots, like the ones in my coffee cup.

One night, after an awful dream, I awoke to find myself in a freshly dug grave. I was merely sleeping there; there was no dirt under my fingernails. I managed to scramble out of the grave before anyone noticed me. Well, almost anyone. A lone woman drove into the cemetery and she saw me, wearing sleep pants and a T-shirt, walking through the dewy grass with clods of dirt in my hair.

I could have seen a shrink then, but I chose not to make the call. Probably be as useless as seeing the doctor. I figured anything a shrink had to say about waking up in a graveyard, I did not want to hear. Besides, I wasn't hurting anyone. Yet.

The next night, in my dream, one of the corpses broke through the dirt wall and I got a brief glimpse of what was behind. Very brief. Just the impression of a lot of heat and motion.

The dreams continued, but I never got a good look at the goal of the corpses' frenzied clawing. Then, one day, I woke up in a sewer. Curled up peacefully in sewage, my head next to half of a dead rat. I resisted the urge to wipe my face, fearing this would make everything worse. I stumbled about for an hour before I found a way out, and when I did, I was horrified to discover I was right next to the funeral home where I had first swallowed the maggot.

I came back later that day, after a shower and a fairly decent night's rest. I knocked on the door. I wanted to look around, to find out where that goddamned maggot came from.

When the elderly man who, I assumed, owned the home, opened the door. He was not sad to see me.

"We were hoping," he said, gesturing for me to come in.

I went straight to the coffee pot and saw three maggots on the floor, near the coffee. I looked at the wall behind it and saw a portion of it that looked both damp and new. Frustrated, sick from the sewer smell I still couldn't get out of my nostrils, I punched the wall and peeled until I could see what was behind it.

"We've been looking for suitable hosts," the elderly man said, unphased by my behavior. "Very few let the maggots into them, let them take control."

I was still gagging because of what I saw behind the drywall.

"You are blessed."

"Because I gave up and let a maggot get in my head?" I asked.

"Yes," the man said. He smiled, his lips wet with drool.

Behind the drywall was a woman's head. I knew it had been there when I drank the coffee. The whole thing was rotted, filled with maggots. The little white worms spilled out of nostrils and lips and eye sockets. They tumbled with chunks of nearly liquid flesh. It was here that the maggot in my head was born.

"Is this what's gonna happen to me?" I asked.

He shook his head.

"Oh no. No, of course not. She gave up. You're still around. Come with me," he said. "Please."

I followed him to a back room where two men, who looked like his sons, were feeding a nasty, flesh-eating thing they kept in a cast-iron pot on an altar. They were taking these chunks out of a body and, through my disgust, I noticed they were careful to pick places the bereaved would not see were missing. The wet, red, angry-looking thing was lunging, trying to escape.

"It's beautiful," the man said. "It will serve you well."

I did not comment. A mural showed a poorly painted vision of squirming worms with angel wings, rising over the planet. Next to the thing's prison was a book bound in some sort of strong animal hide. Next to that was a skull that was being used as a bowl.

"When you become transformed," he said, "we will make a painting of you as well."

I ran then, as quickly as I could.

When I got home, I just locked my doors and hid in my bedroom, only coming out to use the bathroom or raid the fridge. My legs grew number every day, and my arms weaker as well. There were very few lids I could unscrew in my own apartment. I ended up ordering a lot of take out.

I tried to forget about all of it, but after one particular horrid dream, I woke up in a grave again and had to be shooed away by the caretaker, who obviously knew what was going on at the funeral home. This time, I had been digging at the dirt.

I went home and got the message from work that I was fired. I collapsed on the bed and fought to breathe. My arms and legs felt cumbersome and dead.

That night, I finally had a clear view of what was beyond the dirt the corpses were clawing at. It was a room filled with other corpses, bowing down before an empty throne made of bone and swathed in blood.

I fear I know who they believe will sit there.

▲

What Dark Gods Are Friends to Me?
by Chad Hensley

Eidolon sits forgotten, sunken isle;
A cracking obelisk on barren crag.
A monolith grotesque upon the spile?
Tall, woven tiki statues bend and snag

An empty islander and tourists too!
Now midnight ancient masses black far and wide
Will harken calling dark inhuman few
To tread the skies with black, gigantic stride;

A vast necropolis across the land.
Diseased and dying mankind's final out;
Result a very cosmic evil planned
To plant iniquitous hot seeds that sprout

For alien cult messiahs disavow
Their power ushers Earth pariah now.

Baby Mine
by Marilyn "Mattie" Brahen

I was told that Elsa was an Alaskan Husky pup when I adopted her in the late spring of 1998 from the Winnebago Indians at the Black River Trading Post roadside stand off the highway. I was driving from my job at the health spa that Friday to my apartment in Wittenberg, Wisconsin and had stopped there many a time before, as it's about halfway home and the gas and convenience mini-mart are across the side road. The stand has good vegetables and fruit for sale along with the Native American crafts for the tourists. But this time they had a sign that read, "Free Puppy—Needs Good Home."

I fell in love with Elsa the moment she stood up, frantically trying to get my attention, inside the cage Bart Haranga had housed her in. Bart, of the Potawatomi tribe of the Winnebagos, ran the stand. He came over to me and lifted the pup out. He said, "She likes you. Why don't you give her a home?"

"I don't know, Bart. I've never had a dog. Where did you get this puppy?"

He held the squirming pup firmly. "Foundling. Abandoned in the woods near the Black River Falls. I think someone's bitch had a small litter and they only kept one of the offspring. At any rate, this poor thing would have died if I hadn't rescued her. But I've got too many dogs as it is. Why don't you take her?"

He put her in my arms and darned if that little heartbreaker didn't calm right down, nuzzling my chest and neck and giving me that wide-eyed look. Temptation overcame my reluctance. I was divorced and had sold my house. I had no children and the apartment felt lonely. The pup's blue eyes penetrated straight to my heart, as if beseeching me to nurture her.

Bart stroked her soft white silver fur and said, "She needs love. She looks barely weaned. She'll make a good watchdog when she's grown, Carol."

I studied the puppy and then Bart. We were once almost lovers, after my divorce from Peter. Bart was attractive, 29 years old, never married. He was two years older than me, and we had met at a dance in Wittenberg, but I was too skittish about any relationship after Peter dumped me and moved to Florida, when I was 23. Three years of marriage down the drain. When Bart tried to court me little more than a year later, I just wasn't ready for another man that way.

But I did need to feel love, and the puppy nestling in my arms felt like love. "Umm, I don't even know how to train a dog, Bart."

"I'll come over after work and bring puppy chow and newspaper. I'll teach you. Look, she loves you."

The dog was licking my face, its little tongue raspy. "You're just looking for an excuse to get on my good side, Bart."

"Can't blame me for trying. Come on, Carol. I'll just help you get acclimated to the puppy. She just needs a mother right now. And a name." He looked at me with those dark, earth-brown eyes, his hair richly brown and just shy of long, his smile sincere, trustworthy. "I'll even pay for her food."

"Damn, Bart, I think I've fallen in love."

"With me or the pup?"

"With the puppy. Okay, I'll see you tonight. But give me some food for the dog to take back now, so I can feed her if you're late."

Bart put her back into the cage, took a few cans of wet dog food and hauled everything to my car, loading them in the back seat. Then he bagged the produce I'd selected, but refused to take any money. "So what are you going to name her?"

I gave him a cautious smile, still uncertain about taking the pup. "Well, I always wanted to name a daughter Elsa, but didn't have one. So I guess I'll call her Elsa."

"Nice name. Okay, I'll see you and Elsa tonight at 7:30 p.m., soon as I'm done here. Give her some milk if she won't eat the soft food. I'll stop and pick up some proper puppy chow."

* * * *

Elsa was easily trained. I walked her early in the morning and once at night and she never made a mess after the first week. She also loved the toys I bought her and sleeping on my bed at night, although she would paw me as if nursing and I worried that she'd been weaned too early. Bart came over once every weekend to check her progress and probably to check on his own with me. It became a routine, and his presence was becoming enjoyable. We'd watch movies or play cards and he'd act the perfect gentleman. When he left, he'd give me one gentle kiss and scratch Elsa's head.

But the third weekend held a surprise which neither of us expected. Elsa had been asleep on the rug while we watched TV. The sun had gone down, night came and I turned on the living room lights. Then Bart and

I went into the kitchen to make some coffee. A minute later, we heard a baby crying, sounding close.

"What the heck?" Bart said.

"I don't know anyone in the building with a baby. Someone with one must be visiting." But the crying continued, and seemed to be coming from my living room. We started back there, steaming cups in hand, and put them on my coffee table. "Must be directly upstairs."

"Where's Elsa?"

I looked around. "She must have wandered off. She was just there, under the table."

The cry came again, and Bart got up to search for Elsa and froze by the side of the sofa, staring at the floor hidden behind its right arm. "Carol. Look!"

I did. A naked baby lay on the floor, its piercing blue eyes frightened and its silver white hair long and fine against the carpet as it wailed and shivered. A girl child, reaching out its small arms to me.

I reacted instinctively, picking her up. "Oh, God! Where did she come from?"

He stayed silent for a long minute, and then murmured, "I'll get a towel to wrap her in." He went into my bathroom, bringing back a fluffy towel to warm the baby in. But before he covered her completely, he examined her feet. Watching, I sucked in my breath: the baby's feet didn't have soft human skin. It had the pads of a canine.

"What is this?" I asked, "And where's Elsa?"

He hesitated before answering, looking at me directly, reluctant and worried. "This is Elsa, Carol. I've heard of these things, but never saw one before."

"How can this baby be Elsa?"

"Carol, listen to me. There are legends about this. And if I'm right, we have a hard task ahead of us."

I listened. It was hard believing what he said.

* * * *

Bart told me of a sort of reverse werewolf. Wolves are very much like humans: they love, they form family groups, they work together, and they are loyal to each other. They aren't blood-thirsty or violent by nature; they kill their prey for sustenance, never for sport. They respect it and keep its numbers thriving, so that the balance of nature is maintained. And as for their attitude towards mankind, they're both wary and curious about us, knowing us to be superior creatures and possibly more dangerous than any other animal. And so, most of the wolves avoid humans, a species they don't normally trust.

But according to the legends, some wolves became attracted to humanity, so much so, that they would steal among us and shed their wolf pelts and walk in the guise of humans, but only during a full moon when its light allowed that transformation. Then they would clothe themselves in our garments and appear to strangely question the men and women they met and sniff out our ways. Sometimes they became adept at passing as humans. People would make mention of a solitary woman who appeared now and then in town, wandering and mysterious, or a curious man who would nose into late night conversations. And sometimes there was talk of their quiet invitation to bed them and taste their pleasures. But in the morning, they vanished, although they might appear on another night in another month to the same lover, saying they had suddenly had to journey on unexpectedly, but now they had returned, promising to be as faithful as they could be. But they never stayed for more than a season; they knew they couldn't truly mate with us.

Bart called them by a Winnebago name I couldn't pronounce. "They are drawn to humans," he said, "but they know they are wolves, a cousin, but not a brother or sister, and that they cannot live among us as a human. And so their human lover one day wonders why he or she has been abandoned, but it wasn't because the wolf didn't care. The wolf did care, but it knew it must leave its lover for its lover's sake. And once they know this, they know they cannot shift again and must accept their wolf nature completely and leave humans be."

I asked, "What has this got to do with us and with Elsa?"

Bart sat with me on the sofa; I held the baby.

Bart nodded, as if agreeing with something he was thinking. "Carol, we have to find another wolf mother. Sometimes a she-wolf bears a child if she lies with a man. They say a human woman can also bear the child of a transformed male wolf. There are legends about that. But the child always dies and sometimes the mother, too." He shook his head. "Carol, I'm really sorry about this."

"So what do we do now?" I looked again at the baby's feet. "This is unbelievable."

"I know. We'll have to care for Elsa until I talk with the medicine man of my people. The legends say a transformed child-wolf can only be human during the full moon, and according to the lore she must go back to the wild or she'll die."

He took his cell phone from his pocket and dialed the medicine man. They talked for a while. He gave Bart the name and number of another tribal elder, and then Bart hung up. He told me that on the following weekend, when Elsa was once again a wolf—for wolf was what she was and not a dog—we would try to return her to her people.

* * * *

Bart drove us to a forested area farther north in Wisconsin. I held the wolf pup in my arms as we were met by an elderly female Winnebago tribeswoman who led us further into the woods, far away from any marked path. There she instructed me to put Elsa down before a huge tree and made me move away from her. Bart and I were told to stand at nearby trees, and the woman shook tobacco out of a large pouch into our hands. She then went over to Elsa and scattered the tobacco on the ground before the wolf pup.

I watched anxiously for Elsa to bolt, to run away or run to me, but she didn't. She sat down on the leaves and earth, as obedient as a trained dog, watching as the old woman began to sing in Winnebago. She also brought a rattle and moved it rhythmically to her singing, pointing it at Bart and me.

Bart instructed me, "Scatter the tobacco in your hands around the trees and call out to the spirits to have pity on Elsa. Tell the spirits that you are pleading for Elsa to be returned to her true family."

I stared at him.

"Do it, Carol." He pointed at the medicine woman. "She's 'calling down the thunder,' the power of the sky, the power of nature. Only that power can return Elsa to her true form permanently." Bart's eyes pleaded for my understanding. That there were realities beyond those we call normal, and only acceptance could make the magic work.

I flecked the tobacco around the tree we stood beside, and gazed at the pup who had stolen my heart. I had to give her up, caught in a mystery I barely believed in and yet had to believe in.

My mouth dry, I swallowed to moisten it, and I began: "I call down the thunder! Please protect my baby, whom You only let me love for the shortest time." My voice strengthened as a strange breeze seemed to swirl about me. "Please send her another mother to love her as I would have. Please do not leave her alone. Please bring her back to her wolf family!"

Bart scattered his own tobacco and let out a stream of musical words, his voice rising and falling, but I could not understand them, for they were in the Winnebago language.

And then something extraordinary occurred. Elsa began to whimper. I almost ran to her, but Bart quickly stopped me. From out of the woods, a full-grown wolf emerged, halted, and looked at the medicine woman and then at Bart and me. She slowly loped up to me in the forest clearing, leaned back on her hind legs, and then stood up again. She lifted her silver-furred head and bayed in a howl, its pitch unique, melodic.

Somewhere in the distance, other wolves answered her. She gazed directly at me, her blue eyes penetrating.

The she-wolf—I knew the wolf was female—turned and trotted to Elsa. The pup greeted her eagerly, nuzzling against her underside seeking her nipples. The wolf licked Elsa tenderly and swiftly grasped her by the scruff of her neck, lifting her, claiming her as her own.

I wanted to run to the pup, to stroke her, a farewell, a goodbye. I involuntarily called her name. "Elsa."

The wolf-mother turned halfway, her eyes once more on my own, Elsa limply hanging by her scruff, acceptance in her posture, letting this new mother take her to their den. And then the wolf and Elsa disappeared through the thick woods.

The Winnebago medicine woman came over to Bart and me. "This is good," she said. "The child has returned to its true parent." She smiled sadly at me. "You are lonely. You need to have a true child of your own to love."

I nodded.

We walked silently along the forest path back to our cars and parted ways.

* * * *

Bart and I became closer after this. He finally won my love. We now have two sons and a daughter, our true children. Our daughter, of course, was named Elsa.

For years, I thought of the wolf puppy, and I became an advocate for the wolves. Last year, we took the children to a nature reserve where they could watch the wolves from a distance. And as we watched, one female with striking blue eyes and white silver fur came close to us and stood there. She gazed directly at me with open canine curiosity and then turned, moving off, not looking back.

▲

In Blackwalk Wood
Adrian Cole

The old guy who lived at the end of the street was as miserable as sin. Okay, that was just my opinion of him, based on a few meetings, although you could hardly call them meetings—brushes perhaps. These were usually in the local stores. I always say hello to people—it's a small town and not a bad community—I reckon most of its inhabitants would lend each other a hand if the need arose. Maybe my circumstances made me seem more irritable than I realised and maybe that's why the old guy was wary.

I spoke to Dennis, who runs the store, about the old man after I'd said my customary good morning in there one day. I'd got the usual cool stare and nod of the head from the bloke, no more than that. He was big and tall, probably in his sixties, and he was slightly stoop-shouldered. "He's not a bundle of laughs, that guy," I said after he'd picked up his small bag of supplies and moved away before anyone could engage him in conversation. In this town, most people are always glad to exchange at least a few pleasantries. One of the reasons they come to Dennis's store rather than go exclusively to the big supermarket is for the company, the slightly more intimate atmosphere.

"O'Riordan? No, but he's not always been like that." Dennis seemed to be about to enlarge on his remark, but something checked him. The expression on his face was one he usually reserved for me. It was that same look of sympathy, more than that—pity—which I was trying un-comfortably to come to terms with. My wife had been diagnosed with cancer and although a stubborn part of me didn't want to accept it, she probably didn't have long to live. It seemed like the whole town knew it, even though we'd been here less than a year. We'd migrated to this relatively remote spot to try and make the remainder of her time as pleas-ant as we could. We'd always said we'd come here when we retired, expecting that to be a long way in the future. I felt cheated and angry, but I just had to bite the bullet.

"Ten years ago, he was very different," said Dennis. "Affable, very approachable. Nothing he wouldn't do to help people. What you'd have called a pillar of society. Some people tried to get him to run for Mayor, or Councillor, but he just laughed it off. His wife was the same. Very nice lady. Their kids have families of their own now, up country."

"So what happened? Come on, Dennis, I'm not one to blab about things. Tell me about it."

Dennis took my money and rang up the till, weighing his words carefully. "Well, it was a bad business. We had a hard winter. Lot of black ice on the roads. O'Riordan's wife was as sensible a driver as anyone, but she took a bend that bit too fast, slid into the ice and before she knew it, rolled the Land Rover. She was unlucky. Nine times out of ten she'd have got off with a few bruises, a broken arm, maybe. Instead, she hit her head and she was killed outright. A thin skull, apparently."

Dennis wasn't looking at me, as if he'd spoken out of line, cruelly perhaps. I was the last person who'd want to know about someone's wife dying.

"O'Riordan took it badly. The only thing that kept him going was his dog. He had one of those huge beasts—an Irish wolfhound. Man, that was some animal. It stood three feet tall, a grey, shaggy hound that filled the shop whenever O'Riordan came in. A force of nature, but friendly! Jeeze, when that beast licked you, you were just about bowled over. Big softee, he called it. He said it was unusual for its breed because they were usually stand-offish with strangers. Cuchulainn, he called it, after the Irish hero. On the other hand, O'Riordan said if anyone upset the animal, the dog was terrifying.

"After his wife's death, O'Riordan kept to himself a lot more and he was never seen without the dog. Maybe her spirit attached itself to the dog, who knows?"

"I suppose it explains why he's a surly bugger," I said. Like me?

"He was okay while the dog was alive. A year or so ago, it died. It was getting on in years. Went peacefully, but you can imagine the effect it had on O'Riordan. It was pretty devastating. Hard to understand if you've never had a dog of your own."

I had never owned a dog, but I got the idea. And it explained a lot of the old man's moroseness. I felt a slight emotional tremor , as though I could empathise with him, even though he was a complete stranger. However, my own inner despair quickly swamped it, as if O'Riordan was some kind of harbinger, a shadow from the future.

"I'm sorry," said Dennis, genuinely, unsure what else to say to clear the air. He probably wanted to say I was a fine one to talk. If anyone saw through my forced bonhomie, it was him. I knew my anger—fury—at what had happened to Kathy, had made me short-tempered and irritable.

"It's how things go, isn't it?" I said, a bit caustically.

"I must say, I miss that dog, too. It was a monster, but it gave you a warm feeling when it greeted you. And I lost a good account—the amount of food it ate!"

We laughed, but it was a little hollow, not quite easing the tension. I picked up my stuff and waved as I left. Out on the street I glanced in the general direction of O'Riordan's place, about half a mile away. Was that what I was destined to become, once Kathy passed on? That oncoming darkness was inescapable. It took me a while to shrug off the mood. By the time I got home, I had just about put O'Riordan and his tragedies from my mind.

Three days later, in the evening, I was watching something on the television, not taking much in, my thoughts tangled, as they often were at this time of day, after I'd helped Kathy to bed. She retired early now, her strength ebbing almost daily. I'd read her to sleep, holding back the tears that always came until I left her, such a frail form, curled up in our bed, like a child. She still managed to smile.

I was startled by the doorbell. Visitors at this time of the evening were rare. I had even more of a surprise when I opened the door. The old man, O'Riordan, was standing there, an apologetic look on his face.

"I'm very sorry to trouble you," he said. There was a trace of Irish brogue in his voice. "Would it be possible to have a few words with you?"

The October air was cold and I didn't want it to invade the warmth of the house, where my central heating kept the temperature at a steady, comfortable level. "Of course, come on in."

As he crossed the threshold, he seemed bigger than I remembered him, well over six feet and unusually broad. He exuded a natural strength that was mildly disarming. I ushered him into the living room and to an arm chair. Kathy would be fast asleep by now, so we wouldn't be disturbing her.

"Mr O'Riordan," I said, sitting opposite him.

He sat on the edge of the chair and eyed me keenly. He had a thick crop of hair down to his shoulders and it occurred to me he could have passed for the drummer of a 70's rock band. He didn't quite manage a smile—that seemed alien to him—but for once he looked less severe. "Bran," he said. "Please, call me Bran."

"Sure. I'm Phil."

He nodded. "I've seen you about the town. You've been here nigh on a year. It's a good place. A man can make a good life here."

I wasn't sure how to respond, so I just nodded.

"Forgive my presumptuousness, Phil, but I know about your wife. It's a terrible thing."

Again I nodded.

"Listen, I'm not here to offer you religious guidance, or to waste your time with empty words of condolence. I sympathise, as any man would do. But I can help."

I felt myself going cold, as though that October air had slipped in here after all. Over the last year, I had been over this kind of ground too many times. The healers, the God squad, the mystics, the whole band of freaks who offered false hopes and hollow promises. What kind of god would allow this to happen to Kathy? She was twenty-eight, not even half way through her life.

"Bran, I'm sure you mean well, but I can't do this. I'm not a man of faith—if I was, all that would have been kicked out of me by what's happened. I just want to be left with my wife to get through this until she goes. It's kind of you to think you can help, but really, you can't."

"There's a way," he persisted.

"A way?"

"To prevent it. She doesn't have to die."

I would have lost my temper and probably have let him have the rough end of my tongue, but, as I said, I'd been there before. Shouting didn't do any good. I'd done it too many times and it just left me snarled up and even more frustrated. I just wanted to ease him out of the house before he spouted whatever line in mumbo-jumbo he had.

"Just hear me out for a few moments," he said and there was something in his eyes that made me check. I felt an atmosphere that was deeply uncanny, almost as though we had shifted backwards in time and were sitting not in my living room but beside a campfire.

"In a few days, it will be Samhain," he said. "What you probably know as Halloween. October the 31st."

The way he spoke the word—he pronounced it 'Sah-wen'—struck a chord within me, something very deep, a tribal memory, maybe. Whatever it was, it held me there, so I didn't growl an angry dismissal and insist that he leave me.

"There will be celebrations," he said softly. "At Samhain, the walls between our world and what lies beyond are very thin. Remember that, Phil. If you bring your wife to the festival, she can be saved. I promise you." There were tears in his eyes and either madness or a powerful belief in whatever it was he foresaw.

I didn't want to provoke him. "I'll think about it," I said, trying to claw my way back to reality, as if I'd been teetering on the brink of something way beyond my depth.

"Please do," he said simply and rose. He was at the door and gone before I said anything further. I sat down and wondered if I'd imagined the whole thing, but there were a few leaves on the carpet, brought in by the old man's shoes. I picked them up and dropped them in the litter bin.

Halloween, for Christ's sake. Kathy and I usually locked the doors and hid ourselves away from the "trick or treaters" and we certainly didn't carve pumpkin faces and put candles in them. Maybe if things had been different and we'd gone on to have kids. And now this! Take Kathy to the Festival? How bloody ridiculous. I couldn't imagine for one moment it would help her state of mind.

* * * *

The day came, a Saturday as it happened and I fussed around the house, cleaning, tidying, probably creating work, just to keep myself occupied. I'd tried to put my odd conversation with Bran O'Riordan from my mind, but it kept re-surfacing. Kathy was sitting in her usual chair in the living room, the back of which overlooked our garden. Although it was autumn, there was plenty for her to watch, and she sat quietly drinking it in, a small, pale figure. Occasionally she remarking on something, a passing squirrel, or a neighbourly cat stalking invisible prey in the beds.

"You know what day it is?" I said to her over a cup of tea. "Halloween."

She smiled. "Are they celebrating locally? Isn't there something happening on the Common?"

"I think so." I was surprised she'd taken note of it. Maybe she'd read it in the local press. "Why—did you want to go?" The words were out before I thought about it.

"Yes, I think I'd like that."

"You're not just saying it to please me? We don't usually go."

"It'll do me good. I can wrap up warm. And we don't have to stay for long."

So it was agreed. For some reason I felt slightly relieved.

Later, after we'd had tea, I got her into a thick coat and wrapped a blanket around her in her wheelchair and we made our way down the street towards the Common. It was going to be something of a precursor to Bonfire Night, with a few fireworks. People had already set to work hanging up pumpkins, triangular eyes glowing with candle-light, and numerous children ran around, some shrieking with excitement, others wide-eyed and fascinated by events as the time to light the fire drew near.

There was a beer tent, and apart from the alcohol on sale, including a local punch and some mulled wine, there were hot drinks for those who preferred them. I was surprised at the turnout—it was quite a gathering. Fortunately the weather was okay—dry, if crisp and cold. The sky was cloudless, so the stars were in bright evidence, which added to the occasion. Kathy was clearly enjoying it, huddled down in her blanket, but wide-eyed for once. I caught glimpses of the girl I had known in those eyes and had to fight back the anguish of knowing it would be fleeting.

As I stood at her side in the fire-light, watching the flames devouring the heaped branches and stacked wooden crates, I felt a movement beside me. Bran O'Riordan stood there.

"You brought her," he said. "That's good."

I didn't mention our bizarre conversation at the house, just nodding. "It's a nice enough night."

"Perfect," he replied. "Would you and your wife like something to eat or drink?"

"Let me get them," I said, a little too quickly.

"I'll keep my eye on her for you."

I would have refused, but the beer tent was no more than a few steps away, and it would only take me a couple of minutes to get something. I spoke to Kathy, who didn't want anything. I fetched a couple of beers, came back and handed one to O'Riordan.

I kept expecting him to broach the subject of Kathy's illness again, but he was his usual taciturn self, just watching the fire and some dancing that had broken out among one group. I could hear the strains of violins and a drum, so a band must have been engaged, unless it was entirely impromptu. I checked my watch—it was nine pm. I decided to give it an hour before taking Kathy home. She seemed very content. For once I felt a little relaxed.

The night had closed in around the festivities, the far end of the Common blocked off by the doubly dark expanse of woodland there, a natural border to this part of the town. I found myself wondering if this sort of scene had been enacted way back down the centuries, long before modern religions had taken a hold. I could understand people's affinity for the outdoors and the elements, and how they could have imbued them with spiritual powers. Something in that concept tugged at me.

Whether it was the strong beer, a particularly rich brew, or the music and general swirl of activity around me, my mind must have wandered, slightly hypnotised—lulled—by it all. A couple of loud bangs and accompanying sizzles of firework and laughter made me snap back from my reverie. I turned to speak to Kathy, leaning down to her wheelchair.

She wasn't there. The chair was empty.

I looked around, shocked and baffled. People were smiling, laughing, some pointing at the fireworks. I dropped the glass beside the empty wheelchair, panic flooding over me. There was no sign of Kathy. She couldn't have got up on her own. I barged my way through the nearest people, though they took no notice. I found an open space where I had a better view around me, but there was still no sign of Kathy. I didn't see anyone I knew, so I felt impotent, unable to ask those close to me if they'd seen her.

I ran a few steps in one direction and then back-tracked. I was getting desperate, when I saw a movement at the far side of the clearing, beyond the still blazing fire. A tall figure, no more than a shadow, carrying a smaller shape. O'Riordan? Could it be him? Carrying Kathy? It made no sense, but I wasn't in a rational mood. I rushed around the fire.

Beyond the last of the gathered onlookers was the woodland, Blackwalk Wood. It was a wall of darkness, silent and suddenly forbidding. I looked for O'Riordan, but couldn't see him. I studied the impenetrable trees and for a moment thought I'd seen movement. Hurriedly I made my way into the first of them, sure now that something had come this way. Within minutes the bonfire and the crowd were behind me, blotted out as though they were miles away. The night and the chilling air curdled around me. I had no torch with me, but there was a well-worn path.

I almost tripped as I plunged on, shouting Kathy's name. A deep hush had dropped over this enclosed world, muffling my frantic calls. Again I thought I saw movement ahead, a stooped figure. I wanted to believe it was O'Riordan and yet the thought of him abducting Kathy terrified me. She would be far more affected than me, completely helpless.

The darkness had closed in one me like a fist and I had to pick my way more and more carefully through undergrowth that was still waist high, in spite of the season. Brambles tried to snare me, ripping my clothes. I saw vague light ahead, through the packed trees, flickering as if someone carrying a torch was moving away from me. I pushed harder against the raking tendrils of undergrowth, realising I must have come a good half mile into this wood. Whatever I was going to have to deal with, I would be alone.

There was a clearing, a smear of moonlight overhead. That dancing light came from a burning torch—a firebrand—set in the ground at the far side of the open ground. The undergrowth in the clearing had been flattened, unnaturally I thought. My breath steamed in front of me in a white cloud as I panted from my exertions. The figure I had been chasing was in the clearing, standing stock still, head raised to the heavens. I couldn't see more than shadows, but it was big enough to be O'Riordan. And there was something at his feet, laid out on the woodland floor. Christ Almighty—Kathy?

I was about to cry out in rage, ignoring the weird surroundings, and rush forward, but another blur of movement to one side of me snagged my attention. Something among the tree boles had slipped in and out of the darkness. It remained invisible, but I heard a deep-throated growl. It had to be a dog, and a big one. I was certain that it was watching me and I froze. I had no weapons to defend myself with if it attacked. As I waited, I heard a sound further away in the night, partially obscured by distance. I wasn't certain, but I thought it was the sound of baying.

I forced myself to move forward, almost tripping over a fallen branch. I bent down and tugged it free of the growths. I would have felt ridiculous hefting it, but I needed something and the branch was long and weighty enough to do as a makeshift weapon. I felt slightly less vulnerable clutching it. Whatever had made the sounds among the nearby trees was still there—I could feel its presence even if I couldn't see the thing. Mercifully it held back.

"O'Riordan!" I called as I reached the open ground.

The big man turned slowly, his face masked by the darkness.

"What the fuck is going on?" I challenged him.

"It's all right," he called. "I told you she'd be okay."

Was he mad? Dragging Kathy out here into the middle of nowhere! How could she possibly be okay?

Ignoring whatever was skulking in the trees, I shifted forward and stood within a few feet of the old man, although he seemed far too large and powerful to be old—in this grove he had shed his years. I could see that it really was Kathy at his feet, curled up in her blanket, asleep or unconscious, as if readied for what—sacrifice?

I was about to launch an abusive verbal attack, but suddenly I felt the ground tremble, vibrating as though a fast train was passing nearby, except that we were miles from a railway line. There was a distant drumming, coming from the same direction that I'd heard the baying. The sound ebbed and flowed, partially obscured by the forest.

"They're coming," said O'Riordan.

I clutched the branch more tightly. "Get away from my wife."

"You don't understand," he said, holding up a hand. As he did so there was more movement among the nearby trees, where several shapes hovered on all sides. If the idea hadn't been ludicrous, I would have said it was a wolf pack. I might have stiffened to inactivity through fear, but my concern for Kathy overrode all that and I pressed forward. It was obvious that O'Riordan was not going to step aside. Whatever he intended was either insane or unsavoury.

I swung the branch, my meaning clear. There was more baying, excited now, accompanied this time with shouts, again distorted by distance, though not so far away. Riders? Was this some bizarre element of tonight's festivities?

"You mustn't interfere," O'Riordan protested. I couldn't understand his expression, which seemed to be of deep anxiety. Anger flooded me and I stepped in, striking hard with the branch, landing a blow to his forearm that brought a cry from him. There were echoing snarls in the trees and I wondered if I'd unleashed a pack of dogs on myself. O'Riordan rode the blow. I was committed—I struck again, once to his shoulder and again to his side, blows which brought him to his knees. He put his hands to his head, knowing I'd do some real damage if I landed a blow there.

"I'm taking her back," I told him.

"You can't. Not now. She's not in danger."

"You better explain. So help me Christ, I'll split your fucking skull open!" At that moment I meant it, too.

"I know what it is to lose a wife," he said. "I lost my own. She died years ago in an accident, but I could have prevented it. I could have chosen a different fate for her. She could have lived."

"What are you talking about?"

"They gave me a choice, that night. Samhain. They wanted a life. Mine, or one in place of it. It had to be a life I cherished as much as my own." The crashing of the undergrowth and wild sounds of the hounds almost drowned out his voice.

He was crying, tears gleaming in the glow from the firebrand he'd set in the ground. Somewhere out in the darkness, the drumming of hooves grew very close.

"Who? Who wanted a life?" I said, shouting above the din. I glanced at Kathy, but she hadn't moved. She had never looked so small or frail.

"The Wild Hunt. You hear it? Soon it will be here."

He was mad. The things he'd lost in life had fucked his head up. "Get out of the way, or I'll move you, O'Riordan. I mean it."

"I could have given them my wife, or Cuchulainn. They both meant everything to me."

For a moment I wondered what the fuck he was babbling about. Then I remembered his dog, the wolfhound.

"I could not bear to lose Cuchulainn. Perhaps I didn't believe it would happen, that it was a nightmare. I told them to take my wife."

"Your wife died in a car crash," I said coldly, recalling the words of the shopkeeper, Dennis.

O'Riordan nodded. "Yes, it's how they took her. I could have offered myself, or Cuchulainn. I betrayed her, choosing the hound over her."

We were almost surrounded now by the cracking of thin branches, the snorting of horses, the deep-throated growl of hounds. A large body of mounted men was close by. There was a glow among the trees, lanterns or torches, I assumed. Once this party confronted us, as it seemed they were determined to, they'd enable me to get to Kathy and prevent any more interference from this idiot O'Riordan.

"Well, listen, mate, you're not sacrificing Kathy to anyone, so you better get that clear. You touch her and I'll split your head open."

"You don't have to do that," he said. Thankfully he seemed weakened by my blows and made no attempt to rise. It was only now that his age had caught up with him, diminishing his stature.

I stood over Kathy and O'Riordan made no move to stop me. We both waited for the riders to emerge into the clearing. When the first of them nudged their horses into the torch-glow, I felt a sudden gust of frigid air wash over me. If this was an element of the night's festivities, it was extraordinarily convincing. These weren't just riders and horses, dressed up in their annual finery to celebrate the occasion.

If I tried to focus on an individual horse, or rider, I couldn't. They weren't spectral, but somehow their forms eluded the eye. The horses' breath boiled in clouds, like steam released from an engine. The riders wore pelts and woollen cloaks, their arms and legs adorned with silver bracelets and bands of gold, and all were helmeted, some with stag antlers curling over them. Some had drawn their swords—huge, elongated weapons—others hefted axes or spears. Although I couldn't see their faces, I knew instinctively that there were women among them. The hounds that I'd heard, baying in the distance and growling here in the woods, paced about them, huge beasts, teeth barred hungrily as though a word would set them on me.

The riders shouted to each other in a language I didn't recognise.

"The Wild Hunt," said O'Riordan, his voice barely above a whisper. "It has come for another life."

I would have shouted out to the ferocious looking leaders, but then I saw what swung from their belts, the horrendous, grisly trophies of their night's work.

Human heads, freshly dripping with blood that ran down the flanks of the horses like sweat. They weren't fake. I knew that intuitively for a fact. I would have screamed, but terror locked me up.

As I stood there, so impotently, O'Riordan pushed gently past me and put himself between Kathy and the riders. He turned to me and told me not to move. I saw with further horror that he had opened his shirt. Something gleamed on his bared chest, as if he had carved something there, a symbol that leaked his blood. He held out his arms, ironically making a cross of his body. Whatever gods were at work here, pre-dated the Christians by centuries.

I realised what he was doing. He was sacrificing himself, giving himself to these frightful warriors of the night. He walked towards them.

One of them edged his horse forward and swung it around. O'Riordan moved with sudden liveliness and swung up behind the frightful rider, his legs gripping the flanks of the steed. Several of the hounds bayed, as though eager to sink their teeth into human flesh and filling the air of the clearing with the sound. Moments later the whole company wheeled, shouting and waving their weapons at the skies, before plunging back into the forest.

The last of them was a woman rider. I felt her eyes on me before she turned away. Her gaze burned away my anger. Beside her was a huge wolfhound. Then they, too were gone.

I sagged down beside Kathy, drained, my whole frame shaking.

She stirred and sat up. I gave her my arm and she got to her feet, more steadily than I did.

"Darling, why have you brought me here?" she said, laughing softly. "I'm sure it's very romantic, but I can hardly see a thing."

The firebrand had almost burned out, but in its glow I could see her face. There was an unfamiliar energy there.

"It's quite…safe," I murmured. I heard a final flurry of hoof beats somewhere out in the night.

"Really? Come on. Let's get back to the festival. I think I will have something to eat. I don't know why, but I'm starving."

I was about to lift her in my arms, but she demurred.

"What on earth are you doing?" she giggled. "I'm perfectly capable of walking back. I think someone's had too much mead, or whatever you were drinking earlier."

▲

My Longing to See Tamar
by Jessica Amanda Salmonson

I am only rarely certain where my dreams end and realities begin. I had such a weird dream while napping on the davenport. Wouldn't've remembered it if the dogs hadn't decided I had to wake up and take them outside. I was walking naked through a dark labyrinth carrying all my clothes in my arms. I could hear traffic outside, distantly. I had to find a spot to sit down and put my clothes on. I remembered my old fuck-buddy Tamar ran a bathhouse called My Lady of Fatima somewhere in this place.

Through an archway into light, and there I was, walking barefoot, still holding onto my clothes. I strolled between two rows of little squat toilets with high mounted tanks on the walls. About me was a steam cloud populated by young and old women who appeared and disappeared in and out of the whiteness, either naked or partially wrapped in towels, semblances of ghosts, or faded memories of friends once well known.

I skirted the showers and came to a staired pit, hot rocks hissing at the bottom. These were women svelte or lumpy, wet in the heat, beautiful, strange, lounging and laughing along the moist marble stairs. The sound of them was distant, though I stood near. I found a bench against a wall to be alone, and sat thereon to put on my clothes.

I remembered Tamar lived upstairs, which had a difficult entryway from way back of this vaulted, multi-tunneled place. I walked far back until I reached a little bathhouse deli run by a head-shaven dyke named Shorty because she was a short order cook, but was also a short round girl with red stubble on her pate. She remembered me from years ago and waved hi as I was approaching. She had clumsy tattoos and I thought, "If you die before your parents, they'll burn those off and bury you in a wig." A said, "Tamar here?" and she pointed to the steps further back.

The upward stairway was absurdly narrow, hardly wide enough to place a foot; it was a balancing act to use it. It went halfway up and ended midair, where it attached to a big round pipe wrapped in the curly wool hide of a skinned sheep. I spraddled the pipe, scooted across to where I had to stand without losing my balance, and climbed onto a very rickety deck. From there I leapt upward and clung to a window sill. Whew. Made it.

I was wondering how Tamar moved all her stuff in the huge rafters apartment carrying everything along that difficult entrance. She'd lived there for years so I guess she cluttered the place up a little at a time. There were gauzy translucent silken drapes hanging from an uneven ceiling, forming rooms in different cloudy pastels, like tinted mist. The floor was soft with Arabian carpets, the mystic whorls threatening to devour, or leap out of the rugs as fire. Through the hung layers of silk I saw Tamar like a shadow of shifting colors, slinking deeper into her cavern loft. She was gone before I could call out.

I wanted to see her so badly it ached. But in such dreams, the most wanted destination is always further on.

I saw a big dumbwaiter, it's wide short door open in the wall, and I thought, ah, that's how she moved her stuff up here. I could've crowded myself inside that; it would've been easier. I heard a rustling sound, like a kitten's whispering claws on velvet, and looked about hastily for Tamar. I only vaguely recalled she'd died so many years ago. And yet I knew I could see her again, here, now, if I could just find my way through the mazy hazy curtains and drifts of spice-redolent incense.

I began a mental catalog of Tamar's unusual knickknackery and furnishings. There were the camel saddle chairs, huge lounging pillows made from medieval tapestries, a small bookshelf with slim books in leather bindings so old they were going to red dust. A skin-velum lamp-shade with arabesque designs in henna dye was stretched tight over a snail-shaped wire frame, a small-wattage bulb within, like the snail's luminous heart. There stood a grey skeleton that looked to be carved out of hardwood; it might be real though it was only about four feet tall; and I suddenly recalled Tamar called her Princess Mai Cheng Fa, the Patron-ess of Bamboo Rats.

There were several large masks on the wall covered in raven feath-ers, with beaks and eyes made of garnet or emerald, aquamarine or am-ethysts, glowing like christmas tree LED lights and observing me by turns with pity and malevolence.

The skeleton of an enormous but only half-built canopy bed loomed out of the pastel shadows, partially hung with tattered lace and tassels, an equally tattered bedspread unmade and askew. There was so much more, but my mental catalog was interrupted by Tamar's dogs, who be-latedly began to announce that I was present. Slowly they turned into my dogs and I opened my eyes, surprised to realize I was home, upon my davenport.

Logy, my head still in clouds of incense, I stood and exclaimed "Porch!" and three happy dogs raced me to the back door. They ran and I walked down the outside staircase, everyone but me yapping. I walked to the wooden garden chair and sat down as Tsuki, Yukiko, Daigoro, and the ghost of little Okuni explored and pissed. I sat thinking, my god, I really do remember that place.

▲

Scarlet Succubus Shrine
by Frederick J. Mayer

Seek, that which sleep seeks to hide;
beautifully sculpted skull grotto within blackness
'cept for pin prick of living scar tissue there
Cadavere head houses floor for scarlet succubus
who dances to be courted, consummated
in physical devotion of body & soul fair
All ways of the flesh and freshly keen mind
whose true heart shrine adumbrating an essence pumps
*   cardiac mine*
the real self offers...payment for cardinal light
Religiously faithful to burgundy wine giving orichalch
*   delirium eye-les titins de nid aux serpents*
lips' dulcet siren lascivious labial laceration lead to delight
Legs, limbs skin and bone smooth efflorescent hide ridges
chapel fane of curvatious carnivorous desires in growth
*   spread*
dreams coal darkness finally overcome in Nature's baroque
*   ways*
Eyes, sockets, flexible flanks contract west of virgin
rubian sunset brought in close of exquisite even shades
of holy holes, whole inside as without real & brain les frisson
*   cosmique displays*
The scarlet royal hue, oh, scarlet bower of life birth
death bled upon white velveteen bowels bed;
cascading blessed oblivion oblation L'Horloge fare.

▲ *(Inspired by Clark Ashton Smith)*

Gust of Wind Made by Swinging a Blade

by Molly N. Moss

Again, Kinnori strained against the ropes binding him, his muscles already throbbing from exertion. Once again, the cords sliced his flesh and yielded not at all.

It was dark in the hold of the guard-ship *Murakumo*, and a gathering chill numbed his fingers. Rolling waves conspired with exhaustion to make Kinnori's eyelids grow heavy. He shook himself and growled, "Escape or die, Shoji Kinnori."

Visualizing himself forced to kneel, an assistant waiting to behead him if he refused the Ryuzoji daimyo's command to commit seppuku, Kinnori breathed deeply and tried again. With all his might, he struggled to pull his hands free. As the cords gouged his wrists, a warm trickle of blood slid down his left hand.

Kinnori shut his eyes, fighting the urge to weep. Against his will he remembered the weeping of the women whose lives he'd failed to save that afternoon... *How long ago? A few hours? A day?*

Rather than weep, he snarled curses. He cursed the early winter freeze the ship must be coming home to, judging by the cold. He cursed the darkness that matched the souls of the murderous samurai who bound him and tossed him into the ship's hold. As he started to curse Narihiro and the rest of his fellow samurai, he glimpsed a light flaring up near the stairway. His words died in his throat as he watched the flame approaching.

Narihiro must be coming to mock him, again, for throwing away his own life by trying to defend worthless women from a rival clan. Or could it be one of the sailors, coming to give him food and drink? He squirmed, trying to sit up, but that only made his bladder ache with the need to pass water. Kinnori moved his lips in a silent prayer to Kannon, goddess of mercy, begging that his visitor would be a compassionate sailor coming to his aid.

He watched the flare settle into the steady glow of an oil lamp. Kinnori knew every samurai and every sailor serving on the *Murakumo*, but the slim fingers holding the lamp were unfamiliar.

Propping himself up on one elbow, Kinnori whispered, "Who are you?"

The lamp illuminated only a short radius, enough to show Kinnori that the stranger wore a hooded robe. In the prevailing murk, he wasn't certain whether the garment was silver or pale gray.

From fore to aft, the sekibune's hold was filled with baskets of valuables taken in raids of coastal Chinese villages. Yet the hooded person moved with swift and confident steps, picking a safe path through the loot without either slowing pace or shining the lamp around.

"I am nobody," the stranger murmured, kneeling by Kinnori's side.

Kinnori's heart stopped as the unknown person pulled a knife from inside his robe. Could the stranger be an assassin sent by Narihiro to slit Kinnori's throat? *When I prayed for mercy, O Kannon, a quick death isn't what I had in mind.*

The stranger placed the lamp near Kinnori's bound wrists. With a single slash he cut the rope. Kinnori realized he was being rescued, and his heart finally remembered to beat.

He studied his liberator, who moved the lamp near Kinnori's feet and cut the rope that tied his ankles together. His rescuer was short and trim, and the robe appeared to be a kind commonly worn by Buddhist monks. *I suppose he's probably a young runaway from a monastery.*

"You are saving my life. That makes you someone, at least to me," Kinnori murmured. He massaged blood and warmth back into his wrists and ankles, wincing at the agony as sensation returned.

"Call me Tachikaze, then."

Tachikaze—the name meant *gust of wind made by swinging a blade.* Kinnori turned to study his liberator's face, but Tachikaze's features were lost in the darkness of his hooded robe. *What a powerful name for a Buddhist novice! Has he studied karate with the monks? Maybe I've been set free by a gifted knife-fighter.*

Before his rescuer put the knife away, however, Kinnori observed enough to admire it. Long and supple-bladed, on its black leather handle was embroidered a white tiger stalking through a shower of cherry blossoms. Some trick of the lamp's light made the blade appear, for half a breath, to glow with a peculiar blue flame.

Kinnori tried to stand, but the removal of the ropes caused his hands and feet to feel as if hundreds of knife-tips pricked them. Observing his distress, Tachikaze slipped an arm under Kinnori's shoulders and helped him onto his feet. The boy's touch was cold as ice.

How long has Tachikaze been hiding in the hold, a witness to my struggles to get free?

Tachikaze returned to the stairway, weaving through the clutter with that odd grace of his. *I suppose it isn't important how long the boy listened to me fighting my bonds and did nothing. I prayed for help, and he gave it to me. Thank you, gentle goddess Kannon.* Kinnori leaned on the hull to brace himself against the rolling of the ship, and his bladder reminded him of its needs.

As Kinnori relieved himself, Tachikaze returned. The youth carried the oil lamp in one hand and a bundle in the other. "I have something for you," Tachikaze whispered, and he held out the parcel to Kinnori.

It was a wool blanket wrapped around Kinnori's own katana and wakazashi. His swords were taken from him when Narihiro declared him a ronin and took him prisoner. *What stealth this boy must possess, to steal my weapons from Narihiro's keeping!*

Kinnori gazed at Tachikaze in wonder. If Tachikaze noticed Kinnori's awe, however, it meant nothing to him. "You must take a rowboat and escape. To linger would be your death."

A draft of chill air swept around them. Kinnori shivered, but Tachikaze appeared untroubled.

When the icy gust passed, Kinnori thrust his swords through his sash and turned to his liberator. "I know that I am in danger here, but I cannot escape until the sekibune is docked. Where would I go, if I flee while still at sea?"

Tachikaze folded his hands together at his chest. "Please believe me. When the moon sets, everyone aboard the *Murakumo* will die. It is the will of the gods. I wish you spared, Shoji Kinnori, for you are an honorable man."

Frowning, Kinnori asked, "How can you know what fate awaits this ship?"

"Insight was given to me," Tachikaze answered, bowing low from his waist, "when this ship's crew attacked a sekibune belonging to the daimyo of the Imagawa clan."

A fleeting ache panged Kinnori's heart. *That terrible deed must have shocked and saddened this young Buddhist, just as powerfully as it outraged me.*

In late afternoon, hours or a day ago, the *Murakumo's* lookout spied an Imagawa guard-ship trespassing in the outermost waters claimed by the Ryuzoji clan. Narihiro, the samurai commanding the *Murakumo*, ordered his ship's crew to chase the rival clan's ship. When near enough, they'd lowered their main mast for use as a bridging plank, and Narihiro led his samurai aboard the Imagawa vessel.

They discovered that the Imagawa guard-ship carried a bridal party. Only five samurai accompanied the bride and her maid-servants. Narihiro and his Ryuzoji samurai outnumbered them ten to one, and made quick work of killing them. Kinnori didn't protest the slaughter, for naval skirmishes between Nippon's clans were as common as raids against China.

He felt sickened, as always, when next his fellow samurai killed the Imagawa ship's captain, helmsman, and sailors. They were peasants, and therefore unarmed. Although samurai had the right to slay peasants, Kinnori hated seeing warriors cut down men who lacked the training to defend themselves.

When Narihiro proposed to rape and murder the bride and her maidservants, Kinnori could be silent no longer. He looked at the bride, but it was his twin sister's face he saw: Katsuko—pinned down on her back while brutal men took turns ravaging her. Katsuko—forced to kneel and await the fall of a katana on her delicate neck.

Roaring, Kinnori drew his own katana and leaped between the women and his fellow samurai. He knew he couldn't win, for he was one man against forty-nine, but he felt compelled to die fighting for what was right. This innocent young woman had no brother there to protect her. Kinnori *needed* to be her brother and defender, just as he'd want another man to be Katsuko's guardian, if Kinnori's sister were in danger and he couldn't be at her side himself.

"There is no honor in killing helpless women," he snarled at Narihiro, holding his katana ready for a fight to his own death.

Instead of commanding the other Ryuzoji samurai to kill Kinnori, however, Narihiro laughed. He ordered Kinnori held still, forced to watch as one by one the weeping girls were violated and beheaded. *Murakumo's* sailors, unarmed peasants just as their counterparts aboard the Imagawa ship had been, watched the massacre also, powerless to stop it even if they wished to do so.

Kinnori now looked at Tachikaze, probably as innocent as the Imagawa bride whose life he couldn't save. The boy's hood shadowed all his face except his narrow lips and the smooth curve of his chin. "I agree that all the samurai serving aboard this sekibune deserve death," Kinnori told the youth. "But the sailors are sons of merchants, fishermen, and farmers. They did not partake in the murder of the Imagawa women. I must warn them, before I flee the doom of the *Murakumo*."

"You ask to take a great risk."

"And you ask me to believe that you know the future, which can be true only if you communicate with gods."

They faced each other in silence. At last Tachikaze curled his thin, dark lips into a grimace. "Did you not pray for aid, mere breaths before I loosed your bonds?"

A tingly tremor surged up Kinnori's spine. "Yes." He took a deep breath. "So it's true, then. You talk with gods."

"Never before. But tonight I do." Tachikaze's slim shoulders slumped. "As I said, Shijo Kinnori, you are an honorable man. Therefore you believe most other men must also be honorable. I fear you will be often disappointed. Still, warn the sailors, if your conscience demands it. But I doubt they will reward your compassion."

Kinnori said nothing, but only nodded. He led the way as they crept up the stairway, Tachikaze following a few paces behind him. He expected to find at least one samurai at the door to the cabin shared by off-duty sailors, as a precaution against Kinnori freeing himself. None stood there.

They believe I wouldn't trouble to talk to the sailors. A guard is certain to be posted at the door to the deck.

His hand strayed to the hilt of his katana, but he pulled it back and instead pushed open the cabin door. *One task at a time,* he reminded himself. *Waking and warning the sailors will do no good if I'm touching my sword as if I'm thinking of killing them.*

In the cabin the air was warmer, but a frigid draft from the hold followed them. One of the sailors sleeping nearest to the door shivered as the chill reached him, pulling his blanket tighter around his shoulders. Kinnori knelt by the man's side and tried waking him by pulling the blanket away, but the sailor only muttered and hauled the covering over himself again. Then Kinnori shook the sleeper's arm until at last his eyes opened, and swiftly laid a hand over the man's mouth to silence him.

"Please, do not be afraid of me, for I hope to save your life," Kinnori whispered into the man's ear. "A doom has been laid upon this sekibune. Be gone before the setting of the moon, if you wish to live. Warn the sailors, but not the samurai."

He waited a few breaths, then lifted his hand from the man's mouth. For a few breaths more, the sailor neither moved nor spoke, but only gazed at Kinnori with wide-open eyes.

Suddenly the sailor sat up and backed away. "Guards!" he shouted, "the ronin Shoji Kinnori is loose!"

Every sailor in the cabin snapped his eyes open. Kinnori pivoted, drawing his katana, and rushed up the remaining stairs to the deck, trusting Tachikaze to follow. When he dashed through the door he whirled around, ready to fight one or more guards, but again there were none. Tachikaze sped through the door onto the deck, seized Kinnori's free hand, and ran dragging him toward the stern. From the stem came running the few samurai who were on night watch.

At the stern Tachikaze leaped over the rudder and into the port-side takasebune tethered behind the guard-ship. Kinnori jumped after him, and with his readied katana he slashed the rope tying the rowboat to the sekibune.

While momentum and the wind in its sails speeded the ship away from the rowboat, Kinnori hastened to take up the oars and row in the opposite direction. At any moment he expected the samurai to drop their swords and let arrows fly from their bows, and meanwhile he heard orders shouted to the helmsman to turn the ship and pursue the fugitives.

A blast of freezing wind began blowing, and it endured, thwarting the sekibune's effort to turn and give chase. Looking back, Kinnori witnessed arrows blown backward and falling into the rolling waves. When he turned back to the oars he realized Tachikaze still stood, gaze fixed on the vanishing guard-ship, hooded robe billowing in the fierce squall. Neither the swells of the sea nor the blasting wind budged the youth.

Kinnori trembled, though not from the icy gale engulfing them. He'd heard that Buddhist monks wielded powers of a magical nature—from glimpsing the future, to commanding the elements. Such tales, however, always involved men or sometimes women advanced in years. Even if raised by a monastery from birth, Kinorri suspected this boy couldn't have mastered such arts in his few years. *Who are you really, Tachikaze?*

As if privy to Kinnori's thoughts, Tachikaze flashed a small smile and took a seat. He gestured at the moon high overhead. "It will not be long until death comes to the *Murakumo*."

Looking at the starry sky, Kinnori reckoned the distance to Nippon's nearest shores, and a new dread froze the blood in his veins. "Whatever fate befalls the *Murakumo*, we would have been wiser to stay and share it."

Shadowed by his robe's hood, Tachikaze's face was impossible to read. "Why do you think so?"

"We brought no supplies with us, and I cannot row fast enough to reach the coast before we die from lack of food and water."

Tachikaze laughed, though not from merriment. It was a laugh that echoed drought-stricken reeds blown by a hot, dry breeze that gives no comfort to any who feel its passage. "Turn and follow the sekibune, but do not hurry. In a few hours everyone aboard will be dead, and the ship's supplies will have no owners. Who then will stop you from boarding and taking whatever you wish?"

Kinnori turned the takasebune and rowed in the same direction that the *Murakumo* was sailing. As he did so, the wind diminished to the mildest of breezes. Yet he trembled as if still cold.

Beyond doubt, Tachikaze communicated with gods. He knew things no person could know, unless the gods revealed them.

Most gods were indifferent. Some were compassionate. A few were evil.

Which kind of god sent Tachikaze to me, and why?
What is in this boat with me?

* * * *

"Awake, Shoji Kinnori."

Seagulls cried somewhere far away. Tachikaze leaned over Kinnori, his hood an impenetrable void. Dark, too, was the night sky—neither moon nor stars were in view.

Tachikaze pointed at a mote of light flickering ahead. "That is the *Murakumo*."

Closing the distance, Kinnori realized the cries he heard weren't of seagulls. They were screams of men.

Silence fell when the sekibune came into view. He dropped the oars for a few breaths, stunned to see the proud vessel adrift and its sails hanging in tatters.

As Tachikaze tethered the takasebune, Kinnori climbed over the railing and onto the deck. He slumped to his knees and almost retched as the molten-copper stench of fresh blood overwhelmed him. By the light of lanterns hanging from the masts, he witnessed slaughter.

Murderous Narihiro still stood at the ship's helm, somehow. His hands gripped a spear. Upon its tip was impaled his severed head, teeth bared as if in a final defiant snarl—or a terrified scream. Seated around him, the rest of the samurai and all the sailors held their own severed heads in their hands.

His heart thundering, Kinnori leaned against the main mast. "Gods, how did this happen?"

"They died as they chose to live." By his side, Tachikaze bowed his head and folded together his pale, slim hands. "For the gods shape the world as men and women believe should be, and give each of us the life and death our actions deserve."

"How can that be true?" Rage swelled up in Kinnori's gut. Still on his knees, he gripped the hilts of his swords with such force that his knuckles ached. "This fate was well deserved by the men serving on the *Murakumo*, but the Imagawa bride and her maid-servants cannot have earned decapitation."

Tachikaze laughed again, the sound of reeds in a hot wind. By the light of a lantern over their heads, Kinnori now realized Tachikaze's robe was not silver or pale gray. He stared at his white-clad rescuer and trembled. White: the color of death, and of tragedy.

"You are but a man, Shoji Kinnori. Who are you to judge what those young women deserved? Did I not say the gods shape the world as men and women believe should be? Know this: the Imagawa bride had stolen a ship and servants from her grandfather, the daimyo, to go marry her forbidden lover from an enemy clan."

A solution to the riddle of the youth's powers leaped into Kinnori's mind, and he gasped and bowed low, murmuring, "You are one of them, one of the gods, aren't you?"

With a cool hand, Tachikaze raised Kinnori's head so their gazes met. His other hand pushed back his hood. Kinnori yearned to look away, but couldn't.

"No, I am not one of the gods. I am but their servant, only for this night." Dropping the hood, Tachikaze revealed himself to be the murdered Imagawa bride. A ring of dried blood showed where Narihiro's katana cleaved her head from her neck. Her eyes were flat and clouded, her face and hands pale, her lips blue with death.

From the door leading down to the cabins and the hold, the maidservants emerged carrying baskets of food and jars of water. In silence they loaded these provisions into the takasebune Kinnori used earlier to flee. When they passed by him, they bowed their heads. Their necks, too, were ringed with dried blood from their earlier beheadings.

"You must go, Shoji Kinnori." Tachikaze bowed from her waist. "Go to a province where you are unknown. Marry a farmer's or craftsman's daughter, learn his business and make it your own. There is honor enough for any man in the growing of wholesome food or the making of solid wares, but there is no honor in bloodshed. Also," her thin dark lips curled in a smile, "you lack the temperament to be a samurai."

Kinnori opened his mouth to protest, but the words died on his tongue. He indeed lacked the arrogance he'd seen in Narihiro and other samurai. Yet he wondered why a young woman who condemned bloodshed, even between professional warriors, obeyed the commands of gods to slay murderers.

"But you—" he started to ask.

"—are dead." Tachikaze backed toward the rowboat, beckoning him to follow. "What use can the dead have for honor?"

Once again an icy gale blew. Kinnori jumped down into the takasebune and rowed away from the guard-ship, and the bride and maidservants gathered at the stern and watched him go. A white tiger stalked to Tachikaze's side and sat at her feet, and a shower of cherry blossoms fell over all. Before he lost sight of them, the ship and the dead faded to nothing in the rosy sunrise on the horizon.

Kinnori opened a water jar. He washed his face and hands, exactly as the god Izanagi did after failing to bring back his wife Izanami from the land of Death. Thus purified, Kinnori imagined himself cultivating a bountiful orchard. He steered the takasebune toward Nippon and thought: *The life of a farmer must be a blessed life, indeed.*

▲

Penelope, Sleepless
Darrell Schweitzer

Who is this bloody stranger
who lies beside her at night?
Sure, he has washed, but
the stink of death will not leave him,
anymore than it can be scrubbed
from the walls and floor of the hall
where he slaughtered the suitors.

He sleeps with his great bow
always within reach,
murmuring of battles,
or weeping for comrades lost,
or trembling in cold sweat
over something he must have seen
in the Underworld.

Of course their son adores him,
but does anything remain
of the man-boy who left her
nineteen years ago for the war?
She's losing hope,
certain that he is planning
another voyage.

Therefore, silently,
she gets up,
goes to her loom,
and resumes her weaving.

▲

Made in the USA
Middletown, DE
13 August 2016